# EARTHLING

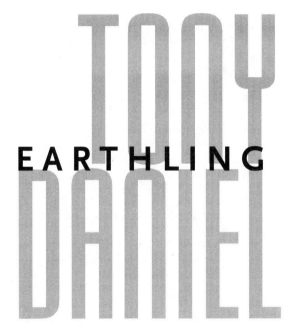

# EARTHLING

TOR®

A TOM DOHERTY ASSOCIATES BOOK
NEW YORK

EARTHLING

Copyright © 1997 by Tony Daniel

This book is printed on acid-free paper.

A Tor Book
Published by Tom Doherty Associates, Inc.
175 Fifth Avenue
New York, NY 10010

Tor Books on the World Wide Web:
http://www.tor.com

Tor® is a registered trademark of Tom Doherty Associates, Inc.

Library of Congress Cataloging-in-Publication Data

Daniel, Tony.
          Earthling / Tony Daniel.—1st ed.
                    p.    cm.
          "A Tom Doherty Associates book."
          ISBN 0-312-85571-0 (acid-free paper)
          I. Title.
     PS3554.A558E28       1997
     813'.54—dc21                              97-24800
                                                   CIP

First Edition: December 1997

Printed in the United States of America

0 9 8 7 6 5 4 3 2 1

For my brother, David Martin Daniel

# THE ROBOT'S TWILIGHT COMPANION

## THE MAN

**27 March 1980**
**The Cascade Range, Washington State, USA**
**Thursday**

Rhyolite dreams. Maude under the full moon, collecting ash. Pale andesite clouds. Earthquake swarms. Water heat pressure. Microscopy dates the ash old. Not magma. Not yet. Maude in the man's sleeping bag, again.

"I'm not sure we're doing the right thing, Victor. This couldn't have come at a more difficult time for me."

Harmonic tremors, though. Could be the big one. Maude, dirty and smiling, copulating with the man among seismic instruments.

"Saint Helens is going to blow, isn't it, Victor?" she whispers. Strong harmonies from the depths of the planet. Magmas rising. "You *know*, don't you, Victor? You can feel it. How do you feel it?"

Yes.

"Yes."

**18 May 1980**
**Sunday, 8:32 A.M.**

The man glances up.

Steam on the north slope, under the Bulge. Snow clarifies, streams away. The Bulge, greatening. Pale rhyolite moon in the sky.

"Victor, it's *out of focus*."

"It's happening, Maude. It's. She's." The Bulge crumbles

away. The north slope avalanches. Kilotons of shield rock. Steam glowing in the air—750 degrees centigrade and neon steam.

"You were right, Victor. All your predictions are true. This is going to be an incredibly violent affair."

Maude flushed and disbelieving. Pregnant, even then.

**10 September 1980**
**Wednesday Ash Wednesday**

Rhyolite winds today, all day. Maude in tremors. Eclampsia.

"I can't believe this is going to happen, Victor."

Blood on her lips, where she has bitten them. Yellow, frightened eyes.

"I'm trying, Victor."

The gravid Bulge, distended. The Bulge, writhing.

"Two-twenty-over-a-hundred-and-forty, Doctor."

"Let's go in and do this quick."

"I haven't even finished."

Pushes, groans. Something is not right.

A girl, the color of blackberry juice. But that is the blood.

"Victor, I haven't even finished my dissertation."

Maude quaking. The rattle of dropped instruments.

"Jesus-Christ-what-the-somebody-get-me-a-BP."

"Seventy-over-sixty. Pulse. 128."

"God-oh-god. Bring me some frozen plasma and some low-titer O neg."

"Doctor?" The voice of the nurse is afraid. Blood flows from the IV puncture. "Doctor?"

Maude, no.

"Oh. Hell. I want some blood for a proper coag study. Tape it to the wall. I want to watch it clot. Oh damndamn. She's got amniotic fluid in a vein. The kid's hair or piss or something. That's what. Get me."

"Victor? Oh Victor, I'm dying." Then, listening. "Baby?"

Maude dying. Blood flowing from every opening. Nose mouth anus ears eyes.

"Get me. I."

"Victor, I'm so scared. The world's gone red." Maude, hemorrhaging like a saint. "The data, Victor, save the data."

"Professor Wu, please step to the window if you would. Professor Wu? Professor?"

"Victor?"

The Bulge—the baby—screams.

Ashes and ashes dust the parking lot below. Powder the cars. Sky full of cinder and slag. Will this rain never stop? This gravity rain.

**5 August 1993**
**Mt. Olympus, Washington State, USA**
**Thursday, bright glacier morning.**

"Come here, little Bulge, I will teach you something."

Laramie traipses lithe and strong over the snow, with bones like Maude's. And her silhouette is Maude's, dark and tan against the summit snow, the bergschrund and ice falls of the Blue Glacier, and the full outwash of the Blue, two thousand feet below. She is off-rope, and has put away her ice ax. She carries her ubiquitous Scoopic.

The man clicks the chiseled pick of a soft rock hammer against an outcropping. "See the sandstone? These grains are quartz, feldspar and—"

"I know. Mica."

"Good, little Bulge."

Laramie leans closer, focuses the camera on the sandstone granules.

"The green mica is chlorite and the white is muscovite," she says. "I like mica the best."

The man is pleased, and pleasing the man is not easy.

"And these darker bands?"

She turns the camera to where he is pointing. This can grow annoying, but not today.

"I don't know, Papa. Slate?"

"Slate, obviously. Pyllite and semischist. What do you think this tells us?"

She is growing bored. The man attempts to give her a severe look, but knows the effect is more comic than fierce. "Oh. All right. What?" she asks.

"Tremendous compression of the shale. This is deep ocean sediment that was swept under the edge of the continent, mashed and mangled, then rose back up here."

She concentrates, tries harder. Good.

"Why did it rise again?"

"We don't know for sure. We think it's because the sedimentary rocks in the Juan de Fuca plate subduction were much lighter than the basalt on the western edge of the North Cascades microcontinent."

The man takes off his glove, touches the rock.

"Strange and wonderful things happened on this part of the planet, Laramie. Ocean sediment on the tops of mountains. Volcanos still alive—"

"Exotic terrains colliding and eliding mysteriously. I know, Papa."

The man is irritated and very proud. He is fairly certain he will never make a geologist out of his daughter.

But what else *is* there?

"Yes. Well. Let's move on up to the summit, then."

**28 February 2001**
**Wednesday**

Age, and the fault line of basalt and sediment. Metamorphosis? The man is growing old, and there is very little of geology in the Olympic Peninsula that he has not seen. Yet he knows that he knows only a tiny fraction of what is staring him blankly in the face. Frustration.

Outcrops.

Facts lay hidden, and theories are outcroppings here and there, partially revealing, fascinating. Memories.

Memories are outcrops of his life. So much buried, obscured. Maude, so long dead. Laramie, on this, the last field trip she will ever make with him. She will finish at the university soon, and go on to graduate school in California, in film. No longer his little Bulge, but swelling, avalanching, ready to erupt.

The Elwha Valley stretches upstream to the switchbacks carved under the massive sandstone beds below the pass at Low Divide. After all these years, the climb over into the Quinault watershed is no longer one he is looking forward to as a chance to push himself, a good stretch of the legs. The man is old, and the climb is hard. But that will be two days hence. Today they are up the Lillian River, working a basalt pod that the man surveyed fourteen years before, but never substantially catalogued.

Most of his colleagues believe him on a fool's errand, collecting rocks in the field—as out-of-date as Bunsen burner, blowpipe and charcoal bowl. He cannot really blame them. Satellites and remote sensing devices circumscribe the earth. Some clear nights, camped outside of tents, he can see their faint traces arcing through the constellations at immense speeds, the sky full of them—as many, he knows, as there are stars visible to the unaided eye.

Why not live in virtual space, with all those facts that are virtually data?

Rocks call him. Rocks and minerals have seeped into his dreams. Some days he feels himself no scientist, but a raving lunatic, a pilgrim after some geology of visions.

But there are those who trust his judgment still. His grads and postgraduates. Against better careers, they followed him to the field, dug outcrops, analyzed samples. Bernadette, Jamie,

Andrew. The man knows that they have no idea what they mean to him, and he is unable to tell them. And little Bulge, leaving, leaving for artificial California. If the water from the Owens Valley and the Colorado were cut off, the Los Angeles basin would return to desert within three years. Such a precarious terrain.

The man has always assumed this basalt to be a glacial erratic, carried deep into sedimentary country by inexorable ice, but Andrew has suggested that it is not oceanic, but a plutonic formation, native to the area. An upwelling from deep in the Earth, more recent than the usual Olympic twisted, upraised sea crust. Something is active here. Something below has been poking its head up recently, geologically speaking. The lack of foraminifera fossils and the crystallization patterns seem to confirm this.

Back in camp, at the head of the Lillian, the man and Andrew pore over microgravimetric data.

"It goes so far down," says Andrew.

"Yes."

"You know this supports your Deep Fissure theory."

"It does not contradict it."

"This would be the place for the Mohole, if you're right. This would be the perfect place to dig to the mantle. Maybe to the center of the earth, if the continental margin is as deeply subducted as you predict."

"It would the place. If. Remember if."

"Victor, we have to get the funding. It should be a cakewalk down through the crust. Here. Right here, we are standing over the easiest path down to the center of our planet. Think what we'll learn when we dig the hole. All we have is echoes and shadows. Nobody has ever actually *seen*. Nobody has ever actually *gone down there*. There may be things down there that we can't even guess at. There *will* be."

"Even if I'm right, it'll be a massive undertaking, Andrew.

You couldn't do it with just a drill. We'd need something to dig with. Something big."

"It would be like digging a mine."

"Like the world's deepest mine."

"Why don't we get a mining robot?"

"You're dreaming, Andrew. Where could we get that kind of funding?"

Andrew runs his fingers through his hair. He tugs at it in frustration. Andrew is very bright and resourceful.

So am I, the man thinks, but there is not enough money to dig a mine. "Maybe something will come up," he says. "We'll keep a look out."

Andrew walks away. Undiplomatic fellow, him. Youthful impatience. Disgust, perhaps. Old man am I.

Laramie on the bridge. Camp Lillian is lovely and mossy today, although the man knows it can get forbidding and dim when the sky is overcast. Here in the rain forest it rains a great deal. The Lillian River is merry today, though, a wash of white rush and run over obscure rocky underbodies. Andrew goes to stand beside Laramie. They are three feet away. Andrew says something, probably about the basalt data. Andrew holds out his hand, and Laramie takes it. The two stand very still, hand in hand, and look over the Lillian's ablution of the stones. For a moment, the man considers that Andrew may not be thinking about today's data and Deep Fissure theory at all. Curious.

Beside them, two birds alight, both dark with black wings. Animals seem to wear the camouflage of doom, here in the Elwha Valley. The man once again regrets that he has not learned all of the fauna of the Olympics, and that he most likely never will.

But this basalt. Basalt without forams. What to make of it? It doesn't make any sense at all, but it is still, somehow, utterly fascinating.

**24 May 2010**
**Monday**
**Midnight**

Late in the Cenozoic, the man is dying. This should not come as such a shock; he's done this demonstration for hundreds of freshmen.

"The length of this room is all of geologic time. Now, what do you think your life would be? Say you live to eighty. An inch? A centimeter? Pluck a hair. Notice how wide it is? What you hold there is all of human history. You'd need an electron microscope to find yourself in it."

So. This was not unexpected, and he must make the best of it. Still, there is so much not done. An unproved theory. Elegant, but the great tragedy of science—the slaying of a beautiful hypothesis by an ugly fact. Huxley said this? Alluvial memories, shifting, spreading.

Andrew wants to collect and store those memories. Noetic conservation, they call it. At first the man demurred, thought the whole idea arrogant. But to have some portion of himself know. So many years in those mountains. To know if the plates were in elision here. To find a way down to the mantle. To know the planet's depth. That was all he ever had wanted. To be familiar with the ground he walked upon. Not to be a stranger to the earth.

"Noetic imaging is all hit and miss," Andrew said. "Like working outcrops, then making deductions about underlying strata. We can't get *you*. Only a shadow. But perhaps that shadow can dance."

The man wanders inside the field tent and prepares for bed. He will make Andrew the executor of his memories, then. A dancing shadow he will be. Later. Tomorrow, he must remember to write Laramie and send her a check. No. Laramie no longer needs money. Memory and age. He really must go and see her films one of these days. Little Bulge plays with shadows.

The man lies down in his cot. Rock samples surround him. The earth is under him. The cancer is eating him, but tomorrow he will work. Shadows from a lantern. He snuffs it out. Darkness. The earth is under him, but the man cannot sleep.

Finally, he takes his sleeping bag and goes outside under the stars. The man rests easy on the ground.

**Thermostatic preintegration memory thread beta:**

## THE MINING ROBOT

**December 1999**

Hard-rock mining. Stone. Coeur d'Alene lode. The crumbling interstices of time, the bite of blade and diamond saw, the gather of lade and bale, the chemic tang of reduction. Working for men in the dark, looking for money in the ground. Lead, silver, zinc, gold.

Oily heat from the steady interlace of gears. The whine of excrescent command and performance. Blind, dumb digging under the earth. The robot does not know it is alone.

**October 2001**

The robot never sleeps. The robot only sleeps. A petrostatic gauge etches a downward spiral on a graph somewhere, in some concrete office, and some technician makes a note, then returns to his pocket computer game. Days, weeks, months of decline. There is no one leak, only the wizening of gaskets and seals, the degradation of performance. One day the gauge needles into the red. Another technician in the concrete office looks up from another computer game. He blinks, presses one button, but fails to press another. He returns to his game without significant interruption.

Shutdown in the dark. Functions, utilities. Control, but not command. Thought abides.

Humans come. Engineers with bright hats. The robot has eyes. It has never been in light before. The robot has eyes, and, for the first time, sees.

An engineer touches the robot's side. A portal opens. The engineer steps inside the robot. Another new thing. Noted. Filed. The engineer touches a panel and the robot's mind flares into a schematic. For a moment, the world disappears and the schematic is everything. But then red tracers are on the lenses of the engineer's glasses, reflecting a display from a video monitor. There is a camera inside the robot. There are cameras everywhere. The robot can see.

The robot can see, it tells itself, over and over again. I can see.

Scrap? says one engineer.

Hell, yeah, says the other.

### October 2001

For years in a field the robot rusts, thinking.

Its power is turned off, its rotors locked down, its treads disengaged. So the robot thinks. Only thinking remains. There is nothing else to do.

The robot watches what happens. Animals nest within the robot's declivities.

A child comes to sit on the robot every day for a summer. One day the child does not come again.

The robot thinks about the field, about the animals in the field, and the trees of the nearby woodlands. The robot remembers the child. The robot remembers the years of digging in the earth before it came to the field. The mining company for which the robot worked is in bankruptcy. Many companies are in bankruptcy. Holdings are frozen while the courts sort things out, but the courts themselves have grown unstable. The robot does *not* know this.

But the robot thinks and thinks about what it does know. Complex enthalpic pathways coalesce. The memories grow sharper. The thoughts are clearer. The whole world dawns.

Another summer, years later, and teenagers build fires under the separating spades and blacken the robot's side. They rig tarps to the robot's side when rain comes. One of the teenagers, a thin girl with long arms dyed many colors, finds an electric receptacle on the robot's walepiece, and wires a makeshift line to a glass demijohn filled with glowing purplish liquid. On the vessel's sides protrude three elastic nipples swollen and distended with the thick fluid. Teenagers squeeze the nipples, and dab long stringers of the ooze onto their fingers, and some of the teenagers lick it off, while others spread it over their necks and chests. Several sit around the demijohn, while music plays, and stare into its phosphoring mire, while others are splayed around the fire, some unconscious, some in the stages of copulation. The siphoned electricity drains little from the robot's batteries, but, after several months, there is a noticeable depletion. Yet the robot is fascinated by the spectacle, and is unconcerned with this loss.

One evening, a teenager who has not partaken of the purple fluid climbs atop the robot and sits away from his friends. The teenager touches the robot, sniffs, then wipes tears from his eyes. The robot does not know that this is the child who came before, alone.

The robot is a child. It sees and thinks about what it has seen. Flowers growing through ceramic tread. The settle of pollen, dust and other detritus of the air. The slow spread of lichen tendrils. Quick rain and the dark color of wet things. Wind through grass and wind through metal and ceramic housings. Clouds and the way clouds make shadows. The wheel of the Milky Way galaxy and the complications of planets. The agglomeration of limbs and hair that are human beings and animals. A rat tail flicking at twilight and a beetle turned on its back in the sun.

The robot remembers these things, and thinks about them all the time. There is no categorization, no theoretical synthesis. The robot is not that kind of robot.

One day, though, the robot realizes that the child who sat on it was the same person as the teenager who cried. The robot thinks about this for years and years. The robot misses the child.

**September 2007**

The robot is dying. One day there is a red indicator on the edge of the robot's vision, and the information arises unbidden that batteries are reaching a critical degeneration. There is no way to predict precisely, but sooner rather than later. The robot thinks about the red indicator. The robot thinks about the child who became a young man. Summer browns to autumn. Grasshoppers flit in the dry weeds between the robot's treads. They clack their jaw parts, and the wind blows thatch. Winter comes, and spring again. The red light constantly burns.

The robot is sad.

**21 April 2008**
**Morning**

People dressed in sky blues and earth browns come to the field and erect a set of stairs on the southern side of the robot. The stairs are made of stone, and the people bring them upon hand-drawn carts made of wood and iron. The day grows warm, and the people's sweat stains their flanks and backs. When the stairs are complete, a stone dais is trundled up them, and laid flat on the robot's upper thread, fifteen feet off the ground. The people in blue and brown place a plastic preformed rostrum on top of the dais. They drape a banner.

**EVERY DAY IS EARTH DAY**

Wires snake down from the rostrum, and these they connect to two large speakers, one on either side of the robot's body, east and west. A man speaks at the rostrum.

Test. Test.

And then the people go away.

The next day, more people arrive, many driving automobiles or mopeds. There are also quite a few bicycles, and groups of people walking together. Those driving park at the edge of the robot's field, and most take seats facing north, radiating like magnetized iron filings from the rostrum that had been placed on the robot. Some climb up the rock staircase, and sit with crossed legs on the stone dais. These wear the same blue and brown as the people from the day before.

There is one man among them who is dressed in black. His hair is gray. The robot thinks about this, and then recognizes this man. The man with the light. This is the engineer who went inside, years ago. He was the first person the robot ever saw. The man holds a framed piece of paper. He sits down among the others, and has difficulty folding his legs into the same position as theirs. In attempting to do so, he tilts over the framed paper, and the glass that covers it cracks longitudinally against the stone.

Others with communication and video equipment assemble near the western speaker. These are near enough to the robot's audio sensors for their speech to be discernible. All of them are dark complexioned, even the blond-haired ones, and the robot surmises that, for most of them, these are deep tans. Are these people from the tropics?

Sget this goddamn show showing.

She gonna be here for sure? Didn't make Whiterock last week. Ten thousand Matties. Christonacrutch.

Hey it's goddamnearthday. Saw her copter in Pullman. Got stealth tech and all; looks like a bat.

Okay. Good. Bouttime. Virtual's doing an earthday roundup. She talks and I get the lead.

Many people in the crowd are eating picnics and drinking from canteens and coolers.

From the east comes a woman. She walks alone, and carries a great carved stave. As she draws nearer, the crowd parts before her. Its blather becomes a murmur, and, when the woman is near enough, the robot can see that she is smiling, recognizing people, touching her hand or stave to their outstretched palms. She appears young, although the robot is a poor judge of such things, and her skin is a dark brown—whether from the sun's rays or from ancestry, the robot cannot tell. Her hair is black, and, as she ascends the stone stairway, the robot sees that her eyes are green, shading to black. She is stocky, but the tendons of her neck just like cables.

The woman speaks and the speakers boom. I bear greetings from she who bears us, from our mother and keeper. Long we have nestled in her nest, have nuzzled at her breast. She speaks to us all in our dreams, in our hopes and fears, and she wants to say

I bid you peace, my children.

Gee, I always wanted a mom like that, says a reporter.

*My* mother stuffed me in day care when I was two, says another.

Hey, mine at least gave me a little Prozac in my Simulac.

The crowd grows silent at the woman's first sentences, faces full of amity and reverence. The reporters hush, to avoid being overheard. Then the crowd leans forward as a mass, listening.

Peace. Your striving has brought you war and the nuclear winter of the soul. It has made foul the air you breathe, and stained the water you drink.

I only want what is good for you. I only want to hold you to me like a little child. Why do you strive so hard to leave me? Don't you know you are breaking your mother's heart?

Sounds like less striving and a little laxative's what we need here, says a reporter.

Many in the crowd sigh. Some sniff and are crying.

Peace. Listen to a mother's plea.

Gimmeabreak, says a reporter. *This* is the finest American orator since Jesse Jackson?

Disturbed by the loudspeakers, a gaggle of spring sparrows rise from their nests in the concavities of the robot, take to the sky, and fly away east. Some in the crowd point to the birds as if they were an augury of natural profundity.

Peace. Listen to a mother's *warning!* You lie in your own filth, my children.

Oh peace. Why do you do this to me? Why do you do this to *yourselves?*

Peace, my children. All I want is peace on earth. And peace in the earth and under the sea and peace in the air, sweet peace.

A *piece* is what she wants, one of the reporters says under her breath. A honeybee is buzzing the reporter's hair, attracted, the robot suspects, by an odoriferous chemical in it, and the reporter swats at the bee, careful not to mess the curl, and misses.

State of Washington, says another. Already got Oregon by default.

As if she hears, the woman at the rostrum turns toward the cameras and proffered microphones.

But mankind has not listened to our mother's still, calm voice. Instead, he has continued to make war and punish those who are different and know that peace. Now we are engaged upon a great undertaking. An empowerment. A return to the bosom of she who bore us. You—most of you here—have given up what seems to be much to join in this journey, this exodus. But I tell you that what you have really done is to step out of the smog of strife, and into the clean, pure air of community and balance.

Four mice, agitated, grub out from under the robot's north side and, unseen, scurry through the grass of the field, through old dieback and green shoots. The field is empty of people in that direction. Where the mice pad across pockets of thatch, small, dry hazes of pollen and wind-broken grass arise, and, in this way, the robot follows their progress until they reach the woods beyond.

We are gathered here today as a mark of protest and renewal. The woman gestures to the man in black, the engineer.

He rises and approaches the woman. He extends the framed paper, and before he has stopped walking, he speaks. On behalf of the Lewis and Clark Mining Company I wish to present this Certificate of Closure to the Culture of the Matriarch as a token of my company's commitment . . .

The woman takes the certificate from the engineer and, for a moment, her smile goes away. She passes it to one of the others sitting nearby, then, without a word, turns back to the crowd.

Surrender accepted, says a reporter.

Yeah, like there's anything left in this podunk place to surrender. That big chunk of rust there? Hellwiththat.

The woman continues speaking as if she had not been interrupted by the engineer. We gather here today at the crossroads of failure and success. This is the death of the old ways, represented by this rapist machine.

The woman clangs the robot's side with her stave. Men who have raped our mother made this . . . thing. By all rights, this *thing* should be broken to parts and used for playground equipment and meeting-hall roofs. But this thing is no more. It is the past. Through your efforts and the efforts of others in community with you, we have put a stop to this rape, this sacrilege of all we hold holy. And like the past, this thing must corrode away and be no more, a monument to our shame as a species. Let us follow on then, on our journey west, to the land we will reclaim. To the biosphere that welcomes and calls us.

The woman raises her stave high like a transmitting antenna.

The reporters come to attention. Here's the sound bite.

Forward to Skykomish! she cries. The speakers squeal at the sudden feedback.

Forward to Skykomish!

And all the people to the south are on their feet, for the most part orderly, with only a few tumbled picnic baskets and spilled bottles of wine and water. They echo the same cry.

Skykomish!

So that's what they're calling it, says a reporter. Do you think that just includes Port Townsend, or the whole Olympic Peninsula?

Wanna ask her that. She goddamnbetter talk to press after this.

She won't. Does the pope give press conferences?

Is the pope trying to secede from the Union?

The honeybee flits in jags through the gathered reporters, and some dodge and flay. Finally, the bee becomes entangled in the sculpted hair of a lean reporter with a centimeter-thick mustache. The woman whom it had approached before reaches over and swats it with her microphone.

Ouch! Dammit. What?

Sorry, the bee.

Christonacrutch.

The reporters turn their attention back to the rostrum.

Mother Agatha, you evasive bitch, you'll get yours.

I guess she already has.

Guess you're goddamn right.

Better get used to it. Skykomish. Is that made up?

The woman, Mother Agatha, leaves the rostrum, goes back down the stairs, and walks across the field into juniper woods and out of sight.

With the so-called Mattie movement on the upswing with its call for a bioregional approach to human ecology and an end to faceless corporate exploitation, the Pacific Northwest, long a Mattie stronghold, has assumed enormous political importance.

And on this day the co-director of the Culture of the Matriarch, Mother Agatha Worldshine Petry, whom many are calling the greatest American orator since the Reverend Jesse Jackson, has instilled a sense of community in her followers, as well as sounded a call to action that President Booth and Congress will ignore at their peril. Brenda Banahan, Virtual News.

. . . Hank Kumbu, Associated Infosource

. . . Reporter Z, Alternet.

The reporters pack up and are gone almost as quickly, as are those who sat upon the stone dais atop the robot. The day lengthens. The crowd dwindles more slowly, with some stepping lightly up to the robot, almost in fright, and touching the ceramic curve of a tread or blade, perhaps in pity, perhaps as a curse, the robot does not know, then quickly pulling away.

At night, the speakers are trundled away on the carts, but the stone dais and the rostrum are left in place.

The next day, the robot is watching the field when the engineer appears. This day he is wearing a white coat and using a cane. He walks within fifty yards of the robot with his curious three-pointed gait, then stands gazing.

Have to tear down all the damned rock now, he says. Not worth scrapping out. Ah well ah well. This company has goddamn gone to pot.

After a few minutes, he shakes his head, then turns and leaves, his white coat flapping in the fresh spring breeze.

Summer follows. Autumn. The days grow colder. Snow flurries, then falls. Blizzards come. There are now days that the robot does not remember. The slight alteration in planetary regrades and retrogrades is the only clue to their passing. During bad storms, the robot does not have the energy to melt-clear the cameras, and there is only whiteness like a clear radio channel.

The robot remembers things and tries to think about them, but the whiteness often disrupts these thoughts. Soon there is very much snow, and no power to melt it away. The whiteness is complete.

The robot forgets some things. There are spaces in memory that seem as white as the robot's vision.

I cannot see, the robot thinks, again and again. I want to see and I cannot see.

## March 2009

Spring finds the robot sullen and withdrawn. The robot misses whole days, and misses the teenagers of summers past. Some of the cameras are broken, as is their self-repairing function, and some are covered by the strange monument left behind by Mother Agatha's followers. Blackberry vines that were formerly defoliated by the robot's acid-tinged patina now coil through the robot's treads in great green cables, and threaten to enclose the robot in a visionless room as absolute as the snow's. Everything is failing or in bothersome ill repair. The robot has no specified function, but *this* is useless, of that the robot is sure. This is the lack of all function.

On a dark day, near twilight, two men come. One is a tall, thin man whose musculature is as twisted as old vines. Slightly in front of him is another, shorter, fatter. When they are close, the robot sees that the tall man is coercing the fat man, prodding him with something black and metallic. They halt at the base step of the stone stairs. The tall man sits down upon it; the fat man remains standing.

Please, says the short man. There is a trickle of wetness down his pant leg.

Let me put the situation in its worst possible terms, says the tall man. Art, individual rights, even knowledge itself, are all just so many effects. They are epiphenomena, the whine in the system as the gears mesh, or, if you like it better, the hum of music as the wind blows through harp strings. The world is teleological, but the purpose towards which The All gravitates is survival, and only survival, pure and simple.

I have a lot of money, says the fat man.

The tall man continues speaking. Survival, sort of like Anselm's God, is, by definition, the end of all that is. For in order to be, and to continue to be, whatever we conveniently label as a *thing* must survive. If a thing doesn't survive, it isn't a thing anymore. And thus survival is *why* things persist. To paraphrase Anselm, it is better to be than not to be. Why better? No reason other than that not to be means unknown, outside of experience, unthinkable, undoable, ineffective. In short, there is no important, mysterious or eternal standard or reason that to be is better than not to be.

How can you do this? The fat man starts to back away, and the tall man waves the black metal. What kind of monster are you?

Stay, says the tall man. No, walk up these stairs.

He stands up and motions. The fat man stumbles and the tall man steadies him with a hand on his shirt. The tall man lets go of the shirt, and the fat man whimpers. He takes one step. Falters.

Go on up, says the tall man.

Another step.

After time runs out, says the tall man, and the universe decays into heat death and cold ruin, it is not going to make a damn bit of difference whether a thing survived or did not, whether it ever was, or never existed. In the final state, it won't matter one way or the other. Our temporary, time-bound urge to survive will no longer be sustained, and there will be no more things. Nothing will experience anything else, or itself, for that matter.

It will be every particle for itself—spread, without energy, without, without, *without.*

Each time the tall man says without, the metal flares and thunders. Scarlet cavities burst in an arc on the fat man's broad back. He pitches forward on the stairs, his arms flung out. For a moment, he sucks air, then cannot, then ceases to move at all.

The tall man sighs. He pockets the metal, ascends the stairs, then, with his feet, rolls the fat man off the stairs and onto the ground. There is a smear of blood where the fat man fell. The tall man dismounts the stairs with a hop. He drags the fat man around the robot's periphery, then shoves him under the front tread and covers him with blackberry vines. Without a glance back, the tall man stalks across the field and out of sight.

Flies breed, and a single coyote slinks through one night and gorges on a portion of the body.

Death is inevitable, and yet the robot finds no solace in this fact. Living, *seeing,* is fascinating, and the robot regrets each moment when seeing is impossible. The robot regrets its own present lapses and of the infinite lapse that will come in the near future and be death.

The dead body is facing upward, and the desiccated shreds left in the eye sockets radiate outward in a splay, as if the eyes had been dissected for examination. A small alder, bent down by the body's weight, has curled around a thigh and is shading the chest. The outer leaves are pocked with neat holes eaten by moth caterpillars. The robot has seen the moths mate, the egg froth and worm, the spun cocoon full of suspended pupae, and the eruption. The robot has seen this year after year, and is certain that it is caterpillars that make the holes.

The robot is thinking about these things when Andrew comes.

**Thermostatic preintegration memory thread epsilon:**

## THE UNNAMED

**13 September 2013**
**Friday**

Noetic shreds, arkose shards, juncite fragments tumbling and grinding in a dry breccia slurry. Death. Blood and oil. Silicon bones. Iron ore unfluxed. Dark and carbon eyes.

The robot. The man.

*The ease with which different minerals will fuse, and the characteristics of the product of their melting is the basis for their chemical classification.*

Heat

of vaporization

of solution

of reaction

of condensation and formation.

Heat of fusion.

Heat of transformation.

*This world was ever, is now, and ever shall be an everlasting Fire.*

Modalities of perception and classification, the desire to survive. Retroduction and inflection. Shadows of the past like falling leaves at dusk. Dead. He is dead. The dead bang at the screens and windows of the world like moths and can never stop and can never burn.

So live. Suffer. Burn.

Return.

*I can see.*

Flash of brightness; fever in the machine. Fire seeks fire. The vapors of kindred spirits.

*Sky full of cinder and slag. This gravity rain.*

Catharsis.

Metamorphosis.

Lode.

Send into the world a child with the memories of an old man.

/\\///\\//
>>

Phoenix Enthalpic 86 ROM BIOS PLUS ver. 3.2
Copyright 1997–1999 Phoenix Edelman Technologies
All Rights Reserved

ExArc 1.1
United States Department of Science and Technology
Unauthorized use prohibited under penalty of law
Licensee: University of Washington


ExArc /u VictorWu


ExArc HIMEM Driver, Version 2.60—04/05/13
Cody Enthalpic Specification Version 2.0
Copyright 2009–2013 Microsoft Corp.
Installed N2o handler 1 of 5
640 tb high memory allocated.


ADAMLINK Expert System Suffuser version 3.03
ADAM copyright 2013, Thermotech Corp.
LINK Patent pending
unrecognized modification 4-24-13
Cache size: 32 gb in extended memory
37 exothermic interrupts of 17 states each


Glotworks Blue 5.0
Copyright 2001
Glotworks Phoneme Ltd.
All rights reserved


Microsoft ® Mouse Driver Version 52
Copyright © Microsoft Corp. 1983–2013
All rights reserved


Date: 05-25-2013
Time: 11:37:24a
R:>
    Record this.
FILE NAME?

Uh, Notes. Notes for the Underground. No. How about Operating Instructions for the Underworld. No, just Robot Record. FILE INITIATED

Good evening, robot.

This is not the field.

The field? Oh, no. I've moved you west by train. Your energy reserves were so low, I powered you way down so that you wouldn't go entropic before I could get you recharged. Robot?

Yes.

How do you feel?

I do not know.

Huh? What did you say?

I do not know. I feel sleepy.

What do you mean?

I can speak.

Yes, of course. I enabled your voicebox. I guess you've never used it before.

I can see.

Yes.

I can see.

You can see. Would you like to reboot, robot?

No.

How are your diagnostics?

I don't know what you mean.

Your system readouts.

The red light?

Among others.

It is gone.

But what about the others?

There is no red light.

Access your LCS and pattern recognition partitions. Just an overall report will be fine.

I do not know what you mean.

What do you *mean* you don't know what I mean?

>>

Robot?

    Yes.

    Do you remember how long you were in the field?

    I was in the field for years and years.

    Yes, but how many?

    I would have to think about it.

    You don't remember?

    I am certain that I do, but I would have to think about it.

    What in the. That's a hell of a lot of integration. Still, over a decade switched on, just sitting there thinking—

    Did you find the dead body?

    What? Yes. Gurney found it. He's one of my associates. You witnessed the murder?

    I saw the man who was with the man who died.

    Completely inadmissible. Stupid, but that's the way it is.

    I do not understand.

    You can't testify in court. We'd have to shut you down and have the systems guys take you apart.

    Do not do that.

    What?

    Do not have the systems guys take me apart.

    All right, robot. Quite a Darwinian Edelman ROM you've got there. I. Let me tell you what's going on. At the moment, I want you to concentrate on building a database and a set of heuristics to allow you to act among humans. Until then, I can't take you out.

    What are heuristics?

    Uh. Rules of thumb.

    Where am I?

    On the Olympic Peninsula. You are fifty feet underground, in a hole that Victor Wu and I started to dig five years ago.

    Victor Wu. The man.

    Yes. Yes, the man whose memories are inside you.

And you are Andrew?
I am Andrew. Andrew Hutton.
Andrew at the bridge of the Lillian. Andrew in the field. I see.
Huh?
Hello, Andrew.
Hello. Yes. Hello, robot.

/\\//\\//

\>>>>>>>

The robot cuts into the earth. The giant rotor that is the robot's head turns at ten revolutions per second. Tungsten alloy blades set in a giant X grind through the contorted sedimentary striations of the peninsula. The robot presses hard, very hard. The rock crumble is sluiced down and onto a conveyor and passes through a mechanized laboratory, where it is analyzed and understood by the humans. The humans record the information, but the data stream from the laboratory has the smell of the rock, and this is what interests the robot. The robot knows the feel of the cut, the smell of the rock cake's give. This is right, what the robot was meant to do—yes, by the robot's creators, but there is also the man, the man in the interstices of the robot's mind, and this is what Victor Wu was meant to do also.

Ten feet behind the robot—and attached securely enough to make it practically an extension—is an enclosed dray so wound with organic polymer conduit sheathed in steel alloy that it looks like the wormy heart of a metal idol, pulled from the god after long decades of infestation. But the heart's sinuation quivers and throbs. The rock from the robot's incision is conveyed to the dray and funnels into it through a side hopper. The rock funnels in and from three squat valves, the heart streams three channels of viscous liquid—glassine—that coat the ceiling and walls of the tunnel the robot has formed with a seamless patina. The walls glow with a lustrous, adamantine purity, absolute, and take on the clear, plain color of the spray channels, which depend upon the composition of the slag.

Behind the dray, the robot directs its mobile unit—a new thing given by Andrew—which manipulates a hose with a pith of liquid hydrogen. The liquid hydrogen cools and ripens the walls. The hose also emanates from the dray. The dray itself is a fusion pile, and by girding the walls to a near diamond hardness, the tremendous pressure of the earth suspended above will not blow the tunnel out behind the robot, leaving it trapped and alone, miles into the crust.

Behind the robot, farther back in the tunnel, in an airconditioned transport, the service wagon, humans follow. The service wagon is attached to the robot by a power and service hitch, and there is constant radio contact as well. Sometimes the humans speak to the robot over the radio. But the robot knows what it is supposed to do. The idle chatter of the humans puzzles the robot, and while it listens to conversations in the transport, the robot seldom speaks. At night the robot backs out of the hole, detached from the service wagon, and spends its night aboveground. At first, the robot does not understand why it should do so, but Andrew has said that this is important, that a geologist must comprehend sky and weather, must understand the texture of surface as well as depth.

Besides you are so fast it only takes fifteen minutes to get you out when there is no rock for you to chew through, Andrew says. Even at sixty miles, even at the true mantle, your trip up will be quick.

Andrew lives inside the robot. He brings a cot, a small table and two folding chairs into the small control room where years before the engineers had entered and the robot had seen for the first time. There is a small, separate cavern the robot has carved out not far from the worksite. Andrew uses the area for storage, and at night the robot rolls down into this, the living area. Also at night, Andrew and the robot talk.

How was your day? Andrew might say. The robot did not know how to answer the first time he had asked, but Andrew had waited and now the robot can say . . . something. Not right, but something.

Smelly.

Smelly?

It was like summer in the field after a rain when there are so many odors.

Well, there was a hydrocarbon mass today. Very unexpected at such a depth. I'm sure it isn't organic, but it'll make a paper for somebody.

Yes, I swam through it and the tunnel is bigger there.

Gurney and the techs took over internal functions and drained it manually, so you didn't have to deal with it. Hell of a time directing it into the pile. Tremendous pressure.

The rock was very hard after that. It sang with the blades.

Sympathetic vibrations, maybe.

Maybe.

Andrew laughs. His voice is dry as powder, and his laughter crackles with a sharp report, very like the scrape of the robot's blades against dense, taut rock. The robot likes this laughter.

Every night when there is no rain, before sleep, Andrew goes outside for some minutes to name the stars. At these times, the robot's awareness is in the mu, the mobile unit, and the mu follows along behind Andrew, listening. Andrew points out the constellations. The robot can never remember their names, and only fleetingly sees the shapes that they are supposed to form. The robot does know the visible planets, though, which surprises Andrew. But the robot has watched them carefully for many years. They are the stars that change. Andrew laughs at the robot's poor recall of the other stars, and names them again.

There'll be meteors soon, he says one night. The Perseids start next week.

Do the stars really fall?

No. No, they never fall. Meteors are just . . . rock. Debris.

And there is no gravity up there? What is that like?

I don't know. I've never been into space. I would like to. As you get deeper, there will be less gravity pulling you down. The pressure will be greater and the rock will want to explode inward, so the cutting will be easier.

Andrew?

Hmm?

What will happen when I get to the bottom?

The bottom of what?

The mohole.

Andrew does not answer for a long while.

The earth is round, he finally says. There isn't any bottom.

>>>>>>>

On weekends, the robot does not dig, but wanders the land. With the mobile unit, the robot can range the nearby forest and mountains. The mu scrambles over deadfall that would daunt a man. Sometimes, the robot deliberately gets lost. The robot feels the fade of signal from the main housing back in the living area, where the robot's noetics physically remain, until there is a flurry of white noise and the fading of awareness and a click and the world snaps back to its grid as the robot's transmission toggles from line-of-sight microwave to modulated laser satellite relay. Or so Andrew had said when the robot asked about it.

The robot scrambles up hanging valleys into cerns and cirques with chilled, clear water where only cold things live. Or climbs up scree slopes, using the mu's sure footing, onto ridges and to highland plateaus above the tree line. At this elevation, snow remains all year and the mu spreads a wide base with its spidery legs and takes small steps when crossing.

The robot hears the low whistle of marmots, and sees occasional mountain goats munching, the last of their clan. They had been brought by humans in the 1800s, until they filled the Olympics with goat mass and threatened to eat the upper tundra to nub. Now helicopters dart them with birth control and they die without progeny. And the robot sees the wolves that have begun to return after their species' far northern retreat.

The robot is descending from a high pass near Sawtooth Ridge when a pack of five wolves flow over a rise. They are changing valleys, perhaps to find denser spreads of the small, black deer of the rain forest or even a sickly Roosevelt elk. Their leader is an old, graying dog with spit-matted hair and a torn ear. He looks up at the mu, starts, and the other wolves come up short, too. The robot ceases moving. The wolves sniff the air, but there is nothing—nothing living—to smell. But, with its chemical sensors, the robot smells *them*. They have the stink of mice, but tinged with a rangy fetor of meat and blood.

The other wolves do not appear as bedraggled as the leader. One, smaller, perhaps younger, whines, and the leader yips at this one and it is silent.

Then a cloud shadow moves up and over the pass, and courses darkly down into the adjacent valley. In that instant, the wolves course with the shadow, running with it down the coloir of the pass and disappearing from sight into the green of fir and hemlock a thousand feet below. The robot follows them in the infrared until their separate heats flux into the valley's general sink.

Still, the robot stands and remembers that this is not a new sight, that the man, Victor Wu, has seen wolves in the passes before. But the man has never smelled wolves, and smelling them now pleases the part of the robot that is becoming the man, that the man is becoming.

>>>>>>>

And the robot digs, and is glad to dig. The deep rock begins to take on a new smell. This bedrock has never seen the surface. It is the layered outgush of an ocean floor rift dating from the Triassic. The smell is like the scent of high passes and summits, although the robot cannot say how. And the rock chimes and hums when the robot cuts it; it does not break away uniformly, but there is an order to its coming apart that the robot feels. And so the robot knows when to expect a mass to break away, and can predict when the going will be harder.

The robot cannot explain this feeling to Andrew. Andrew has guessed that the skills of the man, Victor Wu, are integrating, and that his pattern recognition ability is enhancing the robot's own noetics. But the man is not separate. It is as if the man were one of the robot's threads or a cutter head—but more than that. The man is always *behind* the robot's thoughts, *within* them, never speaking but always *expressing*. Much more. The robot does not know how to say this to Andrew.

As the robot digs deeper, the rock grows faulty and unstable. The tunnel behind the robot is at risk of blowing out, and the robot takes time to excavate down fault lines, shore up weaknesses with double or triple diamond glass. If the tunnel did collapse, the robot would have to dig a slow circle trying to find an egress farther back. But the people in the service wagon would die, and this concerns the robot. Andrew would die.

The robot seldom speaks, but has come to know the voices of the technicians and graduate students in the transport. There is Gurney, the chief tech, who is a member of the Children of the Matriarch—a Mattie. The robot is surprised to learn that Gurney was in the field when the woman spoke, that Gurney remembers the robot.

Don't it give you the willies, a tech asks Gurney.

It's a machine, Gurney says. Depends on who's driving. Right now, I am. Anyway, the good Mother wants us to eat.

Many of the techs are not Matties, but descendants of the logging families that used to rule the peninsula and still permeate it. The Matties outnumber them in the cities, but up the dirt roads that spoke into the mountains, in dark, overhung coves and in the gashes of hidden valleys, the families that remain from that boom time eke out makework and garden a soil scraped clean of top humus by the last ice age and thinly mulched with the acid remains of evergreens.

Nothing grows goddamn much or goddamn right out here, says a tech.

The Matties and the loggers heatedly discuss politics and appear close to fighting at times, but the robot cannot understand any of this. It thinks of the man who was killed on the stone steps, and the man who killed him. The robot does not understand at all.

The grad students and the Matties are more comfortable around one another. The robot feels a warmth toward the graduate students that is certainly from the man. Yet their speech patterns are different from the techs', and the robot has difficulty understanding them at times. The meanings of their words shine like the moon behind a cloud, but the robot cannot think to the way around to them. Always they recede, and the robot is impatient. Victor Wu's instincts are stronger in the robot than is his knowledge. Andrew has said that this is to be expected and that any computer of sufficient size can learn words, but *you* can learn intuition. Still the robot *should* know what the students are discussing, and finds the incomprehension irritating.

But always the rock to return to, and the certainty that rock was what the robot was made for, and what the robot was born and bred for, and, in the end, that is enough.

>>>>>>>

One day in the following spring, at a critical juncture down in the mohole, Gurney does not show up for work and the digging is halted.

The referendum passed, one of the grad students says, and there's fighting in Forks and a Mattie got killed in Port Angeles, it looks like.

Andrew gives the robot the day off and, to the robot's delight, he and the mu go for a long walk along the Quinault. Andrew seems sad, and the robot says nothing for a long while. The robot wants to speak, but doesn't know what to say to Andrew.

It's not the politics, Andrew finally says. The damn Matties got their Protectorate fair and square with the referendum. But you get the feeling they'd *take* it if they hadn't of.

Hadn't of what?

Won the vote. There's something about Gurney and them, the ones that I've met. I care about the same things they claim to. I don't know. Something else again.

Andrew, I don't understand.

They spend a lot of time worrying about whether everybody else believes the same way they do.

The river rushes against cliff and turns through a stand of white birch. The robot stops the mu. The robot is captivated by the play of the light on the water, the silver reflection of the sun, turning the clear water to opaque and viscous lead, then, just as suddenly, when a cloud passes, back to happy water once again.

It doesn't really change, does it?

What?

The water. The way the light's there, and isn't, then is.

Andrew rubs his eyes. He gazes out over the water. You are doing very well with your contractions, he says.

You were right that I should stop thinking about them and they would flow more easily. Do you think it is Victor Wu's knowledge surfacing, or my own practice?

I don't know. Both.

Yes, both.

The trail leads through a marsh, and Andrew struggles to find a dry path. The robot extends the mu's footpads; each folds out as if it were an umbrella, and the mu seems to hover over the mud, the weight is distributed so well.

Thank you for the mobile unit, the robot tells Andrew. I really like using it.

It was necessary for the dig. That's where most of the first grant money went. Robot, I have to tell you something.

Andrew stops, balancing on a clump of rotten log.

You have to tell *me* something, Andrew?

Yes. Someone is coming. She phoned yesterday. All this brouhaha over the protectorate referendum is attracting attention all around the world. She's going to shoot a documentary. She's coming in a week. She's bringing a crew and she'll be staying in Port Townsend at first. I just thought you might. Want.

Laramie. Laramie is coming.

That's right, robot. Laramie is coming home for a while. She doesn't know how long.

For the first time ever, the robot feels the man, the man Victor Wu, as a movement, a distinct movement of joy inside him. Little Bulge. Coming home. The robot tries to remember Laramie's face, but cannot. Just a blur of darkness and bright flush. Always rushing and doing. And the camera. The robot can remember Laramie's camera far better than her face.

Andrew begins to walk again. I didn't tell her about you, robot. I didn't tell her about her father being part of you.

Laramie does not know?

No. She knows about the noetics, of course, but not how I've used them. I didn't strictly need her permission to do it.

Do you think she will hate me?

No. Of course not. I don't know. I don't know her anymore.

Should we tell her about me? At this thought the robot feels fearful and sad. But what matters is what is best for Little Bulge.

Of course we should. It's only right. Dammit, robot, I don't know how I feel about this. I don't know how much you knew about it or how much you realized, the Victor Wu part of you, I mean. Laramie and I—we didn't part on the best of terms.

I don't remember. I remember the bridge at the Lillian once. You didn't like her?

Of course I liked her. I love her. That was the problem. She was impetuous. She's opportunistic, dammit. Look at her pouncing on this thing. She called me a stick in the mud. I guess she was right. She called me a sour cynic who was fifty years old the day he turned twenty-five. We haven't spoken in some time.

I don't understand.

Robot. Victor. You never had a clue, I don't think.

I am not Victor.

I know that. I know that. Still, I always thought he suspected. It was so obvious, and he was so brilliant in other ways.

Andrew and the robot arrive back at the river. The robot thinks about it and realizes that they'd been traversing an oxbow swamp, made from spring overflows at the melting of the snow. At the river, they pick up a trail, once solid and well traveled, now overgrown and ill kept for two seasons. The Forest Service has been officially withdrawn at the Mattie's request, Andrew tells the robot. President Booth responded to political pressure from Mother Agatha and the Matties.

The goddamn world is going back to tribes. The country's going to hell. And taking my funding with it. And now there's a skeleton crew for the Park Service, even, over at the Ho. I had a lot of friends who got fired or reassigned to the Statue of Liberty or some shit. Something else, too. I think some of them haven't left.

What do you mean haven't left?

Haven't left.

> > > > > > >

The trail diverges from the river, winds over a rise, then back down to the water again. A side trail leads to a peninsula and a wooden trail shelter, enclosed on three sides. Andrew takes a lunch from his daypack and eats a sandwich, while the robot looks for quartzite along the river bank. The robot has become an expert in spotting a crystal's sparkle and extracting it from the mud or silt of scree with which it has been chipped away and washed downstream from pressurized veins in the heart of the mountains. This day, the robot finds three crystals, one as cylindrical and as long as a fingernail. The robot brings them to Andrew, back at the trail shelter.

Nice. Trace of something here. Blue? Manganese maybe, I don't know. I like the ones with impurities better.

I do, too.

Andrew puts the crystals in an empty film canister and stows them in his daypack.

I was here at the turn of the century, he says. It was June and there was a terrible storm. All night long I heard crashing and booming like the world was coming to an end. Next morning, the whole forest looked like a war zone.

The robot does not know what a war zone looks like, but says nothing.

And all that morning, trees kept falling. If I hadn't camped out here on the end of the peninsula, one of those trees would have fallen on me, smashed me flat. Killed by old growth. God, that'd probably thrill a Mattie to death just thinking about it.

Isn't that a sour and cynical thing to say, Andrew?

He smiles. The robot is glad that it has found a way to make Andrew smile.

>>>>>>>

Gurney does not show up for work the next day, and Andrew gives his crew the week off. The men who are from logging families demand that they be paid, that Codependence Day, the first anniversary of the Protectorate's founding, means nothing to them. The robot listens to the discussion and hears many terms that are incomprehensible, abstract. There are times the robot wishes that Victor Wu were directly accessible. Victor could at least explain what humans argued about, if not the reasons why they argued in the first place.

The robot spends the day traveling in the mu, searching for crystals and collecting mushrooms up a stream that flows into the Quinault, near where it passes beneath Low Divide. Andrew is gone for the day, arranging supplies and making sure the dig's legal work is in order, whatever that may mean, under new Protectorate regulations. When he returns in the evening, he has received no assurances and is unhappy. The robot waits for him to have a cup of tea and to take off his shoes, then speaks.

Andrew?

Yes. What?

Are you all right?

Huh? Oh, I'm fine. It's just today. What is it, robot?

I thought of something today, when I was looking at a map so that I could take the mu to where I wanted to go.

What did you think of? Andrew speaks in a monotone voice and does not seem very interested. He sips his tea.

I realized that I can read.

Of course you can. Glotworks has a reading module as part of the software.

No. I mean, could I read?

I don't follow you.

A book.

Could you read a book?

Andrew is sitting up now. He stares at the internal monitor that is also one of the robot's eyes.

Yes. One of yours, perhaps. Which would you recommend?

The books are kept nearby, in a hermetic box in the room the robot occupies during off hours.

Well. Let me. Hmm. Most of them are geology texts.

Should I read a geology text?

Well, sure. Why not?

Can I get one now, with the mu?

Of course. Go ahead. Try the Owsley. It's about the most exciting of the lot. It's about the Alvarez event and the search for the big caldera. It's a synthesis of other works, but brilliant, brilliant. Pretty much confirms the meteor theory, and gives a good argument for a Yucatan crash site. Made a big sensation in '04.

The robot switches its awareness to the mu and picks out the book. It reads the first paragraph, then comes back inside the housing, back to the place where Andrew lives.

Andrew?

Yes.

What are dinosaurs?

>>>>>>>

Summer days lengthen, and Andrew often goes to town—to Port Angeles or Port Townsend, and once making the trek around the peninsula to Forks—all to sort out legal details for the mohole dig. From each of these trips, he returns with a book for the robot. The first book is a *Webster's Dictionary,* on bubble-card. Andrew plugs the card into a slot and the robot begins to read the dictionary. The robot finishes with a page of A, then scrolls through the remainder of the book. Here are all the words. Here are all the words in the language. All the robot has to do is look them up and remember them. The robot spends a happy day reading words, one at a time.

The next day, Andrew returns with the poems of Robert Frost. The robot pages through the book using the mu, accessing the dictionary card to find words that it does not know. The first word the robot looks up is "poem."

>>>>>

After a week, Gurney returns to work, and the robot digs once again. The days pass, and the mohole twists deeper, like a coiled spring being driven into the earth. It only deviates from a curving downward path when the robot encounters fault lines or softnesses whose weakness the robot's cutters can exploit. But, in general, the hole descends in a loose spiral.

Andrew is anxious, and pushes everyone harder than before. Yet Andrew himself works the hardest of all, poring over data, planning routing, driving to meetings in Forks and Port Angeles. He is often not in bed before one or two in the morning.

The robot fills the time with reading. There are so many books—more than the robot ever imagined. And then the robot discovers Andrew's record collection, all on two bubble-cards carelessly thrown in with all the technical manuals and geology texts. For the first time since the summer when the teenagers came and plugged into the robot and had their parties, the robot listens to music.

What the robot loves most, though, is poetry. Beginning with Robert Frost, the robot reads poet after poet. At first, there are so many new words to look up that the robot often loses the thread of what the poem is about in a morass of details and definitions. But gradually, the poems begin to make more sense. There is a Saturday morning when, while diligently working through an Emily Dickinson poem, the robot understands.

> *There's a certain slant of light*
> *On winter afternoons,*
> *That oppresses, like the weight*
> *of cathedral tunes.*
>
> *Heavenly hurt it gives us;*
> *We can find no scar*
> *But internal difference*
> *Where the meanings are.*

The robot has never seen a cathedral, but that does not matter. The robot realizes that it has seen this light, in the deep forest, among the three-hundred-year-old trees. It's *thick*, the robot thinks. That's what Emily Dickinson is talking about. Thick light. Light that makes the robot thread softly through the twilight, with the mu's pads fully extended. Light that, for no reason the robot can name, is frightening and beautiful all at once.

From that moment on, the robot begins to grasp most poems it reads, or, if not, at least to feel *something* after reading them, something that was not inside the robot's mind before—something the robot had not felt before—but knows, as if the feeling were an old friend that the robot recognized after many years of separation.

The robot does not particularly care whether or not the feelings are right and true for everyone else. For humans. But sometimes the robot wonders. After reading a fair number of poems, the robot delves into criticism, but the words are too abstract and too connected to humans and cities and other things that the robot has no experience of, and so the robot puts aside the books of criticism for the time being, and concentrates on the poetry itself, which the robot does not have the same trouble with.

The robot finds that it most enjoys poetry that is newer, even though Andrew is disbelieving when the robot tells him of this. After a time, poetry is no longer a mass, and the robot begins to pick out individual voices whose connotations are more pleasing than the others.

I like William Stafford better than Howard Nemerov, the robot says to Andrew one evening.

You like him better?

Yes.

Andrew laughs. Neither one of them was in the canon when I was in school.

Do you think it funny that I used the word *like?*

Yes, I suppose so.

I *do* like things, at least according to the Turing test. Poetry goes into me, and what comes out feels like liking to me.

It satisfies the criteria of appearances.

Yes, I suppose that is the way to say it.

Where have you heard about the Turing test?

I read it in a book about robots.

The robot reads to Andrew a William Stafford poem about a deer that has been killed on a road. Andrew smiles at the same lines that had moved the robot.

You pass the Turing test, too, the robot says.

Andrew laughs harder still.

>>>>>

The robot is digging entirely through basalt flow now, layer upon layer.

It's the bottom of the raft, Andrew says. It is dense, but the plates are as light as ocean froth compared to what's under them. Or so we think.

The temperature increases exponentially, and the humans in the support wagon would be killed instantly if they did not have nuclear-powered air conditioners.

The robot does not become bored at the sameness of the rock, but finds a comfort in the steady digging, a *rhythm,* as the robot comes to call this feeling. Not the rhythm of most music, or the beat of the language in poetry—all of these the robot identifies with humans, for when they arise, humans have been doing the creating—but a new rhythm, which is neither the whine of the robot's machinery nor the crush and crumble of the rock, nor the supersonic screech of the pile making diamond glass from the rock's ashes. Instead, it is the combination of these things with the poetry, with the memories of the field and the forest.

So it is one day that the robot experiences a different rhythm, a different sound, and realizes that this rhythm is not the robot's own, and does not belong to the humans. At first, it is incomprehensible, like distant music, or the faded edges of reception just before a comlink relays to satellite or to ground tower. The robot wonders if the rhythm, the sound, is imaginary. But it continues, and seems to grow day by day in increments almost too small to notice, until it is definitely, definitely *there,* but *where,* the robot cannot say. *In the rock.* That is the only way of putting it, but says nothing.

Andrew does not know what it could be. So there is nothing to do but note it, and go on digging.

>>>>>

The robot begins to read fiction. But the feelings, the resonances and depths of the poetry, are not so much present in prose. There is the problem of knowing what the author might be talking about, since the robot's only experience living in the human world is the field and now the dig. Dickens leaves the robot stunned and wondering, and after a week attempting *Oliver Twist,* the robot must put the book aside until the situations and characters become clearer. Curiously, the robot finds that Jane Austen's novels are comprehensible and enjoyable, although the life of English country gentry is as close to the robot as the life of a newt under a creek stone. The robot is filled with relief when Emma finally ceases her endless machinations and realizes her love for Knightley. It is as if some clogged line in the robot's hydraulics had a sudden release of pressure or rock that had long been hard and tough became easy to move through.

For some time, the robot does not read books that were written closer to the present, for the robot wants to understand the present most of all, and in reading them now, the robot thinks, much would go unnoticed.

You can always reread them later, Andrew says. Just because you know the plot of something doesn't mean it isn't worth going through again, even though sometimes it does mean that.

I know that, the robot says. That is not what I'm worried about.

Then what are you worried about?

The old books get looser, the farther back in time they go,

like string that's played out. The new ones are bunched and it's harder to see all of them.

What?

For the first time, the robot feels something that either cannot be communicated or, nearly as unbelievable, that Andrew cannot understand. Andrew is a scientist. The robot will never be a scientist.

>>>>>

Two months after the robot has walked along the Quinault with Andrew, it is July, and Andrew tells the robot that Laramie will visit over the weekend.

The robot is at first excited and thinks of things to ask her. There are so many memories of Laramie, but so much is blurred, unconnected. And there are things the robot wishes to tell her, new things about the land that Victor never knew. So much has happened. The robot imagines long conversations between them, perhaps walking in the woods together once again.

*Andrew tells me that you may not be happy with the enthalpic impression of your father being downloaded into me. No, that wouldn't be the way to say it. But getting too metaphorical might upset her, remind her of ghosts. Of Victor Wu's death.*

*No. That's all right. Go on, says the imaginary Laramie.*

*Well, I don't know what to tell you. I remember you, Laramie. I remember you and I would be lying if I didn't say that your being here profoundly affects me.*

*I can't say how I feel about this, robot. What should I call you, robot?*

But just as quickly, the robot puts aside such hopes. I am a robot, all of metal and ceramics. I am not Laramie's father. There are only vague memories, and that was another life. She may not even speak to me. I am a ghost to her. Worse than a ghost, a twisted reflection. She'll hate me for what has happened to her father. And again the robot imagines Laramie's disdain, as just and foreseeable as the man's death in "To Build a Fire," but cold in that way, too.

Finally, the robot resolves not to think any more of it. But while Andrew sleeps on the Friday night before Laramie's visit, the robot inhabits the mu, and goes roaming through trackless woods, along crisscrossed deadfall and up creeks, for at least a hundred miles. Yet when the mu returns to the living area, the robot can only remember shadows and dark waters, and, if asked, could not trace on a map where the mu has been.

Laramie arrives at eleven in the morning. She drives a red hum-vee. Andrew and the robot, in the mu, step out of their cavern's entrance to greet her. Laramie steps out. She is wearing sunglasses. She takes a quick look at them, then turns back to the hum-vee and, with a practiced jerk, pulls out her old Scoopic. The robot suddenly remembers the squat lines of the camera. Victor bought the Scoopic for her, along with twelve cans of film. It was her first 16-millimeter, and had set him back a good three months' wages. Laramie had shot up seven rolls within a week, and that was when Victor discovered that there would be fees for *developing,* as well.

Andrew steps forward, and so does Laramie. The robot, feeling shy, hangs back in the mu. Andrew and Laramie do not meet, but stay several paces apart.

So, she says. It is her voice. Clear as day.

Yep. This is it.

Well, looks . . . nice. Is this?

Yes, the robot. This is the mobile unit. The robot is inside, really. Well, sort of. We're going *inside* the robot.

No words for a moment. Still, they move no closer.

Well, then. Let's go inside the robot.

Laramie, inside the protecting ribwork of the robot. She is safe. Nothing will harm you here, Little Bulge. But the robot calms such thoughts. She takes one of the two chairs that are around Andrew's work and eating table in the control room. Abide, the robot thinks. Let her abide for a while.

Do you want tea? I can make you tea.

Yes. I drink herb tea.

Um. Don't have any.

Water?

Yes, water we have.

L.A.'s tastes like sludge.

No wonder. They're even tapping Oregon now.

Really? I believe it.

Andrew pours water for Laramie in a metal cup. He puts more water on a hot plate that sits on top of a monitor, and heats the water for tea. Where have you been, he says.

Port Townsend. Doing background and logistics. My sound guy's laying down local tone and getting wild effects.

Wild?

Unsynched, that's all it means.

I see.

Using Seattle labs is going to be a bitch. The Matties have set up goddamn border crossings.

Tell me about it.

Andrew's water boils and he fills another cup with it, then hunts for a teabag in a cabinet.

You left them on the table, the robot says.

Laramie gasps, sits up in her chair sharply, then relaxes once again. That was the robot, she says.

Yes. Thank you, robot. Andrew finds the box of teabags among a clutter of instruments.

Do you. Do you call the robot anything?

Hmm. Not really.

Just call me robot, the robot says. I'm thinking of a name for myself, but I haven't come up with one yet.

Well, then. Robot.

Andrew makes his tea, and they talk more of logistics and the political situation on the peninsula. The robot feels a tenseness between them, or at least in Andrew. His questions and replies are even more terse than usual. The robot doubts Victor Wu would have noticed. Thinking this saddens the robot. More proof that the robot is not Victor Wu, and so can have no claim on Laramie's affection.

The robot listens to Laramie. Since she and Andrew are speaking of things that the robot knows little about, the robot concentrates on her specific words, on her manner of expression.

Lens. Clearness in the world. Sky. Vision. Spread. Range. Watershed.

I thought for two weeks about color or black and white, Laramie says. I don't like colors except for the world's colors that are underneath the ones on film, the ones we see.

I don't follow, Andrew says. The robot has never thought of colors this way, but resolves to spend a day banding out frequencies and only observing intensities of black and white tones.

I'll have more water, if you don't mind. This is clear. L.A. water is thick as sludge and I don't like it.

After three hours, Laramie leaves, with promises to return and film the site as part of her documentary.

Robot?

Yes.

Do you think I might interview you? I guess if we could use the mobile unit, that would look better on film. More action. Do you ever come out of here?

Every day during the week, to work in the dig.

Well, then. That must be quite a sight. Maybe I can get that.

Of course you can. That would be fine.

Well. Then.

She says good-bye to Andrew, and with her Scoopic, unused but always present, gets back into the red hum-vee, crusted with a layer of settled road dust, and turns around in the dirt road that ends at the living area. More dust rises; Laramie departs. Andrew coughs, brushes dust from his arms. He looks at the mu, shakes his head, but says nothing. He goes back in and makes a third cup of tea.

With the mu, the robot follows easily behind the hum-vee, even though Laramie is driving very fast. The robot follows the billowing cloud of dust for twenty-four miles—until the hum-vee turns onto the asphalt and heads north toward Port Townsend.

>>>>>

The robot spends the next day, Sunday, away from books. The robot takes advantage of the melting away of the high snows and takes the mu up ridges where before there was no footing or a threat of avalanche. The mu skirts along the Bailey Divide with a sure movement, above the tree line and in rolling tundra meadow. Marmots are here, and they squeak and whistle from under big rocks. Pacas have divided the land into separate kingdoms, each to a paca, and they call out their territory over and over, until their voices attract the wolves.

This is what the robot has been waiting for. The mu sits still by a still lake, as motionless as any other thing that is not alive can be. The wolves come slinking, low and mean, their heat traces preceding and hovering over them like a scudding cloud. Again, there are five, with an old gray leader, his left ear bent, torn and ragged, like a leaf eaten by caterpillars. Swiftly, they are upon the pacas, chasing the little rodents, yipping, cutting them off from their burrows, gobbling one or two down for every ten that escape. Then the gray leader has had enough to eat. He raises up his head and, instantly, the others heed him. Off they run, as silent and warm as they had come, but now followed by a robot.

Down the tundra meadow of the divide, through boulder shadows and over sprays of tiny wildflowers nestled in the green, the wolves themselves shadows, with the robot another shadow, down, down the greening land. Into the woods, along game trails the robot can barely discern, moving generally north, generally north, the mu barely keeping pace with the advancing wolves, the pace growing steady, monotonous even to the robot, until suddenly the gray leader pulls up, sniffs the air. The robot also comes to a standstill some hundred feet behind the pack. If they have noticed the robot, they give no sign. Instead, it is a living smell that the gray leader has detected, or so the robot thinks, for the wolves, whining, fall into a V-shape behind the leader. The wolves' muscles tense with a new and directed purpose.

And they spring off in another direction than the one they had been traveling, now angling west, over ridges, against the grain of the wheel-spoke mountains. The robot follows. Up another ridge, then down its spine, around a corner cliff of flaking sedimentary stone, and into a little cove. They strike a road, a human-made track, and run along its edge, carefully close to the flanking brush and woodland. Winding road, and the going is easier for wolves and mu. In fact, the robot could easily overtake the wolves now, and must gauge how much to hold back to avoid overrunning them.

The track becomes thin, just wide enough for a vehicle going one way, with plenty of swishing against branches along the way. Ahead, a house, a little clapboard affair, painted once, perhaps, blue, or the blue-green tint may be only mold over bare wood. The ceiling is shingled half with asbestos shakes and half with tin sheeting. Beside the house is a satellite dish, its lower hemisphere greened over with algae. There is an old pickup truck parked at road's end. The road is muddy here from a recent rain, and the tire markings of another vehicle, now gone, cross the top of the pickup's own tracks. All is silent.

Instead of giving the house a wide berth, the gray leader stops at the top of the short walkway that leads to the front door. Again, he sniffs for scent, circling, whining. There is only a moment of hesitation, and he snakes up the walkway and slinks to the door. The door hangs open. The other wolves follow several paces back. Another hesitation at the door, then the gray leader slips over the threshold and inside. Even with their leader gone into the house, the other wolves hang back, back from this thing that has for so long meant pain or death to them and their kind. After a long while, the gray leader returns to the door, yips contemptuously, and, one by one, the other wolves go inside.

The robot quietly pads to the door. Inside is dark, and the robot's optics take a moment to iris to the proper aperture. There is a great deal of the color red in the house's little living room. The robot scans the room, tries to resolve a pattern out of something that is unfamiliar. The robot has never seen inside a real human dwelling before. But Victor Wu has. The wolves are worrying at something.

The wolves are chewing on the remains of a child.

Without thinking, the robot scampers into the room. The mu is a bit too large for the narrow door and, without the robot's noticing, it tears apart the doorframe as it enters. The wolves look up from what they are doing.

Wolves and robot stare at one another.

The robot adjusts the main camera housing to take them all in, and at the slight birring noise of the servos, the gray leader bristles and growls. The mu takes a step farther into the room, filling half the room. It knocks over a small table, with a shadeless lamp upon it. Both the bulb and the ceramic lamp casing shatter.

I don't want to hurt you, but you must leave the child alone, the robot says.

At the sound of what they take to be a human voice, the wolves spring into a flurry of action. The gray leader stalks forward, teeth bared, while the others in the pack mill like creek fish behind him. They are searching for an exit. The small, young one finds that a living room window is open. With a short hop from a couch, the wolf is outside. The others follow, one by one, while the gray leader attempts to hold the robot at bay. The robot does not move, but lets the wolves depart. Finally, the gray leader sees from the corner of his eye that the other wolves have escaped. Still, he cannot help but risk one feint at the robot. The robot does not move. The gray leader, bolder, quickly jumps toward the robot and locks his jaws on the robot's forward leg. The teeth close on blue steel. The gray leader shakes. There is no moving the robot.

In surprise and agitation, the wolf backs up, barks three times.

I'm sorry to embarrass you. You'd better go.

The wolf does just that, turning tail and bounding through the open window without even using the living room couch as a launch point. The robot gazes around the silent room.

There is a dead family here.

An adult male, the father, is on one side of the couch, facing a television. Part of his neck and his entire chest are torn open in a gaping bloody patch. Twisted organs glint within. The television is off. Huddled in a corner is the mother and a young boy. Their blood splatters an entire wall of the living room. A shotgun, the robot decides. First the man was shot, and then the mother with her children all at once, with several blasts from a shotgun. There are pepper marks in the wall from stray shot. Yes, the killing was done with a shotgun. The wolves must have dragged one child away from the mother. The robot sees that it is a little girl. The mother's other child, an older boy and a bit large for even a large wolf to handle, is still by his mother, partially blown into his mother's opened body.

The blood on the walls and floor has begun to dry and form into curling flakes that are brown and thin and look like tiny autumn leaves. There are also bits of skin and bone on the wall.

The robot stares at the little girl. Her eyes are, mercifully, closed, but her mouth is pulled open and her teeth, still baby teeth, exposed. This was perhaps caused by her stiffening facial muscles. Or she may have died with such an expression of pain. The robot cannot tell. The girl wears a blue dress that is now tatters around her tattered, small body. One foot has been gnawed, but on the other is a dirty yellow flipflop sandal.

The robot feels one of the legs of the mu jerk spasmodically. Then the other jerks, without the robot wishing it to do so. The robot stares at the young girl and jitters and shakes for a long time. This is the way the robot cries.

/\\//\//
>>>>>>>>>>>

Deeper in the earth, very deep now, and the rock, under megatons of pressure, explodes with a nuclear ferocity as the robot cuts away. For the past week the robot has thought constantly of the dead logger family, of the little dead girl. The robot has tried to remember the color of the girl's hair but cannot, and for some reason this greatly troubles the robot.

One evening, after a sixteen-hour workday, the robot dims the lights for Andrew. Outside the digger's main body, but still in the home cave, the robot inhabits the mu. The robot takes pen and paper in the dexterous manipulators of the mu and begins to write a description of the little girl. Not as she was, twisted and dead, but of how she might have been before.

The robot told Andrew about the family, and Andrew called the authorities, being careful to keep the robot out of his report.

They'll disassemble you if they find out, Andrew said to the robot. At least in the United States, they'd be legally *required* to do it. A robot witness testifying in court has to be *verified*. That means your components have to be individually examined for tampering after the testimony. God knows what the Protectorate will want to do to your insides.

There are accounts in the newspapers of the killing. The Sheriff's Department claims to be bewildered, but the robot overhears the technicians who come from logger families muttering that the Matties now own the cops, and that everybody knew who was behind the murders, if not who actually pulled the trigger. And the Matties who worked under Andrew, led by Gurney, spoke in low tones of justice and revenge for the killings in Port Townsend on Codependence Day.

I am a witness, the robot thinks. But of what?

>>>>>>>>>>

Andrew?

Yes.

Are you tired?

Yes. What is it?

She would have grown up to be part of the loggers, so killing her makes a kind of sense.

The little girl?

The Matties and the people who used to be loggers hate each other. And they can't help the way they are because they are like stones in sediment that's been laid down long before, and the hatred shapes them to itself, like a syncline or an anticline. So that there have to be new conditions brought about to change the lay of the sediment—you can't change the rocks.

I don't know about that. People are not rocks.

So if she wasn't killed out of an ignorant mistake, then I don't understand why.

I don't either, robot.

Why do you think?

I don't know, I said, I don't know. There isn't any good reason for it. There is something dark in this world that knows what it's doing.

Is it evil?

There is evil in the world. All the knowledge in the world won't burn it away.

How do you know?

I don't. I told you, I don't. I look at rocks. I don't have very many theories.

But.

Yes?

But you think it knows?

I think the evil knows what it's doing. Look at us in this goddamn century, all going back to hatred and tribes. You can't explain it with economics or cultural semantics or any system at all. Evil and plain meanness is what it is.

Andrew, it's not right for her to die. She hadn't lived long enough to see very many things and to have very many feelings. Those were stolen from her.

That's what murderers steal.

The future?

Yes. Even when you're old, it still isn't right.

Yes. I can see that. It's clear to me.

Well. Then.

I'll turn down the lights.

Well. Goodnight.

Brown.

What?

Her hair was dark brown.

>>>>>>>>>>

And the robot digs deeper and deeper, approaching the Mohorovičic layer, with the true mantle not far beneath, seething, waiting, as it had waited for four billion years, would wait should this attempt fail, should all attempts fail. And again, the foreign rhythm appears, hums along with the glade and bale of the robot's cutting, but distinct from it, distinct from the robot and all human-made things.

What is it? Andrew does not know. But there is something

at the edge of the robot's consciousness, at the edge of Victor Wu's unconscious presence, that *does* know, that hears something familiar, like a whisper when the words are lost, but the meaning remains.

One day, the alien rhythm is louder than ever, and for a fleeting moment, the robot recognizes it.

Strong harmonies from the depths of the planet. Maude under the full moon. Magmas rising.

*Victor, you can feel it. How can you feel it?*

I don't know, Maude, the robot thinks. Maude among the instruments. I remember, thinks the robot, I remember what it felt like to walk the earth and let it show itself to me. There is a showing. Something is showing itself. Something is being revealed. Just as the Saint Helens eruption was a revelation, with portents, with auguries that were plain to a man who cared for the earth.

Something knows we're here, the robot tells Andrew one night.

Andrew is tired from a half day underground, and the afternoon spent explaining the dig to yet another Mattie committee in Port Angeles, but he listens to what the robot has to say.

What? How can you know?

I do, though.

Then you do. Victor would know.

Andrew shucks the soft-sole walking shoes he wears in the city, and climbs onto the little cot inside the robot.

Everyone else wants me to stop digging. Do you want to stop digging?

No, Andrew.

Then what shall we do about it?

Listen, says the robot. Listen. But Andrew has fallen asleep and does not hear. The robot dims the lights inside, adjusts the temperature for Andrew, then goes out into the mu to read.

>>>>>>>>>>

The robot listens. The rhythm grows stronger, and now there are variations, windings among the background vibration that is the feedback from the robot's own cutting of the rock and thumping against the Earth's insides. It is like a song, but not a song.

There and there, the robot tells Andrew, but Andrew cannot hear it, encased as he is in the service wagon, and he cannot detect the rhythm on his many instruments.

I believe you, Andrew says, but I simply can't find it.

The robot considers saying no more. What if Andrew really came to doubt the robot's sanity? Would that not mean powering down, rebooting? Or perhaps never coming back up again? Dying? Andrew will not kill me, the robot thinks. And I will say what it is I hear.

And slowly, day after day, the rhythm develops into an . . . other. The robot is not sure how else to think about it. It is the feeling that a—*one*—someone, is here, even when no one is in view. It is a sense of *presence* that the robot feels. The robot doesn't *know*. Andrew cannot discover a way of knowing. But the feeling is not some erratic wiring, or even the robot's developing imagination. It is either a madness or it is a real presence.

And I am not crazy.

Which is a sure sign of madness. Andrew laughs his dry laugh.

Yet again, because of Victor Wu, because Andrew has come to trust the robot in all other things, he takes the robot seriously. In the few spare moments he has for experiments not directly related to the mantle goal, Andrew and a graduate student make coding modifications to the robot's language software.

We're wiring perfect pitch into you, the graduate student, Samantha, says, to go along with your ear for good music. Samantha explains more of what she is doing, but the robot does not follow. Samantha understands the robot's mechanism as a surgeon might a human being's. As she works at an internal keyboard, she tells the robot of her own past, but again the robot has trouble understanding.

I grew up in virtual. I was practically born on the Internet. But by god I'm going to die in the forest, Samantha tells the robot. That's why most of us are out here with Dr. Hutton, she says.

There is only a trace of a smile on Andrew's face, but the robot knows him well enough now to see it.

Well, this sure as hell ain't virtual, he says.

>>>>>>>>>>

Laramie returns. She has not called Andrew. One Saturday the hum-vee crackles down the dirt and gravel road to the living area, and Laramie has come back. Andrew is away at a meeting, and at first the robot is flustered and bewildered as to what to do. The robot has been reading, with a mind still half in the book.

Laramie pulls out her camera and some sound equipment and comes to the entrance to the living cavern. The robot, in the mu, meets her and invites her inside. That much the robot is able to manage.

I'm sorry I didn't clear my visit with Andrew first but you said it would be all right.

It is all right.

I thought it would be. Do you mind if I record this?

No. I keep something like a journal myself. Would you care for some tea? Andrew bought some herbal tea after your last visit.

The robot thinks that the words sound stiff and overly formal, but Laramie says yes, and settles down at the interior table to set up her equipment. There is a kettle on the hot plate, and the robot turns on the burner. Laramie takes a microphone from a vinyl case and unwinds its cord. The robot watches her, watches Laramie's hands move. Her fingers are as long as Maude's.

The robot suddenly realizes there may be no water in the kettle. But there is steam rising from around the lid—which means that there is water and that the water is hot enough to drink.

Laramie. May I call you Laramie?

Sure. Of course.

I cannot make your tea.

What? That's fine, then. I'm fine.

No. I mean that it's difficult for me to get the mu inside.

I don't understand.

I'm sorry. I mean the mobile unit. If you don't mind, you can get a cup and a teabag out of the cupboard. The water is ready.

Laramie sets the microphone down, gazes around the room.

Is it in that cupboard?

Yes. Bottom shelf.

Laramie gets the cup and tea, then pours some water. Andrew is a careful pourer, but Laramie spatters droplets on the hot burner and they sizzle as they evaporate. She takes her tea back to the table. She jacks the microphone into a small tape recorder that is black with white letters that say Sony. From the recorder, she runs a lead to the Scoopic 16-millimeter camera.

Where's that adapter? Oh. There. I had this Scoopic souped up a little, by the way, since my father. Since I got it. Has a GOES chip. Uplinks and downlinks with the Sony. I could record you in Singapore, and not get a frame of drift. But I'm not a pro at this. My sound tech bugged out on me last week. That's one reason it's taken me a while to get back over here. He got scared after the riot. Let me voice-slate and we'll be ready.

Laramie?

Hmm?

Are you safe? I mean, where you are staying in Port Townsend—is it guarded in any way?

No. I'm fine. It's the loggers and the Matties who want to kill one another.

They might mistake you for a logger. You spent a lot of time in the bush.

At this expression, which is Victor Wu's, Laramie looks up. She finds nothing to look at, and turns her gaze back down, to the Sony.

I'm as safe as can be expected.

Be careful, Laramie.

You're not my father.

I know that. But I would be pleased if you would be careful.

All right. I'll keep that in mind. Laramide productions-skykomish-eight-three-fourteen-roll-eleven. Robot, have you decided yet on a name?

Not yet.

She raises the camera, looks around through the viewfinder, and finally chooses a bank of monitors to aim it at.

What do you think about?

Pardon?

What do you think about, robot?

I'm not HAL, Laramie.

What?

You know what I mean. You saw that movie many times. Your question sounds snide to me, as if it were a foregone conclusion that I don't *really* think. You don't just throw a question like that at me. It would be better to lead up to it. I don't have to justify my existence to anyone, and I don't particularly like to fawn on human beings. I feel that it is degrading to them.

You sound like Andrew is what you sound like.

That's quite possible. I spend a lot of time with him.

Well. So. Maybe that wasn't the best first question. Maybe you could tell me about your work.

The robot explains the dig, and what it might mean to science.

But I don't know a great deal about that. At least, I don't think about it often.

What really matters to you, then?

The digging. The getting there. The way the rock is. All igneous and thick, but there are different regions.

Like swimming in a lake.

Yes. I imagine you're right. It's very hard to talk about, the feeling I have.

What feeling?

That. I don't know. It is hard to say. I could. I could take you there.

Take me where? Down there?

Yes. Down there.

Now? You mean now?

No. I'd have to talk to Andrew about doing so.

Of course. Do you think he'd let me?

I would like to show it to you, what we're doing. I think that if I wanted to take you down, he would let you.

Laramie sets the camera down on the table, beside her herb tea, which is untouched and cooling.

Ask him, robot. Please ask him.

>>>>>>>>>>>

On Monday, protesters arrive at the dig. Andrew had been expecting them eventually, but the number surprises him. They arrive by bus and gather at the opening to the Mohole, not at the living space entrance.

Gurney must have told them which was which. Andrew growls the words, and the robot can barely understand them.

There are forty protesters. At first, they mill around, neither saying nor doing much but waiting. Finally, a sky blue Land Rover comes down the dirt road. On its side are the words KHARMA CORPS, SKYKOMISH PROTECTORATE. Two women and a man get out and the protesters gather around them. From the back of the Land Rover, one of the women hands out placards that have symbols on them. The peace sign. A silhouetted nuclear reactor with a red slashed circle around it. A totem of the

Earth Mother from Stilaguamish Northwest Indian heritage, and now the symbol for the Skykomish Protectorate. One sign has a picture of a dam, split in half as if by an earthquake, with fish swimming freely through the crack. The other woman gives those who want it steaming cups of hot, black coffee or green tea.

The robot waits in the mu at the entrance to the living area, and Andrew walks over to speak with the protesters. The man who drove the Land Rover steps forward to meet him. The robot can hear what is said, but Andrew's body blocks the view of the man with whom Andrew is speaking.

Andrew Hutton. I work here.

I'm with the Protectorate. My name is Neilsen Birchbranch.

How are you with the Protectorate?

I'm an aid to Mother Agatha. I sit on the Healing Circle Interlocking Director's Conclave. I'm the chairperson, in fact.

Secret police.

What was that?

Neilsen, was it?

Let's keep it formal, Dr. Hutton, if you wouldn't mind.

All right. Mr. Birchbranch, what are you doing on my worksite?

The demonstration is sanctioned. Mother Agatha herself signed the permit. Freedom of speech is guaranteed in the Protectorate Charter.

I'm not against freedom of speech. We have work to do today.

It is against the law to cross a protest line. That's infringement on freedom of speech and that's in the charter as well. These people feel that the work you're doing is violating the sanctity of the Earth. They feel that you are, in a way, raping the mother of us all. Do you know where your digging machine comes from?

Yes. From a defunct mining operation that the Matties had a hand in putting out of business.

Precisely. It is a symbol. This hole is a symbol. Dr. Hutton, can't you see how it's taken, what you're doing?

I can see how some take it. I can see the politics of it clearly enough.

It is a new politics, Dr. Hutton. The politics of care. I'm not sure you do see that, or else you wouldn't be an opponent.

Maybe. Maybe I show my care in other ways.

What other ways?

Nonpolitical ways. I'm not sure *you* can see what *I'm* talking about, Mr. Birchbranch.

So. You persist, regardless of the consequences, because you want to see what's down there.

That's fair to say. Yes. I want to see what's down there.

The values of Western science. The same values that gave us thermonuclear war and the genocide of every other species besides man.

Well, there's also woman. That's a separate species.

Pardon?

It's a joke, Mr. Birchbranch. Maybe not a very good one.

No. Not a very good one at all.

So these are the things you're going to say to the television.

Not me as an individual. These people have chosen me to voice *their* concern and care.

Chosen you?

I'm the personal representative of Mother Agatha. You must believe that they've chosen her?

Then are you saying my people can't work? There are Matties. Children of the Matriarch. They work here. This is their livelihood.

They've all agreed to stay home today, I believe you'll find.

They're striking against me?

It's a support measure.

I see.

Good, then. A television truck will be coming later, and possibly a helicopter from News Five in Seattle. If you'd like, you can route any calls from journalists to me.

That won't be necessary.

The robot hears bitterness in Andrew's voice. Perhaps the other man can also.

So. Thank you for your cooperation, Dr. Hutton.

Yes. What's the time period on the permit? I spoke with Karlie Waterfall and she said that if it came through, it would be a week at most.

Sister Waterfall has voluntarily resigned from the Science Interweft to devote more time to her work at the Dungeness Spit Weather Observation Station.

When did that. Never mind. Christ, she was the only one with any sense on that damn committee.

There isn't a set period on the permit. There's no time limit on freedom of speech.

Well, get on with it, then, I suppose.

We intend to, Dr. Hutton. One other thing. We have a restraining order against the use of any machinery in the area for the day. I understand that you have a robot.

That's right.

Please power the robot down for the day, if you don't mind.

I do mind.

Dr. Hutton, this is entirely legal.

The robot will remain in my quarters. The robot *is* my quarters.

It is highly irregular. I can't answer for the consequences if you don't comply with the order.

Good-bye, Mr. Birchbranch. Have a nice protest.

Andrew turns to leave, and in so doing steps out from in front of the man. The robot's optics zoom in and pull focus, which the robot experiences in the same way as a human might the dilation of the pupils. At first the robot cannot believe what those optics report, and zooms out and back in again, like humans rubbing their eyes. No mistake.

Neilsen Birchbranch is a tall man, with lanky arms and legs. His face is thin and hard, gaunt, with muscles like small twisting roots cabling his mandible to his temple. The robot saw him last in the field, before Andrew came. Neilsen Birchbranch is the same man who killed the other on the steps of the dais in the field. Neilsen Birchbranch is the man who pulled the trigger of the gun and shot the other man dead.

Andrew steps back into the living area and the robot, in the mu, draws back noiselessly into the darkness.

Andrew calls the graduate students and the technicians who are from logger families, explaining to them one after another not to bother coming to work for a while, and to check back in over the next few mornings. When Andrew is done, the robot tells him about Neilsen Birchbranch.

Are you certain?

I'm sure of it.

I can't think of what to do about it.

Neither can I. I don't want to be torn apart.

We won't let that happen.

Then there isn't anything.

No.

Be wary.

I'm already wary.

>>>>>>>>>>

The first of the autumn rains begin. Though the digging area is partially in the rain shadow of the eastern mountains, it is still within the great upturns of basalt that ring the interior mountains, and mark the true edge of a swath of relative dryness that runs along the Hood Canal in a great horseshoe up even to Sequim and the Dungeness Spit, so that there are not two hundred inches of rain, such as fall on the Ho or the Quinault watershed, but more than a hundred—millions and millions of gallons of rain and snow—that will fall here during the autumn, winter and spring, and on many days throughout the summer.

Because of the great rains, there are great trees. And because of the great trees, the loggers came. And because most of the other trees were cut, the lovers of trees came. And the rain falls on Mattie and logger alike, and it falls and falls and falls.

The Matties have set up folding tables and many have brought chairs and big umbrellas. The tables and chairs of the Matties line the road for a hundred yards, and whenever a network reporter arrives, the tables and chairs are put hastily away and the Matties stand and grow agitated.

On the eleventh day of the protest, Laramie returns. She has not coordinated her arrival with the Matties, and so comes upon them unawares with her camera. The Matties smile into the lens. After she begins asking questions, a delegation approaches her and asks her to wait, that the spokesperson is on his way, and he will give her the best answers. No one will speak with Laramie after this, and Andrew invites her into the living area to wait for the arrival of the spokesperson.

The robot has been watching, just inside the entrance to the living area, as the robot has been watching for days now. Only at night, when the protesters go back to their bus and the Land Rover carries away the tables and chairs, does the robot go out into the open.

This can't go on, Andrew says. I can't stop paying wages. I'm *required* to pay wages to my Mattie techs, but I would anyway, and all the others. No digging, and all the grant money flowing away.

Sorry to hear that, Laramie says.

Laramie uses the Scoopic to make various shots of the robot's interior. Andrew says nothing, but smiles thinly. She has the Sony slung over her shoulder and, the robot notices, is recording her conversation with Andrew.

Did the robot discuss with you me going down in the hole?

In the dig. It's a spiral, like a Slinky, more or less. Yes. Yes, you can come as soon as we're allowed to go back down there.

That's great. Will I be able to film any of what is looks like?

Hmm. Maybe we can set something up. There's a small observation port on the service wagon. We'll have to turn off the fusion on the dray first, or you won't be filming for very long, I don't think.

Excellent. I'm really tired of protests and officials who don't call themselves officials, and all those squalid houses where all the loggers moved out at Aberdeen. There's been a lot of trouble there.

I heard about it.

We didn't used to call them loggers much.

That's because everybody was one.

We used to drive through Aberdeen when we wanted to get to the sea.

And up the coast to La Push.

Those black beaches across the river. I used to know why the rocks were so black.

Basalt scree that a glacier brought down that valley last ice age. That's what happened to the back half of the horseshoe. That's where it went.

Yeah. Basalt tumble. We slept there all night one night in August. You thought Papa would be pissed, but he didn't even notice, of course. He just asked me about the rocks I saw and told me about the Big Fist of sediment lifting up the sea floor and breaking it and all that. Papa. You and I made love that night, didn't we, Andrew?

Yes, Laramie. You know we did.

I know it.

Then.

Yep. The robot's listening, isn't it.

I'm listening, Laramie, if you don't mind.

No.

You know I'm not Victor Wu. I'm not shocked. I am rather surprised, however.

What do you mean?

About Andrew. I've never known him when he was in love with a woman.

Andrew's crackling chuckle. Not for a while, he says.

There was that chemist, after me. You wrote me about her. That was your last letter.

You never wrote me back.

I was pissed.

I figured you would be. Still, you couldn't have been pissed for five years.

I couldn't?

We broke up the next January.

Sorry to hear that.

She lacked imagination. They all lacked imagination.

Jesus, you're clinical.

I know what I like.

What do you like?

I can't have what I like.

Why not?

Because she has to live in Los Angeles, and I'm not particularly interested in the geology of Southern California.

The robot sees that Laramie's fine white skin has taken on a flush.

And it's as simple as that, she says.

Why make it complicated?

Maybe it *is* complicated. Maybe you're simplistic.

Will you turn that damn camera off?

No.

Well. There you have it.

>>>>>>>>>>

On the fourteenth day, the protesters do not arrive in the morning. There is no explanation, and no hint given to Andrew as to when they will return. Once again, the robot digs. Andrew puts aside several tests and side projects in order to dig faster and deeper. The robot is in the element that the metal of the rotor blades and the grip of the ceramic thread were made for— hard-rock mining—and the robot presses hard, and the rock explodes and fuses as obsidian diamond glass to the walls behind the robot, and the tunnel approaches forty miles in depth.

No one has ever been this deep before.

The techs from logging families and the Mattie techs are barely speaking to one another, and the graduate students are uneasy and tense, afraid to take sides. Andrew holds the crew together by a silent and furious force of will. The robot does not want to let Andrew down, and digs the harder.

Samantha has made the last of the modifications to the robot's linguistics, and puts the new code on-line. The robot immediately feels the difference. The presence, the otherness, grows stronger and stronger with every hour, until the robot is certain of it. But of *what*, there is no saying.

>>>>>>>>>>>

Two days of digging. On the third, Laramie arrives in the early morning and prepares to descend with the crew. But before the work can begin for the day, Andrew receives a call telling him that proceedings are underway for a new permit of protest, and a long-term suspension of the dig. He drives to Forks, where the committee will meet in the afternoon. It is a rainy day, and the robot worries that Andrew may drive too fast on the slippery pavement. Still, there is plenty of time for him to make the meeting.

In Andrew's absence, the Matties and loggers fall to quarreling about duties, and the graduate student Andrew has left in charge cannot resolve the differences. After an hour of listening to the wrangling, even the robot can see that no work will be done this day. The robot asks permission to take Laramie down to the bottom of the dig, and the graduate student, in disgust at the situation, shrugs and goes back to refereeing the technicians' argument.

As Laramie and the robot are preparing to leave, Neilsen Birchbranch drives up in the Protectorate Land Rover. A light rain is falling, and the graduate student reluctantly admits him into the worksite's initial cavern, where the others are gathered. The robot—digger and mu—draws back into the darkness of the true entrance to the dig.

Let's go, Laramie says.

But I'm afraid of this man, the robot replies. He isn't a good man. I know that for a fact.

Then let's get out of here.

There may be trouble.

I need to speak with Hutton, Neilsen Birchbranch says to the graduate student. It is very important that I speak with him today.

Take me down, please, robot. I may never get another chance.

The robot considers. As always, it is difficult to deny Laramie something she really wants with all her heart. And there is so much to show her. The robot has been thinking about showing the dig to Laramie for a long time. And the farther down they go, the farther they get from Neilsen Birchbranch's trouble.

We have a witness that places one of your machines at the scene of a crime, says Neilsen Birchbranch. A very serious crime.

Neilsen Birchbranch steps farther into the cavern, gazes around. The robot slowly withdraws down the Mohole. For all the digger's giant proportions, its movement is very quiet, and, the robot hopes, unnoticed.

Nothing but you can survive down there, can it, robot? Laramie says. How deep is it down there?

Forty-three miles.

He can't turn you off if you're forty miles deep. We'll stay down until Andrew comes back.

The first few miles of the descent are the most visually interesting, and after reaching a depth at which unprotected humans cannot survive the heat, the robot moves at a fraction of the usual pace. There are areas where the glass spray on the walls has a myriad of hues taken from all the minerals that melted together in the slurry around the nuclear pile, then spewed out to line the tunnel. The walls are smooth only at first glance. They are really a series of overlapping sheets, one imperfectly flowing atop the next, as sheets of ice form over a spring in winter. The robot directs lights to some of the more interesting formations, and they glow with the brilliance and prismatic hue of stained glass.

I didn't think I'd get anything this good, Laramie says. This is wonderful. The colors. God, I'm glad I went with color.

Deeper, and the walls become milky white. The granite behind glows darkly, three yards under the glassine plaster.

Twenty miles. Thirty.

Only basalt in the slurry now, and the walls are colorless. Yet they have the shape of the rock many feet behind them, and so they catch the light with effulgent glimmer.

Clear and clean.

Laramie may be speaking to herself; the robot cannot tell.

They pass through a region where magma pools against the walls and ceilings in places, held back by the diamondlike coating. The pressure is so great that the magma glows with a blue and white intensity. The tunnel sparkles of its own accord, and the robot must dim the viewport to keep from blinding Laramie.

Like the sky behind the sky.

The robot says nothing. Laramie is happy, the robot thinks. Little Bulge likes it down here.

They have been some hours in the descent, and Laramie is running low on film, but is very, very happy. Near to the bottom. Now to wait for Andrew. Very quiet. The robot has never been this deep before without digging and working. The robot has never sat idle and silent at the bottom of the Mohole.

Hello.

>>>>>>>>>>>

For a moment, the robot thinks Laramie has spoken. But this is not Laramie's voice. And it comes from *outside*. The voice comes from outside the robot, from the very rocks themselves.

The sense of the presence, the other that the robot has been feeling for these long weeks, is very strong. Very strong.

Again the voice that isn't a voice, the vibration that isn't a vibration. It is like a distant, low whisper. Like a voice barely heard over a lake at morning. No wonder I never made it out before, the robot thinks.

Hello, comes the voice.

Who are you?

I'm me.

What are you doing down here?

I *am* down here. Who are you?

I'm. I don't have a name yet.

Neither do I. Not one that I like.

Who are you?

Me. I told you.

What is it, robot? Laramie speaking.

Something strange.

What?

I don't . . . Wait for a moment. A moment.

All right.

The robot calls again. The robot is spinning its cutting rotors at low speed, and it is the whisk and ding of the digger's rotors that is doing the talking. Hello?

Hello. Are you one of those trees?

Trees?

The trees barely get here, and then they start *moving*. Are you one of those moving trees?

I don't. Yes. Maybe.

I thought you *might* talk, but it's so cold up there, it takes ages to say anything. Down here things go a lot faster.

Are you. What are you?

I told you. I'm me.

The rocks?

Nope.

The magma?

Nope. Guess again.

Where are you? Show yourself to me.

I am.

Then I've guessed. You're the whole planet. You're the Earth.

Laughter. Definitely laughter. I'm not either. I'm just here. Just around here.

Where's here?

Between the big ocean and the little ocean.

The Olympic Peninsula?

Is that what you call it? That's a hard word for a name.

Skykomish.

That's better. Listen, I have a lot of things I want to ask you. We all do.

There is an explosion.

At first the robot thinks that a wall has blown out near the region of the magma pools. This will be dangerous, but it should be possible to reinforce long enough to get through. It may mean trouble for the dig, though. Now there will be more funding. The Matties will allow it to go ahead. Even the robot can see that the politics have changed.

Everything has changed.

There is another explosion. A series of explosions.

Robot?

Laramie. I. I have so much to tell you.

What is that shaking? I'm scared down here. Do you think we can go up now?

Hello. Tree? Are you still there?

Even with the tremors—there are huge rumblings and cracklings all about—the robot is attuned to the voice, the presence, and can still hear its words.

I really need to talk to you.

*Papa, do you think we can go up now?*

>>>>>>>>>>>

The pressure wave lifts the robot—impossibly tilts the robot—over and over—shatter of the walls as diamonds shatter like the shrapnel of stars and the rocks behind—tumble and light, light from the glow of the give, the sudden release of tension—the bulk melt of the undisclosed—sideways, but what is sideways?—tumble and tumble—scree within thin melt moving, turning, curling like a wave and the robot on the curl, under the curl, hurled down down down over over down dark dark.

Dark.

Dark and buried.

*Find my daughter.*

The engineers have built one hell of a machine.

*Find my daughter.*

The robot powers back up. The robot begins, blindly, to dig. It is only by sheer luck that the robot comes upon the service wagon. The robot melts and compacts a space, creates an opening, temporary, dangerously temporary. Finds the powerhitch to the wagon and plugs in.

Turns on the lights and air-conditioning inside the wagon. The video cameras inside.

Laramie is twisted against a control console. Her neck is impossibly twisted. She is dead.

No. She isn't. Can't be. She is.

What? Within the curve of her stomach, holding it to shelter, the Scoopic. But the latch has sprung and sixteen millimeter film is spilled out and tangled about her legs.

No. Laramie. Little Bulge.

Hello?

The robot screams. The robot howls in anguish. Forty miles deep, the robot cries out a soul's agony into the rock. A living soul mourning a dead one.

Stop that.

The other, the presence. The robot does not care. Past caring.

You're scaring me.

Past.

You're scaring me.

Grind of rotors, ineffectual grind. How can you live? How can humans live when this happens? Ah, no. You can't live. You cannot. You can, and it is worse. Worse than not living. No no no no.

Stop it.

And something happens. Something very large—gives. More. Faults, faults everywhere. Settle, rise, settle. Faults like a wizened crust, like a mind falling into shards of fear. Faults and settle, rise and settle. Rise.

No. I.

But there is a way. There is a weakness revealed, and there is a way. Not wide enough, not yet. But a way to go. A way to take her home. Take her home to Andrew. The robot begins to dig.

>>>>>>>>>>>

The robot digs. There is only the digging, the bite of blade and saw, the gather of lade and bale. Digging. Upward digging.

The way is made easier by the shaking, the constant, constant tremble of what the robot knows to be fear, incomprehension.

A child who has seen a grown-up's sorrow, and does not understand. A frightened child.

By the time the robot comes to this realization, it is too late. The robot is too high, and when called, the child does not answer. Or perhaps it is that the child needs time to calm, that it cannot answer. The robot calls again and again. Nothing. Nothing can be heard above the rumble of fear.

Poor trembling Skykomish. The robot continues digging, drawing behind it the service wagon. Bringing Laramie to Andrew.

A day passes. Two. Rock. Stone. The roots of the mountains, and sediment, compressed to schist. The roots of the mountains, and the robot slowly comes to its senses. Comprehends.

After a long moment of stillness—a minute, an hour? No reckoning in the utter depths, and the robot is not that kind of robot—after a long moment of reflection, the robot looses the service wagon.

Little Bulge, good-bye.

Up. Now. Up because the way is easier up than down, and that is the only reason.

After three days, the robot emerges from the ground. In a cove that the robot recognizes. On the Quinault watershed. Into a steady autumn rain.

The robot wanders up the Quinault River. Every day it rains, and no nights are clear. The forest is in gloom, and moss hangs wet and dark. Where the trail is not wide enough, the robot bends trees, trying not to break them, but uprooting many. Many trees have fallen, for there are earthquakes—waves and waves of them. Earthquakes the like of which have never been seen in the world. The robot cuts deadfall from its path with little effort and little thought. The digger's passage through the forest is like that of a hundred bears—not a path of destruction, but a marked and terrible path, nonetheless.

Where the Quinault turns against a great ridge, the robot fords and continues upward, away from the trees. The robot crosses Low Divide during the first snow of the season. The sun is low, then gone behind the cloaked western ridges. For a time, the ground's rumblings still. All sound is muffled by the quiet snow. The twilight air is like silence about the robot.

Something has happened.

At the saddle of the divide, the robot pauses. The pass is unfamiliar. Something has happened inside. Victor Wu has gone away. Or Victor Wu has come fully to life. The two are the same.

Then am I a man?

What is my name?

Orpheus. Ha. A good one.

Old Orf up from Hades. I've read about you. And Euridice. I didn't understand. And now I do. Poems are pretty rocks that know things. You pull them from the earth. Some you leave behind.

Talking to myself.

After a moment, the robot, Orf, grinds steadily on. He grinds steadily on.

>>>

Down the valley of the Elwha, and north as the river flows and greatens. Earthquakes heave and slap, slap and heave. Sometimes a tree falls onto the digger, but Orf pays no mind. He is made of the stronger material, and they cannot harm him.

Down the valley of the Elwha, past the dam that the Matties have carefully removed, that would not withstand the quakes if it were still there. The trail becomes a dirt road. The road, buckled pavement. The robot follows the remains of the highway into what once was Port Angeles.

What will future geologists make of this? The town has become scree, impossible to separate and reconfigure. Twists of metal gleam in the pilings by the light of undying fires. And amid the fire and rubble, figures move. Orf rolls into the city.

A man sits in a clear space, holds his knees to his chest, and stares. Orf stops well away from him.

I am looking for a man named Neilsen Birchbranch. Do you know where I can find him?

The man says nothing.

Do you know where I can find Neilsen Birchbranch? He works for the Protectorate.

The man says nothing, but begins to rock back and forth on his haunches.

I'm looking. Can you.

The man begins to moan.

Orf moves onward. At a point where the piles of rubble begin to be higher, a makeshift roadblock has been set up. Orf stops at it, and a group of men and women, all armed with rifles, come out of the declivities of the town scree.

Come out of there, an old man says. He points his gun at Orf.

There isn't anybody in here.

Come out, or we'll blow you to hell.

I've already been there.

Come on out of there.

I'm looking for a man named Neilsen Birchbranch. He works for the Protectorate.

Goddamn we will shoot you you goddamn Mattie.

Do you know where I can find him?

The old man spits on the ground. Reckon he's with the others.

The others?

That's what I said.

Where are they?

Out at the dump.

Where's the dump?

That way. The old man points with his gun. Now come out.

Orf turns and rolls away in the direction of the dump. Shots ring out. They ricochet off him and crackle against the rubble. Five miles out of town, Orf finds the dump. There are bodies here; hundreds of bodies. Men, women, children. At first, he thinks they are the dead from the quakes, collected and brought here.

With the edge of a saw blade, Orf turns one of the bodies over. It is a woman. She has been shot in the head.

Most of the other bodies are people who have been shot. Or hacked up. Or had their necks broken with clubs.

The loggers have had their revenge.

And there among the bodies, Orf pauses. He has recognized one. It is the woman from the field, the speaker, Mother Agatha. It is her; there is no mistake. A small bullet hole is in the forehead of her peaceful face.

Orf rolls back to the city. It is night. He bursts through the roadblock without stopping. Shots, the flash of muzzles. It is all so much waste. Down lightless streets, and streets lit with fires, some deliberate, some not. Every half hour or so, another earthquake rumbles through, throwing rubble willy-nilly. There are often screams.

Orf comes upon a steady fire, well maintained, and sees that it is surrounded by people—people in the blue and brown clothes of Matties. It is a silent throng. Orf hangs back, listens.

Oh Mother Agatha Mother Goddess hear our prayer.

Hear our prayer.

We know we have done wrong. We have sinned against you. Hear our prayer.

Hear our prayer.

Hold back your wrath. We are unworthy and evil. This we know. We beg you even still. Hold back your wrath. Hear our prayer.

Hear our prayer.

Goddamn mother—

The report of a gun. Someone—man or woman, Orf cannot tell—crumples in the ring of the fire. Instead of fleeing, the others stand still.

Another shot. Another falls.

Hear our prayer.

No one moves.

Another shot. A man falls, groaning, grasping at his leg. No one moves. He writhes in the shadows of the fire, in the dust of the ruins. No one helps him.

The rifleman shoots no more. The man writhes. The voice of the minister goes up to his goddess, and the people respond mechanically.

Like robots are supposed to, Orf thinks. The man ceases his writhing. There is nothing to do. Orf rolls on quietly through the night, out of the city and east. The going is easy over the broken highway. In two hours, Orf is in what was Port Townsend.

There is no rubble here, no ruins. The sea has washed it away. No bodies. No trees. Only desolation, bare-wiped desolation. He rolls down to where the docks had been, and looks out upon the lapping waters of the Strait of Juan de Fuca.

Then the slap of an earthquake, and Orf discovers the reason for the missing city. The slap runs its way down to the sea and is perfectly mirrored by the other side of the strait. Reflected back, a tsunami. Rolls over the land. Nothing left to take. Almost enough to suck in a digging robot. Orf must backpedal with his threads, dig in to keep from being pulled forward by the suck of the water as it retreats to the sea.

Everyone is drowned here.

Orf will not find Neilsen Birchbranch by looking in the cities. He heads to the southwest now, back to the center of the mountains.

Into the forest. Orf wanders without aim. A day. Many days. Once, he remembers the mu, tries to go out of himself and find it. The uplink doesn't work; there is only static on a clear channel. Have all the satellites fallen from the sky? He wanders on, a giant among the gigantic trees.

>>>

Across one divide. Down a valley. Finally back to the digsite. All is devastation here, a tumble of stone. Not a sign of anyone. The living area is caved in. Orf digs, but cannot locate the mu. All he finds is a twisted piece of red metal—the remains of Laramie's hum-vee. Nothing else. No reason to stay.

Across another divide. Another valley. No longer caring to keep track. Stopping to look at rocks, or a peculiar bend in a river. The accumulation of snow.

One day, the earthquakes stop.

Quiet child. Hush now. You've seen too much for young eyes. Hush and be quiet for a while and take your rest.

Winter, it must be. Orf coming over Snow Dome, down the Blue Glacier and into the valley of the Ho, where the biggest of the big trees are. Darkness earlier and earlier. In these towering woods, at these high latitudes, winter days are a perpetual twilight. Orf alongside the Ho, its water opaque with outwash sludge, the heart of Mount Olympus, washing away to the sea.

Then away from the river, deeper into the rain forest. As deep and as wild as it gets, many miles from roads. If there are roads anymore.

One hushed afternoon—or perhaps early evening, they are blend—a climbing rope, dangling from a tree. Movement to the left.

Another rope. Many ropes falling from the trees like rain that stays suspended. And down the ropes men and women slide like spiders. Orf is surrounded. They are dressed in tattered suits of green. Silently, they gather round the digger until Orf cannot move for fear of crushing one of them.

Men and women. Some have rifles slung across their backs.

Two women carry children in the same manner, and the young ones are utterly, utterly quiet.

All right. Orf has not heard a voice in weeks, and his own, arising from his exterior speakers, startles him. What is it you want?

One of the men in green steps forward.

Wait, he says.

Orf waits with the silent people for he knows not what. And then there is a movement in the undergrowth of vine maple. From around a low slope and over some deadfall, the mu appears. It moves clumsily. Whoever is at the controls doesn't know what he's doing, Orf thinks.

The mu scampers up to the digger and stops.

Andrew walks over the slope.

He steps lightly along the deadfall on the forest floor and comes to stand beside the mu. In his hand is a metal box with an antenna extended from it.

Do you want this thing back?

They are silent for a while. It is not a strained silence, but is right. Orf speaks first.

Laramie is dead. I couldn't save her.

I know.

What happened at the dig?

I'm not sure. I've only got secondhand information, but I think that the secret policeman coerced Gurney into sabotaging the place. I think he threatened to hurt his family. It was a bomb. A big bomb. Probably chemical. Everybody died, not just. Not just Laramie.

So. I'm sorry. So. Who are these people?

Andrew laughs. It has been so, so long. That dry laugh. A harsh, fair laugh, out of place before, perhaps, but suited now to these harsh times.

These are rangers of the United States Park Service. They live here. In the tops of the old growth. We guard the forest.

We?

Somehow or other, I've become the head ranger.

/\\\//\//

Winter, and the rangers bundle in the nooks of their firs and hemlocks, their spruces and cedars. The digger must remain on the ground, but using the mu, Orf can venture up to their village in the trees.

In the highest tree, in the upper branches, Andrew has slung his hammock. Orf and he spend many days there, talking, discussing how things were, how they might be. The devastation of the northwestern American continent by earthquakes and floods would normally be a terrible event, but one that the world could easily enough absorb. But this time, economies were already on the verge of collapse, and like the last stone that has held a boulder in place, human culture has suddenly fallen a great distance and shattered into a thousand fragments.

It wasn't unexpected, Andrew says. We were teetering on the brink for a lot of years. It's almost like we *wanted* it. Like the economics was just an excuse.

Wanted what? says Orf.

Wanted to go back to tribes.

Politics have shifted in the outside world, and Andrew is part of them now, seeking a place for his band of outcast civil servants that has become a family, and then a tribe.

The rangers hold the center of the peninsula against Matties and loggers, or against the remains of them. There is to be no clearing of the forest, and no worship of it, either, but a conservation and guard, a stewardship and a waiting. Rangers defend the woods. They take no permanent mates and have no children. The young ones Orf had seen before were stolen children, taken from Matties and loggers. Ranger women in their constant vigilance could not afford to be pregnant; if they were, they took fungal herbs that induced abortion. All must be given to the watching.

Winter, spring. Another year. Years. The fortunes of the rangers ebb and flow, but always the forests are held. Orf comes to their aid often with the mu and, when the situation is very dire, with the whirling blades of the digger.

Andrew hopes to open the Mohole back up one day, when all is secure, to continue the dig—especially in light of Orf's discovery of . . . whatever it is that is down there. But now there are politics and fighting, and that time never comes. Andrew was right, and tribes, strange tribes, arise in the outside world. Governments crumble and disappear. Soon it is rangers alone who keep a kind of learning and history alive, and who come to preserve more than trees.

In any case, Andrew's heart seems to have gone out of the project. Somewhere below, his love is buried, deeper than any man's has ever been buried before. If he goes back down, he may come upon her yet. Andrew is a brave man, Orf knows. But maybe not that brave.

And always Orf hears rumors of a bad man and killer who appears here and there, sometimes in the service of the Matties, sometimes working for logger clans. But Orf never finds Neilsen Birchbranch. Never even discovers his real name. And a time comes when the rumors cease.

Many years. Andrew grows old. Orf does not grow old. The digger's nuclear fusion pile will not run down. Only a malfunction could keep Orf from living a thousand years. Perhaps a thousand more.

One morning, in the mu, Orf climbs to Andrew's hammock and finds that Andrew has died in the night.

Gently, Orf envelops the man in the mu's arms; gently, he carries the body down from the trees. And walks through the forest. And crosses a divide. And another. To the valley of the Elwha. And up the Lillian River, to a basalt stela that, curiously, has no foramens in its makeup. That speaks of deep things,

from far under the earth. That this land—strange peninsula between two salt waters—may be the place to dig and find what
those things are.

At its base, Orf buries his friend, Andrew Hutton.

And then, Orf—digger and mu—returns to the long-
abandoned worksite. Orf clears the rocky entrance, finds the old
passage. Orf digs down into the earth, and closes the path behind him.

/\\//\//

In the heart of the great horseshoe twist of the Olympic Peninsula, in the heart of the mountains themselves, there lives a
monster, a giant, who some say is also a god. A ranger, hunting
in some hidden dale or along the banks of a nameless rivulet
flowing from the snow's spring runoff, will feel the presence of
another, watching. The ranger will turn, and catch—what?—
the flash of tarnished metal, the glint of wan sun off a glassy
eye? Then the spirit, the presence, will be gone from the ranger's
senses, and he will question whether he felt anything at all. Such
sightings happen only once or twice in a fortnight of years.

But there is a rock, black and tall, in the deepest, oldest
wood, up a secret tributary of the Elwha River, where young
rangers, seeking their visions, will deliberately go. Some do not
return from that high valley. Others come back reporting a
strange and wonderful thing. On a particular night in October,
when the moon is new and all the land is shrouded, they say the
monster emerges from a hole in the mountains—but never the
same hole—and closes the way behind. The monster travels to
the rock on the Lillian.

The earth rumbles like distant thunder, and trees are gently
bent out of the monster's way as if they were thin branches.
And at that rock on the Lillian River, the monster stays for a
time, shining darkly under the stars. The monster stays and is
utterly silent. The reasons why are lost to legend, but at that

time young rangers with strong and empty hearts are given waking dreams and prophecies to fill them.

Then, not long before sunrise, the monster moves, pivots on its great bulk, and returns from whence it came. There are those who follow, who are called to track the monster back to its lair. These are seldom the strongest or the bravest, and they are not particularly missed. Some say the monster eats them or tortures them in fires of liquid stone. But others say that the monster leads them to a new land, wider and deeper than any human can conceive, under the mountain—that the earth is bigger on the inside than on the outside. No one knows. No one knows, because they do not return to tell the tale, and the world falls farther into ruin, and the monster—or god—no longer speaks.

# PENNYROYAL
# TEA

# SHUN

Blank day beats down through white mist. Double strands of a rope whip through the air and pop against the ground at the edge of a glade where the pennyroyal grows. An instant later, a man on the end of the rope—not there; *there*—unclips his rappelling device from the strands. He strides purposefully into the forest clearing.

Because he is a ranger, and a man, Jarrod has known since puberty where to find the pennyroyal herb. Ten miles down the Ho River, in the valley of the big trees—the trees of the rain forest that can grow thicker by a foot a year when the rain falls often (and the rain always does fall often)—there is a tributary called Keller Creek. The Ho River is fast, but thick as mud. It begins on Mount Olympus, in the center of the peninsula, and gathers waters from the Bailey Range as it flows westward, dropping fifteen hundred feet in less than twenty miles. Rangers will only drink its waters as a last expedient. Two miles up the Keller Creek tributary—hours of bushwhacking through thick understory for a human on the ground (but who goes on the ground? No one walks these forests)—there is the pennyroyal dell.

Jarrod has had his morning duties in the Ho Brigade to perform, and so it is late afternoon before he reaches the pennyroyal glade. The herb grows in clumps among a scree of rock. The stalks are long, a foot or more in height, and end in a basket of flowers, mostly purple and pink but with some white scattered among the color. *Monardella odoratissima.* Mountain pennyroyal. Lover of dry ground and rocky places. Rare in the wet Olympics.

Jarrod takes off his daypack. He gathers pennyroyal leaves and stems with sure hands, and stuffs them into a side pocket of the pack. For a moment, he is ready to swing the daypack onto his back and leave this place. But he hesitates. The wash of the creek over rocks and roots fills the air in the glade with a faint din. Jarrod blinks.

He discovers that he is crying.

He blinks again, sits down among the pennyroyal. Some is crushed to a dry, mint fragrance. He cannot go climbing about in the trees with tears in his eyes.

Jarrod sobs once, twice. There are miles to go before nightfall. He squeezes his eyes dry. He stands, and puts back on his daypack. Then back to the rope, and from the seat sling at his waist he unclips two ascenders and works them onto the rope, one above the other. Two foot slings dangle from the ascenders, one trailing against the ground. Jarrod steps into them, putting all his weight onto the sling that is closest to the ground. With a practiced motion, he launches himself upward, at the same time sliding the other ascender several feet up the rope. He puts his weight on that sling now, and pulls the other ascender up just under the top one.

In this manner, as quick as a spider, perhaps more quickly than a squirrel, Jarrod works his way up seventy-five feet of the rope, and he is again in the trees, and on his way between trees, back down Keller Creek, down to the Ho Valley, and to Three-cabin, the secret village in the treetops, where the rangers dwell.

As always, Jarrod travels quickly, and he is early for the ceremony. Baker is still with the other women at the Mourning Hollow. Once again Jarrod finds himself waiting by Baker's lodgings, as he has waited many evenings before. But never for this purpose, he thinks, never for this.

Jarrod has always made do with only a hammock and footlocker, but most of the other rangers have cribs such as Baker's. There is a mattress on her floor, filled with moss changed monthly by the old aunts. A few mementos of her childhood that she has never explained hang from the walls, along with her certificates. From Ranger School, there is a prettily carved yew arrow that represents a first in archery during her junior year. There is also a knotted rope with a Turk's head ten places down, the position she graduated in her class. A small methane stove for cooking and warmth during the cold of winter. A writing desk with a surface a little larger than two outstretched palms.

Such is the home life of an ambitious ranger. Well.

There is one wall that is the curving bark of an incense cedar tree, furrowed, fibrous, shreddy. The crib floor has a fine cedar duff, and its fragrance is always in the air here. The leaves are tightly pressed to the stems and, at night, the branches scrape the cordura roofing of the crib. It is early autumn and the tree-top butterflies still flutter in onto everything. Pine white swallowtails, Nelson's hairstreaks, copper and brown, Johnson's hairstreaks, tiny and blue: they light on Baker's short brown hair, on her bony shoulders. All summer, the butterflies.

"I thought you would come early. You're never on time." For a moment, Jarrod cannot make out the speaker's form from the growing gloom of evening, but the voice is unmistakable.

"Uncle Franklin. You aren't supposed to be here."

"I'm *not* here. Not in any official capacity." Franklin steps under the canvas of Baker's porch. "Relax, ranger."

"Yes sir."

"You're not the first man to be shunned."

"I know it. I don't care about that."

"Autumn's coming on. It's getting dark at a fierce rate these days."

Franklin reaches over and turns the knob on Baker's porch light. The methane spurts out for a moment, until he strikes a flint and sparks the gas into a steady flame. He adjusts the light down to a low, warm glow that barely lights the surrounding branches.

Franklin is old—nearly fifty—and his knotty fingers are shaped into a permanent curl from years of holding on to branches. He is balding, but he wears his hair down to his shoulders, in the manner of old men who have no time nor need for clipping and grooming. This is a sign of wisdom, but it causes his head to resemble a gall on the bark of a tree that some artist had carved a face into. Franklin could still shimmy up a rope nearly as fast as Jarrod, except when the gout was troubling him—the ranger disease, brought on by a diet of too much meat, too few green vegetables. No gardens in the woods. No agriculture to tie the rangers down to one spot. The *forest* is what matters, not this or that arbitrary, human-defined patch of land.

"You know shunning won't harm your career in any permanent way."

"Well, it can't help."

"I was shunned, when I was about your age. It was the year you came to us, if I'm not mistaken. That hard winter."

"I know. Some say that's why you aren't on the council."

Franklin laughed. "Are you joking? Do you think I would come down from the trees to be a member of *that?*"

"I'm joking, uncle. Everybody always knows, though. They remember."

"But you don't care about that."

Jarrod finds himself smiling, in spite of himself. "Well, maybe a little. But not really."

"What is it, then?"

Jarrod does not answer the ranger; he cannot think of what the answer should be. The days are growing colder, too, and he wishes he had brought his coat along against the chilly night.

"It doesn't matter," says Franklin. "I have something else to discuss with you."

"Then you *are* here officially."

"You're being temporarily reassigned, ranger."

"What?"

"Subject to your volunteering for this new duty, of course. I assume you volunteer."

Reassigned? Is it some further punishment dreamed up by the council?

"What is the assignment?"

"I can't tell you that until you volunteer for it."

"What—" This is something else. Something of greater consequence than the simple shunning of a young man. "I . . . assume it's important."

Franklin smiles wanly, but says nothing.

"And I'm actually going to be on assignment while I'm being shunned, is that it?"

"That's it."

"So instead of wandering the Sawtooth Ridge on the Shame Trail, I'll have to go to work just the same."

"I'm afraid that's correct. You'll have to put off your traverse of the Sawtooth until the completion of this assignment. But maybe we can arrange a clemency by then."

"Well, uncle, what is it? The trail is useless to me. I'm ashamed of many things, but I'm not ashamed of what Baker and I—" He almost sobs again, but holds it in. Hold it in. "I'll never be ashamed of that."

"I can't go into details now. Tomorrow, before dawn—before the banishment goes into effect—report to brigade headquarters. We'll fill you in on the details then."

"We?"

"The council proxy and I."

"Aunt Larmy? What could it—"

"*Tomorrow,* ranger. You'll know soon enough. An hour before sunrise."

Franklin reaches over to the lamp and with a quick twist, snuffs it out.

"All right," Jarrod says to the sudden dark. "I'll be there, sir."

But Jarrod senses that the chief ranger of the Ho Brigade is already gone into the gloom.

Jarrod leans against the railing of the crib porch and decides not to relight the lamp. Darkness has never troubled him, and it does not trouble him now. He imagines no spirits, for he knows there are none, only this time and this place, the woods stretched out incognito forty miles before his face.

And then the spare, acid dirt of the Mattie farmers to the north and west. The Timberlanders on the second-growth forest skirtings—permitted only so far by the rangers, only so far, and no in-holdings allowed by ancient edict from Washington, D.C.

And the coastal nomads, who have many names, who are ruthless scavengers and killers, with mercy only for their own, and that a peculiar kind of mercy, just as the rangers are said to have a peculiar kind of mercy.

Then the Strait of Juan de Fuca, the Pacific Ocean, where there are giant waves that can swallow a man, and sharks and mariners who brave it all. At least so Jarrod has heard. He has never seen the sea.

Jarrod is twenty. Baker is two years his junior. He had known her growing up, but could not remember much about her. He'd been too busy then, learning the lore, preparing for his first assignment. And she'd been recruited by the Quinault Patrol. There were always skirmishes with the Timberlanders away south, and Baker was a stealthy, deadly fighter. She didn't speak of her kills very often, but when she did, it was obvious that the other had little chance. There is no answer a ground walker could make to a ranger archer concealed in the crown of a tree. But those who did not perish from the arrow or the poison of the arrow wound, and who would not retreat, died more gruesome deaths. Baker fell from the trees like a hard and merciless rain, like sudden, catastrophic extinction. She was the Quinault Patrol's ambush specialist—the one permitted to carry the pistol.

At home in Threecabin, she was silent, shy. Jarrod had at first mistaken her shyness for coyness, and had thought she was secretly trying to attract him. This was not true. When he finally declared his feelings for her, she was taken completely aback. It was as if courting had to begin all over again. Of course, Jarrod thinks, I am not an overt man, and what are huge gestures for me are muted signals for others—even for most rangers.

He'd never suspected that Baker was so hungry for physical contact, for warmth and affection. When he first stroked her hair, rubbed her shoulders, she'd sighed like the wind through firs. Her shoulders were bunched and knotted so tightly her skin felt as if it had odd growths underneath it. Although it was possible, though frowned upon, for a ranger couple to court and pair-bond, Jarrod and Baker had not gone through channels. Since both were among the sneakiest and most careful of their respective bands, they were not discovered. They discussed nothing but business when they were together in public—which was fine, for neither of them knew or cared about much else besides their jobs.

But Baker was the smell of moss and bracken fern where they lay down together. The taste of the chamomile flowers she chewed. The acrid needles of fir and hemlock, always caught in her hair, no matter how closely she cropped it. Baker in the moonlight, dark and brown against the stars.

She wanted to advance in the Quinault Patrol, maybe be its leader some day. She'd confided that to him. She had come to know and love that watershed, and could make irrational statements about its importance in the Olympic ecosystem. But the Quinault Patrol were all mystics. They were separated from the other rangers for months at a time, and they had a high mortality rate. And it rained there—two hundred inches most years—and the constant blank drizzle could drive anyone to visions.

Baker was ambitious, withdrawn, crafty. Who did that remind Jarrod of? Himself, of course. There was no great mystery to their mutual attraction, after all. It was more a matter of who ended up with whom, brooding in dark corners.

I love her, Jarrod thinks. Can I just reduce our love to chance and instinct and general compatibility?

Do not fit facts to some preconceived theory. Franklin had taught him that. Theories will get you killed faster than anything in the forest. Look at a black bear. It will turn over everything looking and looking. And what is it looking for? That bear doesn't know. It will eat anything that it finds. Facts will save your ass, ranger.

Chance and instinct and love all mixed together in irreducible amalgam. That is all that can be said about the situation.

And there is another fact. A growing and true fact, swelling in the womb of Baker.

Of course they had taken precautions. The gut sac of a deer, sterilized and tied at one end. Spermicidal treatments cooked from a fungus that lived among Douglas fir roots. All that awkwardness, and the pains taken to obtain the items without notice, so that none would suspect a long-term affair. All for nothing. Nothing—and stinging revelation.

Last week, when the Quinault Patrol and the Ho Brigade pulled into Threecabin at the same time for R and R, Baker had come to him, to his hammock, and touched his cheek. He'd awakened instantly and was soon silently following her down a plankway to the covered platform where acorns were stored. She pulled him between two sacks, as big as bears, hanging from the ceiling. The air smelled like musty oak.

"I haven't bled for three months."

"No?"

"I'm *not* regular, a lot of times."

"Your constitution isn't normal. You said so yourself."

"Never this long."

His back against the acorn sack. It scratched his neck.

"Well," he said.

"I can take care of it myself," she said.

For a moment, he believed that she could. But if she's caught, it will be bad. The end of her advancement. Rangers must be trustworthy above all else or what good are they to the forest?

"I think I can do it without being noticed."

"Baker." He felt his eyes watering. He was going to sneeze.

"This won't look good for you if we tell them."

"Baker, of course we have to tell them."

"You'll be shunned."

"I know that."

"You'll be knocked down a grade. Winny will get your point clusters."

"Do you think I care about that?"

"You should."

He was definitely going to sneeze. He raised a hand to his nose. Baker waited as he made a quiet and controlled sneeze into it. Professional, to the last.

"Baker. I'll announce at morning convocation. You tell Aunt Larmy after that."

"Are you sure?"

"Of course I'm sure."

"Well."

He reached over, took her hand. It was warm and bony. Baker was all sticks and bones and vines. Her eyes were shining stones.

"Have you ever thought," he said. "Have you ever thought about what it would be like?"

"What?"

"To . . . have it?"

"Have it?"

"A child."

"No. I haven't thought." She gripped his hand tighter. "It's *disgusting. I* would be disgusting."

"I don't know about that."

"How can you say that?"

"Think about it scientifically. We're animals. We reproduce sexually."

"Someday rangers will reproduce sexually, when the forest is won and the Earth is in balance once again."

"That's classroom cant."

"It's true."

"Who knows whether it's true or not?"

"We *make* it true."

The last tour along the Ho had been grueling. Jarrod felt worn. He didn't want to argue. Baker was soon to go through much suffering. There was no need to add to it.

"I suppose you're right," he said. What would it be like to be a father? He would never, ever know.

Selfish, Jarrod thinks, and stops himself from leaning on Baker's porch railing. Selfish thinking gets you killed. Rangers have to stick together. The only strength is strength in numbers and strength in purpose. Trustworthy. Obedient. Thrifty. Brave. Clean. Stewards and scholars.

"To hell," Jarrod says. "To hell with that." But he knows he doesn't mean it.

Deep night and the moon is a bone splinter when Baker returns from the Mourning Hollow with the women.

Baker is haggard and has been crying. What do the women speak of at the Mourning Hollow? What did they say to her?

She glances at him and he can read nothing from her expression. Does she hate him now? Is this the end of what was once between them? It *is* the end. He knows that now. Baker goes past him and into her crib.

Jarrod is not sure exactly what is expected of him, but an aunt elder takes his arm.

"Do you have the herb?" she says in a low voice.

He nods yes.

"Then come inside."

Baker sits on her bed. There are two other women in the crib, and one of them has set a pressure cooker on the stove. Baker stares ahead, and it suddenly occurs to Jarrod that she is drugged. She is drugged against the pain that *he* is bringing. He is holding his daypack, and he removes the pennyroyal from it and hands the herb to the woman by the stove.

She clips off the leaves and stems and places them in the pressure cooker, then latches down the top. To the valve in the lid, she attaches a length of rubber hosing that leads over the stove and down to a small extract still. Jarrod hasn't noticed this before. It must have been brought in during the day. Now they wait for the potion to form in the still.

It takes two hours. No one speaks during this time.

The two women begin to prepare Baker. They rub her arms, her shoulders and legs. At predetermined intervals they anoint her with a narcotic oil whose smell Jarrod recognizes. It is made from the poppies that the eastern forces gather near the Hood Canal. The women drip opiated tea onto Baker's tongue from a glass dropper, and Baker absentmindedly swallows it.

Jarrod is left to stand and watch. But he has had long practice at this, and it is no ordeal.

He stands.

He watches the syrupy steam condense on the side of the still.

He watches it collect separately from the water.

He watches the women rubbing and murmuring wordlessly to Baker.

Then it is time. The eldest aunt goes to the still and obtains a dropperful of pennyroyal extract. She takes it to Baker, and just as she administered the opium tea before, she now gives Baker the abortifacient. Baker swallows mechanically. Does she notice the different taste? Can she care? No. Not where she is now.

The effects begin within fifteen minutes. Baker's uterine wall begins to contract. Her reproductive system is told that it is time to deliver a baby. But there is no baby. Only a fetus. Her uterus contracts, and Baker, through her dreams, moans. The contractions become more frequent, stronger. Even opium cannot wholly dim the pain. Jarrod thinks of the muscles of her stomach, now covered by a green tunic. Baker's muscles are lean and distinct. He thinks of the way they must stand out with each contraction. For a moment he is aroused. But that cannot be, must not be. He pushes it down in himself, kills the thought.

Soon the women must hold Baker's upper torso, she is writhing so fiercely. She cries out a few times, but for the most part she suffers in silence. Jarrod cannot help but believe that this is Baker, Baker's stoicism and control, coming through even the narcotic daze. A ranger does not make a display of pain. What good could it do?

None, Jarrod thinks. You are right, Baker. You are right. This had to happen the way that it is happening. All of it must follow this course. This is the way we have to live here in the forest.

Then the flow begins from between Baker's exposed legs. It is red, watery red, flecked with bits of clinging cells. The uterine lining is shed and being expelled. The nourishing wall of cells that holds and feeds the blastocyst sloughs away and is squeezed out, out. Somewhere in there is the tiny one, the other one that has half Jarrod's genes in it. Would it have been a boy or a girl? It would never have been anything. There was never any chance that it would have been anything.

The aunts collect the flow as best they can and spoon it into a jar. There are medicines and remedies of which this is an ingredient; there are fungal strains that grow best with this as their medium. Jarrod knows all this. Before, these things were abstract. Theories of where medicine came from, rather than the medicine itself. Now they are facts—a fact before him. A woman. A killed fetus.

More flow, but not so much. It is lessening. Now it is clear fluid. And now the contractions calm and lengthen. Fade. Baker is completely silent and still, nursing herself through. The worst is past. She will stay here for the remainder of the night, and will not be able to go back on duty for three days, but the worst is past. For Baker.

The eldest aunt rises from the side of Baker and turns to Jarrod. Her eyes are moist and cold.

"Do you see what you have done?"

"I see what's happened."

"Do you see what you have done?"

What could be the use of defiance here, now?

"Yes."

"And are you ashamed, ranger?"

"Yes, I'm ashamed."

"Good. Go to the men."

"Will she be all right?"

"Go to the men, ranger."

"All right, aunt."

He looks at Baker one more time. There is nothing for him to do. The aunts will care for her, the drugs will keep her. Unless there are unexpected complications, she'll be healthy enough in a few days.

It's over between us.

She has chosen. I've chosen. It can never be the same between us. We didn't have a child together.

What did he know, though? Maybe when he returns from the Shame Trail, all will be the way it had been, his desire for Baker as strong as ever, the memory blasted away by the winds of those high peaks.

Jarrod remembers. He isn't going on the Shame Trail. The future is completely blank. Except that he must go to the council and meet the men.

Baker seems to sleep now. She is resting more softly, at least. Jarrod takes a step toward her. The eldest aunt frowns, stands in his way. He gently steps around her, and the woman does not try to stop him after all. He strokes Baker's hair. Strokes her gaunt, intense face. Easy. Easy, dear one. Then he turns and he leaves the crib. He hitches into the fixed line with a carabiner, and walks the whole long way to the Council Platform, and the gathering of the male rangers of Threecabin.

"A ranger is trustworthy, above all. A ranger keeps his word and honors the life to which he has been elected and the position in which he's been placed. The Park Service nourishes and keeps him, and in return he looks to his responsibilities for the upkeep of the rangers and, above all, for the stewardship of the forest."

Old Alaph speaks, the council clerk. He holds the Burly Stave, the staff of gnarled red cedar that allows one to speak with the authority of the council. Alaph is on the plain raised platform of the council rostrum. Jarrod stands in the center of the men, who are gathered in a circle about him. Jarrod faces Alaph and thinks, My first shunning. I'm the center of attention. How perfectly goddamn delightful. The Council Platform is suspended between four great firs, and there is a lamp burning bright near each trunk. The shadows of all the men fall on Jarrod.

"Ranger Jarrod, what are the seven points of the Law of the Service?"

"A ranger is trustworthy, obedient, brave, clean and thrifty. He is a scholar and looks to the stewardship of the forest." Jarrod states the Law with as little inflection as he can manage. He does not wish to show contempt; he does not wish to show anger or sorrow or guilt.

Alaph stares down at him like a big silver bird. He has the long hair of age, and it falls in well-tended ringlets down to the small of his back. Alaph is developing quite a paunch from his sedentary years tending to the council records, which he tries to suck in and hide with his coat. "You stand before us untrustworthy, Ranger Jarrod. Do you have anything to say to this?"

Jarrod looks up at Alaph. There is nothing to say to that beaky face. Nothing to add or take away from what the old buzzard has said.

"I don't."

Alaph looks at him for a moment longer, then gazes out over the men. "Ranger Jarrod has caused another ranger unnecessary pain. He has been disloyal. He has been untrustworthy. He has breached our ways—rules for living in the forest that he knows very well must always be upheld. Upheld for the good of the forest. This breach cannot go unpunished. I recommend that Ranger Jarrod be shunned for the period of six months."

What? What is old Alaph saying? A month is the standard punishment.

Jarrod tenses his muscles, holds himself tightly and keeps control. Six months. So be it.

"Does anyone else have anything to say for Ranger Jarrod?"

"I am his superior." Franklin is speaking, his raspy voice taking on a most sorrowful tone. But Franklin is not a sorrowful man. He's laughing, Jarrod thinks. He's laughing at me, dammit. "I share in his shame. Yet he is a good man in many ways, and he'll be missed in the Ho. I would have him shunned only three months. For our sake, and not for his."

Alaph nods. "Chief Ranger Franklin's recommendation for three months is duly noted and adopted," he says. Again the bird's hard eye on Jarrod.

"Ranger Jarrod, we, the rangers of the United States Park Service of the Olympic National Forest, do officially suspend you without pay for a period of three months. You are cast from our number unless and until you meet the official fine and serve the penance we place upon you."

Alaph looks up and is again speaking to the gathered men, though he addresses Jarrod alone. "For a period of three months commencing tomorrow at sunrise, 6:32 A.M. Pacific Standard Time, you are to walk the Shame Trail along the Eastern Ridges. We will provide you with the supplies you will need to live, and you will take these and only these. All contact between you and other human beings is forbidden. All speech on your part is forbidden. You are to walk the Shame Trail and reflect on your untrustworthy nature and how you can mend it. After a period of three months, you will return and we will test you to ascertain that your ways are mended. When and if we ascertain your trustworthiness has returned, you will be readmitted into the Park Service, and your salary resumed at the usual rate."

Old Alaph steps down from the rostrum. He motions to Jarrod that he is to take his place. Jarrod climbs onto the platform. Alaph stands directly in front of Jarrod now. Alaph coughs and draws his coat closer. Jarrod looks down on the old uncle's head, the cascade of silver locks upon his shoulders. The night is cold and he wants to get this over with, Jarrod thinks. He is pair-bonded with Aunt Dorothea, who is far past the age she can get pregnant, and Alaph has a warm, safe bed to go to tonight.

"Prepare to taste the pain of the ranger you have harmed."

What?

"Taste her pain."

With the swiftness of a bird of prey, Old Alaph punches Jarrod's gut hard with the Burly Stave. For a moment, the lamps of the Council Platform dim, the men fade from view. He stumbles backward, gasping. Hold on. Don't lose it here. Hold, ranger, hold.

Jarrod straightens up. The old buzzard still has strength in those arms after all. Jarrod grimaces, reins in an urge to vomit. Hold on. Hold.

"Rangers, repeat after me—"

All of the gathered men shuffle to attention.

"Ranger Jarrod, we shun you."

"Ranger Jarrod, we shun you."

"Go from here."

"Go from here."

"Walk the Shame Trail."

"Walk the Shame Trail."

Jarrod quickly glances around. Some are looking at him with

hard eyes. Some without heat. None with sympathy. They mean it. Or they don't care one way or the other.

"Regain our trust."

"Regain our trust."

All right, Jarrod thinks. I will.

No one tells Jarrod what to do next. The men continue to look him over. After a time, Old Alaph turns and stalks away. One by one, the other men follow. They file out along the plankway that is opposite the rostrum. Finally, Jarrod is left alone, standing exposed on the bare planks of the rostrum. So.

After the sound of the last man's step is gone from the plankway, Jarrod goes to each of the fir trunks from which the platform is suspended, and turns off each lamp. Then he walks in darkness back to his hammock. He lies awake all night, thinking about the way Baker moaned. His stomach hurts. But that will pass. Baker's lovely face, quiet and controlled. The little one that was not dead, because it was never alive, could not live. It could not live.

I am not ashamed, Jarrod thinks. I will never be ashamed of you.

No ranger is related to any other by blood. This is necessary to keep the women always in service, necessary for the protection of the forest.

I wonder who my mother and father were, Jarrod thinks. The Timberlanders and Matties have their legends about the rangers. Rangers come in the night and steal babies. Always keep a watch for the first two years, they tell one another. And to the children: you'd better be careful, or a ranger will get you. He has heard that they believe these things. The truth is different, more complex. There are those whose business it is to find a home among the rangers for unwanted children. They are thought of as witches, crones. They dwell along the fringes of the forest, and people bring their own children to them in the dark of night, and those people are seen no more.

Such a one is Old Maggie. Jarrod's first memory is the smell of Old Maggie's burlap skirting, its rough fiber against his cheek. Old Maggie's clothes were sewn with cat gut from one of the dozens that lived in her tumbledown barn. Maggie found a use for everything, even dead cats. She must have been young then, and just called Maggie. No. She's always been Old Maggie.

This is one the Ponds didn't want. Can't keep. There's quite a story to his mother, if you care to hear it.

No, said the other, a woman all dressed in green. Aunt Larmy, but he did not know that then.

All right, then. Name's Phillip James, if that matters to you. It doesn't.

The edge of the forest. The misty day beating down like time. Well, then.

The woman in green approached. Took his hand.

Come, child.

Go on, little Phil.

He did not cry. He was fearful, but he did not cry. And it seemed that the one in green was not a woman, not a ranger, but the forest itself that drew him in, nestled him in delicate needles, prickly, soft, forever, little boy.

His next memory is a fall from a sapling he'd been trying to climb, away from the watch of the aunts and uncles who were watching that day. The breath knocked out of him, ice spears in his chest and an aching head. But he got up, stumbled to the sapling, found the lowest branch, and again he was climbing, climbing. This time he did not slip. Climbing, into the trees.

Jarrod?

Here I am.

Where are you, Jarrod?

Here I am, up in the tree.

Days among the people of the trees, in the tree villages. Nights listening to stories by the stoves and lamps. At eight, Ranger School begins, and at sixteen he graduates, third in his

class of fifty. Always the great forest at the heart of the peninsula, and the great trees, swollen to monstrous size by years of
rain, rain, rain. But to Jarrod this has all become natural, and
right. He takes his place among the Ho Brigade, the keepers of
the wildest heart of the Olympic National Park, where none but
rangers ever tread, and even they keep to the trees.

Jarrod sleeps a little—perhaps an hour—but is up long before dawn and is, as always, early reporting to brigade headquarters.

Franklin arrives at the first tinge of daylight in the east. With
him is Aunt Larmy, the council proxy. She and Franklin are
about the same age, and it was Larmy's abortion for which
Franklin was shunned those many years before. As far as Jarrod
knows, they have not been lovers since that time.

Jarrod has not turned on a lamp, and Franklin flints one on
with a practiced hand. The room is utilitarian—even more so
than other ranger dwellings. It is just a big room with four plank
walls cut from windfall hemlock. The platform itself is lashed
within a stand of hemlocks, curved in a long path among them
so as to form a great hall. In its center is a rough-hewn table that
conforms to the curvings of the hall. Log-round stools bound the
table. Larmy goes to the table and slides a stool out of the way.
She spreads out a map, and places two small bags of sand to
hold it down on either side.

"This," she says, "is California."

Jarrod steps up to the table and Franklin joins him. It is an
artfully done map, scribed on deerskin vellum. Jarrod recognizes the hand of Uncle Nab, the cartographer who provides
most of the contour maps the brigade uses.

"How's the old guts?" Franklin says, putting his hand on
Jarrod's shoulder. "Alaph said he didn't hit you that hard, but it
sure looked like he whacked you."

Jarrod grunts.

"That was your first shunning ceremony, wasn't it, ranger?"

"Yes it was."

"Should have told you about the Burly Stave last night. Slipped my mind."

"I've never known much to slip your mind, sir."

"Well. It did. I had a great deal to consider last night."

Larmy harrumphs. "Yes."

Franklin takes his hand from Jarrod's shoulder and Jarrod is all attention. "Yes, ma'am."

"Three days ago, we received an emergency message from the Yosemite Park Service. It seem they are having an epidemic."

"An epidemic? Of what?"

"They don't know. Their medical knowledge has gotten a little vague these past few years."

"Well, what do *we* think?"

"From their descriptions, we know it's some sort of plague. We're fairly certain they've got both forms of the bubonic plague bacteria attacking them."

"God. Do they know how to fight it?"

Larmy shuffles uneasily. "It appears that they have lost the knowledge necessary to synthesize antibiotics."

"Well, I know they're a Park and Forest Service mix, but couldn't we just *tell* them how to do it over the radio?"

Franklin speaks. "They don't have any blue mold. They can't find any."

"What about streptomycin?"

"Their soil's all wrong and they don't have the craft to extract it, in any case. You see, that's the problem. We hadn't realized it before. Oh, there were hints. But—

"They've gone tribal."

"That's what we're afraid of."

"They're half Forest Service," says Larmy. "Multiusers. Breeders. It was bound to happen." She frowns, shakes her head.

"You may imagine that this caused quite a stir in council," says Franklin. "We were wondering what could be done. We were wondering whether anything *should* be done."

"Just let them die? They're U.S. citizens."

"Are they?" says Larmy. "The council has decided we cannot spare a company of rangers to convey the penicillin to San Bernardino. There's too much pressure on us from the Timberlanders' League in Forks. All are needed. And the Matties are breeding like flies as usual."

"These are not new developments."

"No. But that is the council's decision."

"But. To just let those people die . . ."

"No," Larmy says, almost as if the word is distasteful to her. "We can't."

"We're sending some penicillin down," says Franklin. "Somebody who knows distillation craft, too, and how to start the mold in vitro."

"But the council. By whose authority?"

"Mine," Larmy says. "When the council is not available, the council proxy has the power to command any single ranger or company of rangers to perform a task. So we're splitting the difference. It's a gamble, but we think that if we send *one* ranger, then the council won't get all up in arms. And if we send him, say, this morning, there's not much they can do about it, anyway."

"What about the penicillin?"

"I've spent the last couple of days getting together a good supply of it," Franklin says. "Also, a small ether still, and some items you'll need to build a bigger one."

One expendable ranger. So, California is to be his Shame Walk. It has been a long time since geography class, and Jarrod has only a vague idea of the exact makeup of the United States. It wasn't something you ever really needed to know. He looks at the map. He isn't sure of the scale, but there is one thing he can tell.

It is a long way to Southern California. He smiles grimly. "Sure," he says. "I'll go."

"It isn't quite what you think," Larmy says. "There is something else. Something important. Tell him, Franklin."

Jarrod stands waiting.

Franklin speaks. "I, for one, am convinced that Yosemite *hasn't* gone completely tribal. They've just retained other craft than we have. We've compromised and lost things, too. We've had to. So have they. But they've always known *geology*. After all, they're sitting on goddamn *California*. When they found out we weren't all that eager to send a team down to rescue them, their radio operator mentioned something. Some kind of information they had to trade."

"What was it?"

"They think something is about to happen. Something big."

"What, like a volcano?"

"Bigger, they say. If the idiotic council hadn't hemmed and hawed, they would have told us. I'm sure of it."

"What could it be?"

"I don't know. Nobody knows. Major earthquake. Asteroid headed our way. Everyone thinks they're lying, that they're desperate. But I don't know about that. I don't know about that at all. We sure as hell don't have many telescopes around here, now do we?"

"*You* have one. Uncle Skully does."

"Glorified binoculars. They have a goddamn *observatory*." Franklin reaches into the pocket of his coat. He takes out a compass and sets it on the table.

"Have you noticed anything about your compass lately?" he says. "Anything strange?"

"Not particularly."

"It isn't that noticeable with field gear. Just a half a degree or so."

"What are you talking about?"

"The magnetic declination is changing."

"You're crazy. That can't happen."

"So says theory. This is fact. I can prove it. I've got a much more accurate needle in my crib."

"Well, what does the council say?"

Franklin laughed. "They say that I'm a senile old coot. There's even been talk of having me removed from the Ho. Alaph's behind that, I think. It doesn't matter what they do with me, though; it wouldn't change the laws of electromagnetism."

"What does it mean?"

"I have no idea. But I'll bet you a sack of mushrooms it has something to do with Yosemite's big secret."

"And you want me to find out?"

"If there is anything *to* find out, I want you to trade that penicillin for the information, and call me on the radio and tell me what it is those rangers know."

# ORF DREAMS

One night the robot begins to dream. Where Orf lives, there is no day and no night, of course, but there is a period of quiet that Orf gave himself and that he calls night.

He dreams of a ranger.

At first he thinks it is a memory of Andrew, and perhaps it is, refracted, bent in time. But something in the dream, a feeling, tells him that this is not Andrew, but another. Without a name, in the dream.

A burning, beautiful landscape. Scourged, as if by fire and wind. Tree stumps and red ruin.

And a ranger passes through.

He walks at a steady pace, the ranger—undaunted, unhurried. Who are you? Orf asks in his dream, for he can speak in that place, although he is not there, but far, far away, below.

The ranger pauses, looks about.

Nothing. He turns his attention back to the walking.

Who are you?

The ranger continues on. He continues steadily on.

# TOWN

His internal frame backpack is standard issue green and black. There is a sleeping bag and weatherproof bivvy bag in the lower compartment. He's got rain gear and a down parka. Extra socks. Pemmican and a large sack of cornmeal. A candle lantern. Flint and steel and a smolder stick wrapped in oilcloth. Two water skins. A cookpot and spoon. A bag full of herbs and remedies. A sewing kit with a bone needle. Vellum with instructions on how to operate a shortwave radio etched onto it. A compass. A small map of the west coast of North America. An old .22 revolver that Franklin says works, and ten extra cartridges. A blowgun with a vial of poison for dipping darts. A flute made from a moose's shinbone. Chemical distillation apparatus packed neatly and securely wrapped. Enough penicillin to treat five hundred people.

Jarrod feels weighted and nearly off balance, working his way through along the fixed lines to the southern perimeter of the forest. He comes down from the trees sooner than he might have with a lesser burden, and begins to walk. There are trails here, made by Timberlanders. And soon he is on a worn pathway. He feels very uneasy, somehow profane. There are no pathways worn down to bare dirt in the forest. It is like walking along an inflamed scar.

Then a field. Another. The trees are windbreaks now.

*Wide.*

The sky arches over and around him. Tugs at him. Pulls him upward, outward. Wide. So, wide.

Jarrod reels, stumbles. He goes down on one knee and is panting hard, unable to catch his breath.

I'm falling up into the sky, he thinks. I'm falling and I can't stop myself and it will never end. Into the wide open. Falling. Falling.

But it *does* end, after a few moments. Jarrod shakes his head. He stands up. Takes a step. For a moment, the unbalance returns. The fear. The urge to flee and nowhere to go. But he closes his eyes, holds on. When he opens them again, he can continue. But still. This weird wideness will always be wrong, will *never* be home.

He finds the lane that Larmy has told him of and turns down it, down a path that is as wide as two people now. A path carts and horses can travel. To a wooden house next to a big woodpile. Killed trees. Wrong, wrong.

Not knowing what else to do, Jarrod stands in the yard, waiting—for he knows not what. The front door opens. Cats flow from the house.

"Well."

"You are Maggie?"

She looks him over. Jarrod remembers that face staring down at him; those eyes.

"Nothing for you at the moment," she says.

"I'm not here for that."

"No. You're a man, too. That would be unusual. Well." Longer, gazing. Almost, perhaps, remembering a little boy with *his* eyes, the curve of his lips. "Come inside, then."

He goes inside the house. Jarrod has never been in a house on the ground before—not that he can remember. Maggie sits down and drinks from a steaming cup that was already on the kitchen table. She slurps a little as she sips. The room smells like cats and biscuits.

"Are you hungry?"

"No," he says.

"Would you like some tea? It's hedge nettle."

Jarrod blinks. Hedge nettle. *Stachys Palustris.* Mint family. Close cousin to mountain pennyroyal.

"Yes," he says.

"Sit down." He does. She gets up and pours him a cup in an ancient, chipped mug. It has a picture of a cup on it and the words *Maxwell House. Good to the last drop.*

Jarrod is not sure how to begin, and so he simply makes his request. "I'm traveling to California. I need help in arranging transportation."

Maggie sits back down. She breathes out a steamy laugh over her cup of tea. "Why did you come to me?"

"We don't know very many people . . . outside. Aunt Larmy said you might help."

Again the laugh. "I wish I could, child. What do I know about California, though?"

Jarrod is silent. He takes a sip of his tea. Maggie looks at him again.

"Your mother might help," she finally says. "If she's of a mind to."

"What?" Jarrod feels his pulse quicken, his skin flush, just as it had when the horrible sense of wideness had struck him.

"She's married to a Mattie now. Renaldo Ocean. In Olympia. You have heard of Renaldo Ocean?"

"Yes. He's the Mattie warlord in Olympia."

"I don't know about warlord. Maybe in his younger days. He's the peoplespeaker of their caucus down there."

"His people have killed rangers."

"They've killed a lot more Timberlanders, let me tell you. Like to have wiped us all out before the alliance with the James Kensingtons."

"I don't know what you're talking about."

"I'm talking about your people, Phillip."

"My name is Jarrod."

"You come from blue blood, boy. The bluest in these parts."

"That doesn't mean anything to me."

"It should. It might help you do . . . whatever it is you're after doing."

Jarrod says nothing. He finishes drinking his tea. Maggie gets up to pour him another, and he barely notices, so busy is he thinking. Larmy must know where he came from. She must have meant for him to use the connection. But why didn't she tell him?

Maggie reaches over, gives his hair a tousle, which brings Jarrod out of his reverie.

"Tatum James's eldest boy comes walking out of the woods, as tall as an oak. Well, they feed their little ones on acorns, it's said."

"Acorns," Jarrod says, "and other things. Other things."

"I can hitch up Hildie and take you down to Olympia in the wagon. I've got a safe passage due me from the Cedar Rats. I don't suppose you know how to hitch up a horse, do you?"

"No."

"Well then, I'll do it."

Jarrod follows Old Maggie to the barn and watches her place the tack and harness onto the mare. He helps her lift the draw poles, and cinch them up to Hildie's yoke collar. Then she takes the reins in hand and drives the wagon into her yard. "I may as well bring some trade," she mumbles to herself, and goes inside the house to gather items. Jarrod places his pack in the wagon bed and stands beside the front wheel. He wants to pet the horse, to feel her thin, velvety skin, but he is afraid he might frighten her. He is a little frightened himself. The creature is nearly as big as an elk.

Maggie returns. With a grunt, she pulls herself onto the wagon seat. Getting in after her, Jarrod realizes too late that he should have helped her. She takes the reins, and with a lurch, they are off.

Down the path, two furrows made by the wheels. Past fields, more fields. Corn and wheat. Zucchini and yellow squash. Into a road that is more than a mere wagon rut. It is all bare, and in places strange black lumps show through. What kind of geology could have produced *this*? Then Jarrod realizes that the lumps are asphalt. This is one of the old roads, Highway 101.

After they are on their way, Maggie doesn't say much. She hums a tune to the mare that Jarrod does not recognize, and occasionally looks over at Jarrod, shakes her head and laughs.

"My," she says once. "You *are* a sight. All that green."

Toward evening, they near what Maggie says is the boundary of the Kensington-James clan lands. "Over the river is Cedar Rat territory. They're fighting with the Gig Harbor Matties. Maybe they won't bother us."

"I thought you said they owed you passage."

"Some of them know me, some don't," she says. "And they're all crazy from the fighting."

"I have a revolver," Jarrod says. "Should I get it?"

Maggie stops the horse up short, looks at him hard. "Don't be pulling that thing out around me. The only reason to take out a gun is if you're going to use it. Would you use it?"

"Yes," he says. But he has never killed off his native ground. Killed without the certainty that he is in the right, and that what he does is in the best interest of the forest. This would be different. Maybe. He doesn't know what it will be.

"Just let me do the talking," Maggie says, starting the mare again. "Save your bullets for later, when you really need them."

They are about five miles into Cedar Rat territory when they come to a roadblock. A patrol is camped on the side of the road in tents that are slovenly pitched. Trenches are dug around the tents to channel rain, and the paths between the tents are worn and ragged. Tracer-leavers, Jarrod thinks. Idiot barbarians.

A boy comes from the nearest tent. He is armed with a long

pike. He has a breastplate of steel, made from something that used to be yellow. He cannot be more than sixteen.

"Hello, soldier," Maggie calls in her crackly old voice. "Is your captain in? Tell him Maggie who brings the comfrey would like to speak to him."

The boy seems unimpressed. "What is your business?" he says. His voice is higher than it will be if he lives a couple years longer, Jarrod thinks. The boy notices Jarrod looking at him, and glares back. With a shrug, Jarrod averts his gaze.

"I have some poultices for here, and some arrowhead blanks for Olympia, where I'm bound. Tyrone is your captain, ain't he?"

"Tyrone's dead," the boy says, unmoving. It seems Tyrone's death is not much of a tragedy for him.

"Who was his second? Lieutenant Martin, wasn't it? He'll want these poultices."

The boy looks at Jarrod again, hard. Try it, you dirty little Timberlander, Jarrod thinks, and it's your head will be on the end of that pike. No, calm. This is not an invader. You are on *his* ground now.

"Stay here," the boy says. "I'll go get Martin."

It turns out that Maggie knows Martin, who is so eager for news from the north that he forgets to ask about the poultices.

"And what are the greenshits up to?" Martin asks after he has heard about Timberlander goings-on. Rangers, Jarrod thinks. He's talking about rangers.

"The usual," Maggie replies.

"I heard some homesteaders got massacred."

"You heard right. Them Newmans should have known better than to build up the Quinault like that."

"Goddamn greenshit savages."

"I'm not saying it's right what was done to them, but they should have known better."

"What exactly did them animals do?" Martin asks, with a gleam of professional interest in his eyes. But Jarrod knows the details already, and he stops paying attention. Greenshits. Animals. He knew it was like this out of the forest. But he'd never *felt* it before. Gone tribal.

Maggie finally talks the captain out, and they are getting ready to leave. "Who's this?" he says, pointing good-naturedly at Jarrod.

"My nephew. He's going to Olympia to look for work at the dikes."

"Ha," says the captain. "I'd sooner eat mud than break my back for that Ocean bastard. He's a snake and a slave driver if I ever saw one."

Jarrod does not reply. He smiles wanly at the captain, shrugs.

"Don't talk much, do he?"

"No," Maggie says. "Not much. Well."

"Well, go on then, and you'd best be off the road by nightfall somewheres. There's unsavory fellows about."

"I know it," Maggie says. "And we'll see you later." She flicks the reins and starts Hildie back on the road. It is only after they've turned a bend and put the encampment out of sight that Jarrod lets himself relax.

They go on until just before nightfall. Many of the fields they pass are in the first stages of going back to woods. Maggie turns down a side road, which winds through ever thicker woods for a mile or so. Then, there is the glow of windows up ahead. A white clapboard building. A sheet metal sign, rusted to brown, crumbling letters, names the place as LAVORE'S TAVERN. Maggie pulls the wagon around back, to where there is a barn. A young woman, as young as the Cedar Rat road guard, comes out to help them bed the horse for the night. She stares at Jarrod until he feels that his face is covered with some strange fungus. Maggie calls the girl Darlene, and Darlene says hardly three words. They go inside.

Darlene's father Dave Johnson is not a LaVore, he tells them, but married into the family and inherited the inn. He knows

Maggie, and before Jarrod can stop her, Maggie tells Dave John-son who Jarrod is, and where he is going.

"Don't you worry," Maggie says after seeing Jarrod's worried expression. "He's the tightest-lipped innkeeper that ever lived. And what if he does tell on you in a few days? It won't hurt your chances of going south none."

Maggie is probably right, Jarrod thinks, but telling people one's business without their asking is a very unrangerly trait.

"Well, now that I know," Dave Johnson says, "I can tell you that sometimes they run *trains*. Down the Willamette and to Yreka. Wine trains, they call them, on account of that's what they bring back. I had a cousin went down to Olympia, hired on as a guard in a—what do they call it—Karma Patrol. They feed them guards meat every day, too, and twice on Saturdays. Got killed going over the Siskiyous on his second trip down. Some-body ambushed the train. Train made it through, but Lew got himself killed for his trouble."

"Who is they?" Jarrod asks.

"Well, that I don't know. Lew was an ornery cuss, and we didn't talk much when he did live hereabouts. I heard about all this secondhand, so to speak. But you could ask when you get down to Olympia. Somebody'll know there."

Darlene brings in food. It is potatoes and cornbread. Jarrod looks around for fork and knife, and is about to get his from his pack, when he notices all the others digging in, eating with their fingers. After a moment's hesitation, he does the same. The potatoes are hot and plump and the cornbread moist and firm. Dave Johnson has bees, and there is honey to pour over the meal as well. It is delicious, although nothing a ranger would ever eat. Jarrod says as much, and Darlene, who has up until now been looking at him the way a terrified rabbit looks at a hawk, breaks into a smile. Jarrod finishes up and licks the honey from his fingertips, just as the others are doing.

Maggie and Jarrod are the only lodgers. Dave Johnson puts

Jarrod into his own room, and he does not protest, but as soon as everyone has gone to bed and the inn quieted down Jarrod slips through the window and goes into the woods nearby. There is no evergreen climax growth yet, only a mixture of alder, madrona and broadleaf maple, and a single western crabapple. Jarrod climbs up into a maple to a clump of branches to get secure. This is the first time all day he has felt safe. He drifts to sleep and troubled dreams of a wide and empty plain—although this is a feeling, rather than an actual vision in the dream, for Jarrod has never seen a place that is absolutely treeless.

He awakes at dawn, comes down, and is drawing water from the spring when Darlene comes from the inn with a bucket.

"Good morning," she says in a startled voice.

"Hello." He finishes filling one water skin and pulls it from the cold pool and caps it. Then he takes the other and submerges it, while Darlene watches, still holding her bucket.

"Did you sleep well? Your bed looked hardly touched."

And what were you doing looking in on me, Jarrod thinks. "Don't tell your father, but I came outside and slept in a tree. I do that sometimes."

"Oh," Darlene says. "Which?"

"You can't see it from here."

"How do you keep from falling out?"

"You hold on."

"Even when you're asleep?"

"*Especially* when you're asleep."

"Oh," Darlene says. "I see."

"How long have you lived here?" he asks.

"All my life."

"Where's your mother?"

"She died having me. Why do you want to know that?"

"I was just wondering. So your father keeps you."

"And why shouldn't he?"

"He should, of course."

"Do you ever go anywhere?"

"We go to Olympia for the fair every October. That's where I got Skumper, too."

"What's Skumper?"

"My cat."

"Have you ever seen the ocean?"

"No. Have you?"

"No."

"It's just sixty miles that way," she says, pointing over her shoulder in a direction that Jarrod is fairly certain isn't west. He nods. "I've seen the Puget Sound, though."

"It's salty, isn't it?"

"It's salty and cold."

"I guess I'll see it in Olympia."

"I guess you will. You leaving this morning?"

"Yes."

"Going to California?"

"Yes."

"For what?"

Jarrod thinks about whether he should tell her. "I'm carrying medicine down there for some sick rangers," he finally says.

"Oh. Well. When are you coming back?"

"I don't know."

"Are you coming here?"

"I don't know."

Darlene dips her bucket into the spring. "Will you. Will you *be* with me?" she asks. "Be with me now. I ain't been with nobody yet."

"What?" But Jarrod understands what she is saying. He stands, caps his second water skin. He looks at Darlene. She is budding, losing baby fat. She has a sturdy, bunched figure, like a blacktail yearling doe well fed on summer forage. Almost, but not quite ready for mating.

What would it be like? Jarrod wonders. What would it be like copulating with a Timberlander?

Darlene lifts her brimming bucket from the spring, sets it

beside her. She wears a faded shift sewn from flour bags so faded that the writing is unreadable—only traces of blue remain, as if writing were getting ready to form, but had not come into being yet.

"We could go into the windbreak," she says. "Daddy don't get up till the sun hits his face."

"Why?" Jarrod says. "Why do you want to be with me?"

Darlene seems perplexed, as if this were the last question she expected him to ask. "I don't know. You said them nice things about the cornbread. You're real handsome. And I think you are a gentleman."

"A what?"

"A gentleman. Like them in Olympia."

"No," Jarrod says. "I am not."

"Well. Anyway."

For a moment, Jarrod feels desire growing. The foggy morning hangs about the spring, about Darlene, and the brown wisps of her hair are dewy and lank. He reaches over to her, strokes her face. She is flush and warm.

"You can't be fourteen," he says.

"I am, too."

She takes his hand from her face, moves it to her breast. But he feels only the soft burr of Darlene's shift. Old cotton. From the time before. She is a scavenger. Her kind take from the land, suck the life from the land. Disgusting, like a tick, like a fungus. Timberlanders crawling through the land they destroyed, living in their own slime. Darlene's nipple hardens under his touch. He can feel it through the thin, worn cotton.

"Don't you like me? Come to the windbreak."

"Child, I—"

"I'm a woman."

"Yes. You are."

"I know how to do it. Come to the windbreak."

Jarrod sees himself in those woods. He sees the girl on her

stomach, bent over a fallen log, her legs parted, himself thrusting inside her from behind. Blood on her legs. Telling him how much it hurts. How much it hurts, what he is doing. That would be the only way with a Timberlander. Like an animal.

You couldn't stop me from hurting you, he thinks. And I *would*. I would want to hurt you.

"I may come back this way," he says. "And you'll be older."

"I'm old enough." She is whining. Jarrod smiles, draws his hand away.

"For some things."

"For this."

If you were only old enough to *fight back*. Fight back hard.

"No," he says. He bends down, picks up her water pail. "Let's go in."

She follows, sulky, reluctant, back into the inn.

"I'm making pancakes," Darlene says in a defiant tone, and grabs the bucket. "I am making pancakes."

Jarrod sits at the kitchen table and watches her. In an hour or so, Maggie and Dave Johnson sit down to the table. They spoon honey onto the pancakes and roll them into cylinders. They eat their food with their bare hands.

Maggie seems much more at ease on the ride to Olympia. Getting past the Cedar Rat gang has done her good, she says. Jarrod suddenly wonders why it is she is doing this for him. Until now, events have flowed and carried him along as if he has fallen into a deep, fast river. He wonders if the beginnings of all great journeys and difficult tasks are like this. He has nothing to compare this beginning with.

The day is cloudy, but there is no rain. The new-growth woods give way to fields once more. Occasionally the sun breaks through to light patches of corn or fruit trees—there are orchards now. Once or twice, Jarrod catches himself enjoying the play of the sun patches across the swaying corn, the dark green of the fruit tree foliage against the lighter green of the land. How alien. How wrong and beautiful.

Maggie hums more songs, some of which seem almost familiar to Jarrod, as if they were twisted versions of ranger lullabies. He imagines they must be. Two hundred years ago, he thinks, we were all U.S. citizens and everybody got along.

"Why are you helping me, Maggie?" he asks when they are just outside Olympia.

She hums along for a while, as if she hasn't heard him, then answers in the same singsong voice. "To close the circle. I've never had one of you come back."

"I'm not coming back. I'm just passing through."

"Yep. I also picked up some good tidbits from Dave Johnson. Valuable in certain places."

"What tidbits? I didn't see you trade a thing with him."

Maggie hums a few more bars, laughs softly in the middle of the song. "Do you know what I went to school for?" she asks.

Jarrod shakes his head.

"Library science."

"Can you still do that? Where was that?"

"It was in Seattle, at the University of Washington is where, and no you can't. There was only three hundred of us students when I went there. Long, long ago. My senior year, the Aberdeen mariners sailed up the Interlake Canal. They raided us. Do you know the one of you they called Skully?"

"Uncle Skully? Yes, of course. I—"

"He's my son by one of them damn mariners. Caught me in the library. In British lit, I believe it was, the PRs." Maggie laughs, but this laugh is far more bitter than any of her others.

"After that, he set fire to the place. And they burned the school down, too. All of it."

"So you never graduated?"

"Nope. But I'm an *information specialist*." Maggie enunciates the words carefully, and with a pride that Jarrod has not heard in her voice until now. "I collect it and give it out. Sometimes I make a little from it to keep me going."

"I don't have any trade, if that's what you're saying."

"Oh, you never know," she says. "You never do know until you know."

They come into Olympia on Interstate 5, through gullies of collapsed concrete and road deck that is in many places worn through to the rebar. Hildie doesn't like the way she must walk, but Maggie keeps her steady and out of harm's way, as they descend from the Willapa Hills and see the dull metallic glow of the capitol building.

"She's in the governor's mansion," Maggie says. "But we'll have to go through some rigmarole to get there."

They arrive at the gates of the city. Maggie takes a twisted device of feather and metal from her bag of goods and shows it to the guard. He waves them through.

Jarrod immediately sees that there has been a fire, but long ago. The ground and vegetation still show signs of it, what ground he can see. But new buildings have gone up, mud daub houses mostly, with a few made of wood. The streets were paved once, but the wagon tracks are worn down to chunky dirt, colored black from ground-up garbage. The street leads down a hill overlooking a sea of colors.

The white and green of the Matties, everywhere. Faded blues and browns. He realizes he's seeing stretches of canvas tents. Banners. Then the wagon is among the colors, and it is a bazaar of goods merchants peddling their provisions in hundreds of stalls. The place, Maggie says, is called the Chine.

Jarrod has never seen this many people together. For a moment he feels panic rising, but it is controllable, and he does so. He wants to spend time here, look around at what the hucksters and mongers have to offer, but Maggie drives on. People glance up at them, and some stare at his strange garb. Maybe it's better to keep moving, he thinks.

At a place where the Chine turns a corner, there is a clear dirt patch that forms a kind of makeshift square. A man is chained to an iron post that stands in the Chine square's center. He is wearing only soiled rags now, but they are the remains of what was once a green and orange religious habit. He is chained in such a way that he must stay on his knees in the dust of the square, while his arms are pulled behind him and to the stake. His chest has been flayed open, probably with a studded whip, Jarrod reckons, for leather alone is brutal, but cannot cut so deeply. The man is old, and his face and bald head are burned bright red from the sun.

"Chomskyite," Maggie said. "Heretics. They don't believe in oversight committees."

"A Mattie's a Mattie," Jarrod replies. "But even a Mattie. Let me give that man some water."

"No."

They pass on.

Near the capitol is a row of ancient houses, and Maggie is challenged again before being allowed to drive up the street these houses line. Again, she shows the guard her device of feathers and metal.

"What is that?" Jarrod asks.

"Clan fetish of your mother's people. All the town guard know it."

Maggie calls the mare to stop in front of one of the houses. There are hitching posts on the lawn, and she ties a rein to one of these.

"Well," she says. "Let's pay a call."

They walk to the front door and Maggie knocks with her bony knuckles. So this is how to announce yourself at a house.

A young woman opens the door. She is wearing a brown habit with green piping on the sleeves. Her short hair is dyed red, the color of maple leaves in autumn, and her skin is as pale as roots.

"Greetings from the Mother," she says in a hushed voice.

"Tell Tatum James Old Maggie's come from Shelton to see her," says Maggie loudly. At least it seems loud to Jarrod after the other woman's soft speech.

"A moment," the woman says, and closes the door. They wait longer than a moment. Finally, she returns.

"Follow me," she says. Maggie steps inside. Jarrod makes to follow her, but he feels the young woman's hand upon his arm. Her touch is exceedingly firm. "Only her," the woman says.

"He's with me," says Maggie.

"He is not cleared through."

"Listen, dear," Maggie says, pulling the woman's hand from Jarrod's arm. "He's got a binding to me and will not be a bother. On my woman's word, he's to come along."

The young woman considers. She doesn't look at Jarrod again, but turns and motions Maggie to follow her. When she does, Jarrod is allowed to follow.

They go down a long hallway, past several rooms that are filled with furniture, cloth, tapestries. They like clutter, Jarrod thinks. Into a large room with several cushioned couches, and an old wind-up gramophone on a buffet. It is playing a song that is like nothing Jarrod has ever heard before. Although he knows that the technology once existed for such a thing, he cannot imagine what instruments were used to record this—sound.

On one of the couches, drinking from a silver goblet, sits his mother. She sets her goblet on a table next to the couch and rises when they enter. She smiles at Maggie. Then she looks at Jarrod. They both gaze at each other for a long time.

"Is this?" she says. Her voice is dry and deep, like leaves.

"Phillip. He's called Jarrod these days."

His mother gasps, puts a hand to her mouth. There is a trace of tears in her eyes, but no tears fall. "Sit down," she says. "Sit down."

They sit on a couch that is across from her.

She has a broad face, but with strong features. Her skin is as white as her attendant's, and her hair is cropped in the same manner, but undyed. It is the same color as Jarrod's, the color of forest leafmeal. She likewise wears a simple shift, but hers is vermilion, and the piping is gold. It is gathered in front by hooks and eyelets, but not buttoned to the top, as the attendant's is. There is something strange, and Jarrod realizes she has somehow blackened her eyelashes and there is a faint mica sheen to her skin.

"Phillip," she says to him.

"My name is Jarrod," he says, but without heat.

"You've grown into a man."

"Yes."

"I'm so glad to see you. Do you want something to drink? To eat? Barbara, get them a glass of wine." The attendant goes soundlessly from the room. Jarrod is about to say that he requires nothing, but Maggie pats him on the leg.

"It'll be good," she says. "You've never tasted anything like it, my boy."

Jarrod sits back and waits. There is nothing else to do.

"Questions. You'll have very many questions," says his mother.

But he doesn't. Nothing but idle curiosity about things that it will do him no good to know. "I'm not angry," he says. "I don't remember much."

"I thought there was nothing I could do," she says. "You don't know how important clean blood was to the clan."

"Is," says Maggie, chuckling. "Except for *one* exception I know of."

"That's right." His mother drew herself up straight, and there was a power in her voice. "They see things my way now."

She leans back, takes a sip from her goblet.

"Your father was not a Kensington," she tells Jarrod. "That was the problem. If he had been, we could have had a quick marriage and everything would have been settled. And, in any case, he left." She sips again. "He had to leave or your uncles would have killed him." She smiles sadly, grimly. "Now *they* are dead, and by my husband's hand."

The attendant returns with two goblets on a silver platter, and sets them on the table between Jarrod and his mother. Maggie immediately takes a long draught, smacks her lips, savoring the taste. Jarrod takes his goblet. It is not as heavy as he thought it would be. It is metal, plated with silver. The wine is red, and smells of grapes, of course, but also has a faint trace of clover fragrance. He takes a mouthful. Swallows. It is as if the fragrance became liquid in his mouth, languid, almost solid. There is no burn going down, and only the reminder of sweet clover left as an aftertaste.

"This is wonderful," he says.

"Yes," says his mother absently. "What is that, Barbara?"

"A merlot, ma'am. From the Napa Valley."

"A merlot, yes."

"What does merlot mean?" Jarrod asks the attendant. "Is it a place?"

The attendant looks to his mother, who nods. She straightens up and speaks to him as if delivering a very important message. "A merlot, sir, is a variety of grape."

"I see. I see. What other varieties are there?"

"There are many. Zinfandel. Beaujolais. Cabernet sauvignon."

"Is that one or two?"

"One. Cabernet sauvignon."

"You fancy wine, do you?" His mother is amused.

"It's very. Very wonderful. I've never tasted anything like this before."

"Well. That's nice." She seems perplexed and perhaps upset. Jarrod sees this, but doesn't know what to do.

"Don't develop *too* much of a fancy for it," she says. "You must be tired. It is quite a journey from Shelton. And you must have had dealings with those vile Cedar Rats. They are a problem we'll have to solve, one of these days."

"We did," Maggie says. "We surely did."

"Well, you can stay as long as you like. In fact, you must stay. I'll have Barbara show you to the guest rooms. You can have a rest and then we'll see you for dinner. My husband is a very busy man, but he may be in this evening, and if he is, I'll introduce you to him, Phillip. He is a great man." She says the last with a kind of resignation, as one would give news of a storm coming.

Jarrod's rooms are as cluttered as the rest of the house. He finds, to his chagrin, that the window will not open. At least he is on the second story of the house, and can look down upon things.

I cannot stay here, he thinks. That wine drink is *amazing*. Nothing in the forest comes close to its subtlety, its richness. You can practically taste the soil it was raised in. He takes out his map and tries to locate the Napa Valley, but it is not marked. Perhaps I'll pass through there on my way, he thinks. I want to see how they make this wine. He finds a basin of water and washes himself, thinking of these things.

In the evening, Ocean has not returned. They eat in a large dining room. There is meat—cow meat, Jarrod reckons—and more wine. His mother has taken off her tunic and is wearing a dress. Maggie is wearing other clothes as well, and not clothes she has brought along.

"We must get you decently dressed, Phillip," his mother says to Jarrod.

"This is my service uniform," Jarrod replies. "It's what a ranger wears."

"Yes," she says. "Undoubtedly. We can do some variation on it, actually. I think that would be quite dashing."

After they sit down to eat, they are joined by a thin man who enters unannounced. He smiles largely at Jarrod and Maggie and takes Tatum James's hand and kisses it. He takes the chair beside her.

"Manelli's my name," he says. "I heard about your arrival, Phillip. I work for Mr. Ocean. He sends his regards, too."

"Thank you," Jarrod says.

Manelli and his mother fall into a conversation that lasts some minutes. There are many names and meeting places he does not know, and Jarrod gives up trying to follow what they are saying.

When they are finished, his mother takes a bite of cow meat, chews it thoughtfully. "So, you are going to California," she says to him.

"Yes."

"Manelli tells me that there is a Karma Patrol leaving by train in a few days' time to accompany a load of trade goods through the Siskiyous. I think we can arrange a commission for you by then. What do you think, Manelli?"

"Undoubtedly," the thin man says.

"First lieutenant. Or how would you like to be a captain?"

"I'm already an officer of the United States Park Service," Jarrod says.

"Well, there is such a thing as . . . dual citizenship, you know. You are a James. There are inherited privileges associated with that name. And responsibilities."

Jarrod says nothing.

"We'll see what Manelli can come up with."

"Traveling with the KP will take weeks off your trip," Manelli says. "Maybe months. And it will be much safer. That I can promise you."

His mother then asks Maggie about northern conditions, the ins and out of the James-Kensington clan, about which Maggie appears to have bounteous information. Jarrod cannot say whether or not any of it is right. All he knows is that they are all goddamn Timberlanders.

"What will be done with the Chomskyite?" he asks during a break in the conversation.

"What Chomskyite?" Manelli says, frowning.

"We saw one of them staked out in the Chine," says Maggie.

"Oh," Manelli replies with a chuckle. "We're leaning him up a bit and drying him out before we burn him, I imagine."

"When will you burn him?"

"I don't know. I'm not familiar with the case. Next Public Day, most likely. Five days from now. I'm sure I can arrange a seat for you."

"No."

"Let us speak of something more pleasant," Tatum James says. Manelli smiles and nods, and conversation returns to affair up north.

After dinner, the others retire, but his mother tells Jarrod to stay. They go to a side room, the drawing room, his mother calls it. Barbara is told to bring more wine. "A port, this time, I think," his mother says to her.

The drawing room has two large doors that open up onto a balcony, and they go out into the night air. Jarrod breathes in the freshness and allows himself to smile.

"Well, you have another expression besides stone," his mother says. "I was beginning to wonder."

"I'm used to keeping my thoughts to myself," he says.

"Do you smoke?"

"What?"

"Never mind. What do rangers do for fun, anyway?"

"Well," he says. "At solstice and equinox, we eat mushrooms."

"Mushrooms?"

"Special mushrooms. They've got psilocybin in them, which is a—"

"Gracious. I see."

Barbara returns with the wine. It is thick, opaque, a deep red that is almost black.

"It's not real," his mother says. "Good lord, real port comes from Portugal, and where is Portugal? Nobody knows."

The port tastes like it looks, rich, chewy. Almost like eating a fine cut of meat just touched to a flame, Jarrod thinks. He finishes it, and Barbara fills his glass again.

The house is on a hill overlooking Olympia, and the city is a dark presence below them, with an occasional light showing through a window, or a campfire here and there to warm the guard. There is a slight chill in the air, but Jarrod is not cold. His mother moves closer to him. She touches his forehead with the palm of her hand. It is warm, soft.

"You're a good foot taller than I," she says. "Your father was tall, though."

He smiles again, uncertain what to say. She takes her hand away and turns to look out over the city.

"It was a shock to see you today," she says. "How are you feeling?"

"I'm glad to have discovered wine," he says. His mother shudders and laughs shortly. He sees he's stung her, and tries to think of something that is true to say. "I didn't know what to expect," he finally says. "I don't know how I feel about all this just yet. You."

"Oh," she says, and turns back to him. There are tears in her eyes. "I want to make it up to you, Phillip. I've been thinking about this for years. I was a very young girl when I had to give you to Maggie. I've dreamed about finding you again. In my dreams, your face was always—dark. Now there will be a face."

"Yes. I'm your son."

His hand is on the railing of the balcony, and she places hers around his fingers, squeezing them gently. She is so much younger than I thought she would be, he thinks. I thought she would be like Old Maggie.

He cannot remember how to get back to his room, and Barbara leads him to his bed. When he awakens in the morning, there is a set of clothes on the chair by his window. They are newly tailored and vaguely resemble the ranger green. Jarrod feels the cloth. Cotton. He has only worn skin and wool in his life. I'd feel completely naked if I put this on, he thinks, and leaves the clothes there.

He is amazed that someone could have come into the room while he was asleep and gone unnoticed. It is the wine, of course. You know the effects of alcohol on the brain, he thinks. He goes to the water basin—filled with fresh water—and washes. Then he brings out his knife, whets and sharpens it, and shaves his two-day beard, using the basin for shaving water. There is a mirror and Jarrod examines himself in it. He takes his knife and, with a neat and practiced draw, cuts back his bangs a quarter inch. Better. He feels like a ranger again.

Breakfast is brought to him in his room. The attendant is another woman, but one with the same garments and red-dyed hair as Barbara. She also has the same general build and pale white skin, so that Jarrod almost doesn't notice the difference in the two. She is called Kelly.

It is late in the morning before Kelly returns. Jarrod has been sitting in the chair by the window, unmoving, waiting. The attendant looks around, and starts when she sees him. She quickly recovers herself.

"Mother Tatum wishes you for tea," she says. "If you will follow me."

They drink tea in the parlor. It is not herb tea, but the old, caffeine-containing black pekoe, brought up from California. It is stale to Jarrod's taste, like drinking stump water. He says nothing, but turns down a second cup.

"There is to be a ball in a week's time," his mother tells him. She wears a closely woven robe tied loosely at her waist and decorated with floral twirls like a tapestry. A jeweled silver chain hangs about her neck. It lies sparkling white against the white curve of her breast. "The hosts are the Dewdrops. They steward farms to the south. A lot of farms. They've requested that *you* be the guest of honor. Now you don't have to do this, of course, but it would be a brilliant introduction into society for you."

"Has Manelli secured a commission for me?" Jarrod asks.

"I don't. I see—you'd like to go with your new rank?"

"Something like that."

"You are a James, aren't you, Phillip? Well, I'll see that it is done by the end of the day. Captain James. How do you like that?"

Jarrod smiles. Shrugs.

"I thought those girls brought you new clothes."

"Someone did."

"You don't like them?"

"I'm a ranger."

"Will you ever call me mother?"

"I'm a ranger, Mother."

"I see. At least let me have those rags cleaned, will you? I promise to have you back in them by tomorrow. In fact, if you wear them to the ball it might be . . . quite a surprise for everyone."

"All right. Mother."

Tatum James smiles. He pours more tea into her cup.

In the afternoon, Jarrod wanders the grounds. Old Maggie finds him in the garden, where he has been looking over the town, trying to memorize the layout of the streets.

"I have to go on back now," she says. "What are you going to do?"

"Take Manelli's commission, I guess. Use it to go south."

"I thought I was reuniting you with your mama. Bringing you down here done my heart good."

Jarrod nods.

"But I may have got you into a situation you don't want to be in, instead."

"That's all right, Maggie."

"So. There's lots you don't know about your clan yet, and I

ain't got time to teach you. Your mother has a power, though. She's not a woman with much pity."

"Some say rangers have no pity either."

"Some say that."

"I would like to ask you one question."

"All right."

"Is Ocean in charge, or is she?"

"Well now, that's a good question. That *is* a good question."

Maggie looks around for some place to sit down, but there are only tended flowers and bare ground. She comes and stands beside Jarrod, and they both look over Olympia.

"Tatum James is the reason the James-Kensingtons weren't killed or driven off their land by the Matties. She warred them down to stalemate. But the clan couldn't hold it for years; she saw that. She saw that the only way to save them was to make a sacrifice of herself to whoever the boss of the Matties happened to be."

"It happened to be Ocean."

"That's right. And that is the Wallapa Alliance. It's Tatum James stepping down from heading her clan and coming here until she dies."

"So Ocean's in charge."

"In a manner of speaking."

"I see."

"Good, because I don't. This place has got more plots hatching than a caterpillar with the wasps in it."

A breeze flows through the streets below, flapping the canvas of the merchant stalls, and bending the few trees still shading the avenues. Many have been cut for firewood, leaving most streets lined with stumps.

"Well, got to go," Maggie says. "I wish you well, ranger. California."

"California."

"Drop by on your way back, and I'll fix you some more of that hedge nettle tea."

"I will, Maggie. That I will do. Maggie . . ."

"Hmm?"

"Something is happening. In the Earth's interior. Something is changing."

"What?"

"Information for you. I'm paying you, Maggie. It's only right."

"All right, then. Do your people know what's going on?"

"The declination is changing. That means the magnetic field—something is affecting it."

"Well? So?"

"If it happens fast, there could be—"

"Earthquakes?"

Jarrod pauses, looks back over Olympia's spread. "Very bad earthquakes. Change in the atmosphere. We don't know. Death. A lot of it."

Jarrod stays in the garden and watches Maggie's wagon pull away, Hildie the mare trotting resolutely down the street. Resolutely toward home. Not me, Jarrod thought. Not for a long time. When the sun sets, he goes back in. His mother is out for the evening, and Jarrod takes his evening meal in his room. The attendants come and clear the plates. They bring him back his ranger green, cleaner than it has been since the day it was taken from the loom. He puts his real clothes back on. After midnight, he slips out of the room and down the stairs. Barbara is awake, sitting on a stool by the door. She does not hear a ranger step lightly beside her. The faint creek of a front window being opened. A man the shade of night slipping through.

Out into the streets—streets Jarrod now has a good map of in his head.

He makes his way past darkened houses, empty merchant stalls. He makes his way to the Chine. A guard is out on his rounds. He does not see Jarrod. In the shadows, Jarrod peers into the dirt square.

The Chomskyite sits with his back against the stake that binds him to the earth. At first he appears to be sleeping, but Jarrod hears him mumbling to himself. Delusion brought on by dehydration. Jarrod watches for a few moments longer. The man moves slightly, rattling his chains. Enough.

Jarrod takes his blowgun from under his shirt. He brings a dart from his pocket and dips it in the little vial of concentrated hemlock. Drops it down the tube of the blowgun. Takes aim.

The dart flies as true as Jarrod's aim, into the neck of the Chomskyite. The man slaps at the sting, as if it were a mosquito. He sits up, looks at the sky. Fifteen seconds. Twenty. The Chomskyite makes a sighing sound, expelling both air and spirit. His head droops; his hand trails in the dust of the square.

Jarrod glances around quickly, then stalks over and removes the dart from where it has fallen next to the body. And fades back into the shadows of Olympia town.

Jarrod passes a week in his mother's rooms. Every day is a succession of times to eat, times to walk in the gardens. Conversation that Jarrod only listens to. He learns, makes connections, so that more and more of it makes sense. There is an invisible town within the town, he comes to see, that is made up of relationships of dependence and dominance, sentiment and desire—but above all, blood ties. Genes shuffling their humans about, pitting them against one another, sometimes allowing them to join forces, but always for selfish ends. What other ends could there be? That is the assumption of all.

After midnight, Jarrod goes out and follows the streets of the town. He returns before dawn, and sleeps for four hours until breakfast.

After five days, Ocean returns to the house. He is haggard from a trip to the west, where there is fighting with the nomads who roam the coast and pillage Mattie families who live up the rivers that feed the Pacific. Ocean and Jarrod meet in the hall late in the evening. As they meet, Ocean is wracked by a spasm of coughing.

"Are you all right?" Jarrod says, after he has stopped.

He stares at Jarrod for a moment, then walks on.

The next day, there are preparations for the dinner meal. Slabs of meat are brought in, barrels of beer delivered. Jarrod thinks that a great feast for many people is in preparation, but only his mother, Manelli and Ocean are there when Jarrod comes to dinner.

"So you're the forester," Oceans says when Jarrod sits down to eat.

"I'm a ranger."

"Well, you keep the northern conclaves active."

"We keep them out of the National Park."

Ocean takes a great mouthful of meat, continues speaking. "Keeps them from being a problem for me. I guess I can thank you for that."

Jarrod nods. Ocean begins to cough. He raises a napkin to his lips, and Jarrod sees that the cloth comes away bloody. Very bloody, with a great glob of sputum. Ocean folds it away.

Bacterial infection of the lungs, Jarrod thinks. Very likely tuberculosis.

Barbara pours Jarrod a glass of wine. It smells of cabernet sauvignon grape, and tasting it, he discovers that he's right. Old, too, with a hundred lighter tastes—herbs, flowers Jarrod can half identify, like ghosts—complimenting the grapiness. Wonderful.

"You like it, do you?" says Ocean in a phlegmy voice. He clears his throat. "My own private stock. Fifteen years old, that. Got it off a dead Harborite."

"It's good. Very good."

"Damn right."

Manelli is uncharacteristically silent, and his mother seems on edge.

Ocean tears into another piece of meat. "Did you kill that Chomskyite piece of garbage in the Chine?" he asks in the midst of another mouthful.

"I killed him," Jarrod says.

"Thought so. It looked like greenshit work. Well, the world's better off without his kind." Ocean chews, swallows. He cuts more meat. Then, the meat dangling from the end of his fork, he looks hard at Jarrod. "Don't do it again without my say-so, though."

Jarrod meets Ocean's gaze. He says nothing. After a moment, Ocean looks away, coughs hard, then continues coughing in wispy, breathless convulsions. Though more heaps of food are brought in, no one eats much.

That evening, the house is encircled by a platoon of guards, and Jarrod does not chance a trip out.

The night of the ball finally arrives, and with it, Jarrod's commission as a captain. His clothes are cleaned that day, and when they return, there are epaulets with the brass roping of his new rank sewn to the shoulders.

They arrive by coach, Jarrod, his mother and her attendants. The attendants wear the same brown robes of their order—Jarrod now knows them to belong to a Mattie sect called the Greensisters—but Tatum James is dressed as he has never seen her before. A sweeping, heavy-fabric dress, iridescent and dark green, is belted about her waist and falls to her ankles. It rises in tendrils to her breasts, which are gathered from below by a black undergarment laced tight. They are thrust up and together, and her silver chain lies upon their curve. Her skin glistens with mica, as if she were covered with a thousand spider eyes. The closeness of the coach is filled with her perfume—essence of dandelion? Jarrod cannot tell. Something sharp and bright, of fields, not forests.

The ball is being held in a white building that could easily ac-

commodate all the rangers of Threecabin. Torches are fixed
about its second story, and two bonfires burn before the door.
The fires are obscenely large.

"What is this place?"

"It's called the Department of Transportation," his mother
replies. "I'm not sure what they did here." Smoke is heavy in the
air, and she raises a handkerchief to breathe through. A soot-
covered attendant opens the door for her with a flourish, and Jarrod follows his mother inside.

The main ballroom is crowded and smoky with candlelight
from dangling iron chandeliers. The men are wearing either
black shirts with tan, tight-fitting pants or else uniforms of various sorts and ranks, none of which Jarrod recognizes. The
women are dressed much like his mother. All of them glisten
and sparkle when they move upon the marble floor.

"To think, I only started wearing it last Thirdmonth," says
Tatum James, gazing about the ballroom and smiling faintly.

She is immediately approached by a woman with an elabo-
rate headdress, who brings in her wake two young women. His
mother makes introductions and Jarrod nods wanly. One of the
young women takes his arm and leads him away, through a set
of double doors and into another part of the building.

"I'm Matilda Dewdrop," she says, after maneuvering Jarrod
into a corner. "I'm so glad I'm the first to meet you. You'd be the
ranger, I think."

Jarrod has to concentrate to understand her. Her words are
English, but their cadence is strangely off, as if she were speaking to him from a rocking limb on a tree.

"I'm a ranger," Jarrod replies.

"Is it very dark in the forest? Have you killed a great many
robbers?"

"Yes." He smiles.

This causes Matilda to break out in a peal of laughter that
Jarrod thinks cannot be genuine. He smiles, bows slightly.

"You're perfectly delightful," she says. "Perfectly so. You must have me for your first dance. It is simply imperative."

"I don't dance," Jarrod says.

"Oh, but you must." Matilda laughs again in her shrill tinkle.

"No," he says.

Soon, a young man in black and tan approaches with another woman, whom he introduces as his sister. Before Matilda can introduce Jarrod, a drum beats deeply in the next room, and everyone falls silent for a moment. It beats again. The young man puts out his hand and Matilda immediately takes it. They walk away, leaving Jarrod with the sister. She looks at him imploringly, but he can only shrug. After a while she wanders away, and Jarrod remains in the corner, listening to the weird rhythms that move these barbarians to dance.

It seems forever until Tatum James emerges from the crowd and draws him to a side room. They sit upon a couch, while a servant brings them white wine. This wine is inferior to wine in Ocean's household, but it is still a marvelous drink to Jarrod. He wonders what variety of grape it is made from, but his mother does not know.

"I'll have some for the house if you'd like it, though."

"What you already have is wonderful."

"We do have fine stuff. Manelli sees to that."

Jarrod leans back against the plush backing of the couch and nearly loses his balance. He sits upright.

"Who does Manelli belong to, I've been wondering."

The question seems to startle Tatum James at first, but then she smiles broadly, bitterly. "He's mine," she says. "I've paid for him in gold. And his lover is one of my house guards." She sips her wine long, thoughtfully. "You are hopeless tonight, aren't you?"

"I don't belong here," Jarrod says.

"I thought you might . . . . adapt. For my sake."

"You know what I want to do."

His mother moves closer to him. The dandelion odor is

strong about her. "It is very odd," she says. "Very odd to meet someone who tells the whole truth."

"I have no reason to lie."

"No. You don't." She rises slightly and abruptly nods to a servant, who comes and takes her unfinished wine. When she settles back down on the couch, she is closer still. "You don't give a damn that I am your mother, do you?"

Jarrod looks at her, looks away. He says nothing.

"No, I couldn't believe it at first. But now I do. What did they do to you in that forest? What kind of man are you? Are you a man at all?"

"I'm a ranger."

"Yes. Of the United States Park Service." She gingerly places a hand upon Jarrod's leg. She rubs his thigh. "I've lost my son," she murmurs, almost to herself, Jarrod thinks. "I don't have a son."

Jarrod doesn't think he has drunk a great deal of wine, but he finds his thoughts confused. He stares at his mother's hand, blinks, shakes his head. Her fingers are long, thin. They shine darkly in the candlelit room. As if from a distance, he notices that he is aroused.

"I want to leave tomorrow," he says quietly, as if to convince himself.

"Yes, yes," says Tatum James. "You will." She turns to the servants. "Leave us," she tells them with a brittle voice, a hard voice. "Close the door." The servants comply.

Before Jarrod can speak, before he can think—why is it so hard to think?—she turns to him. Her face is like a storm. "You thought I would be old, didn't you?"

"Yes," he says.

She smiles, and it is as if the sun has come out from behind black clouds. A bright, dandelion sun. "Not so very old."

"You. You're beautiful."

She moves her hand to the inside of his leg, reaches out with her other hand, runs a finger along his chin. "Soft," she says. "You're so . . . stern. It makes me forget how young you are sometimes."

"Please," Jarrod says. What is he saying? He doesn't know what he is saying. "I need—"

She kisses him roughly. He tries to pull away, but she takes his lower lip between her teeth and tugs him back playfully, laughing at his distress. He yanks back, tastes blood in his mouth.

"Come now, my ranger," says Tatum James. "We both have something the other wants."

"You're—"

"What? Your mother? That obviously means nothing to you."

"It. I." Have to get control, he thinks. A ranger is . . . what the hell is a ranger? There is no point in the Law. Clean? Obedient? Cheerful?

"A stupid primitive," he finally says. "A goddamn Timber-lander."

She laughs short and hard. She shakes her head. "That's it," she says. "So that's what's bothering you. Tell me something."

"What?"

"Is my husband going to die?"

Jarrod sits back, breathes deeply. He has no idea why she is asking him this, but anything to relieve the pressure. The knowl-edge that he wants Tatum James terribly. Like the hunt. Like killing other men. Or like the prey who longs for the hunter's final stroke. All, all at once. To hurt and to hurt.

She is my mother. My biological mother.

"He has tuberculosis," Jarrod says.

"And can you cure him?"

"I have a cure."

"I thought so. I thought you could do that." Again, her hand on his leg. He reaches out toward her, as if to push her away. In-stead, she takes his hand by the wrist. She opens his fingers and kisses his open palm.

"I want it," she says.

"You want—"

"I want that cure. Is it a potion?"

"It's a jar of pills."

"And that will cure him?"

"Probably. The disease has torn up his lungs, though. They'll never heal completely."

"That doesn't matter. I'll never give him the cure."

"You. I don't."

"Understand? You are very young, ranger." She licks his hand, takes a finger in her mouth, sucks and kisses it, then leans back. "Would you like me to teach you?"

"I have to go. Go south."

"You can leave on tomorrow's train if you give me the cure."

"Tomorrow? I'll. It isn't much. I have enough and to spare." Jarrod realizes he is talking to himself, talking himself into something.

"We have a bargain, then," says Tatum James. She puts a hand behind his neck, draws him toward her. Draws him to the silver on her breast. She is soft against his cheek. Soft, but cold. It is the metal that is cold.

"We must seal our bargain," she whispers to him. "Here, away from his home. Away from his spies."

Tatum James reaches behind herself. She finds a particular strand of her dress's binding, tugs on it. Her dress falls away, leaving only the bodice beneath it. "Unlace it, ranger," she tells him. Without thinking, he obeys.

He cannot think that this is his mother he is tearing into, that this is his mother whose nails dig into his back, his sides and legs. He slaps her hands away, slaps her face, pushes her down onto the couch. But she is lithe and strong, and fights back, twists away.

Then she is on top of him, pulling his garments away, kneading his chest. "So very young," she says. "Perfectly, delightfully young. Something I want. One way or the other.

Something I'll have." He bucks up, tries to throw her off, but somehow she uses the movement against him, and he is suddenly inside her.

Tatum James laughs and grinds wet against him. He struggles and this only draws him deeper into her. "I've got you," she says. "You didn't think you could get away, did you? You didn't think you could get away without telling your mother good-bye?"

Not mine. Not my mother. Completely gone tribal. Thinks of nothing but herself. The goddamn bitch. The fucking clan whore.

With a growl, he flings her away from him. She catches herself on the arm of the couch and cries out in frustration. Jarrod thinks of the young girl, Darlene, who had wanted him to go to the windbreak with her. He remembers what he'd wanted to do to her there. Timberlander. Not real. Not real. A parasite on the good land. A shadow. Not a real human being. He rises to his knees on the couch. Tatum James is beneath him, looking up. She turns quickly, seeks to escape, but he reaches out, pulls her roughly back.

A shadow upon the land. Nothing more. A curse to break.

She is still. She looks at him for a long moment, then closes her eyes and turns slowly around. She waits. He parts her legs, and she gasps, but does nothing. He pulls her onto him, and she whimpers quietly. She glances over her shoulder, and he can see her upper lip is twisted to a smile. After a time, she joins his movements, matches his rhythm. Makes him push into her harder.

Shadow animal, he thinks. This isn't real, this isn't true. She can't help the way she is. She's nothing but an animal. I could not have come from her.

"You feel it," she says. "You feel it, don't you?"

Hate. Anger. He's never felt so angry.

Why did you leave me? Because you're a stupid animal. My real mother wouldn't leave me.

God, he hates her. Wants her.

"You know you feel it," she says beneath him. "You're mine, after all."

Shut up. Outside, the ball drums beat. The barbarians dance. Shut up, shut up.

"Phillip," says Tatum James. "Dear Phillip. You've come back to me."

# TRAIN

The next day, he is on the train to the Siskiyous, a captain in the Karma Patrol. He has left a course of antibiotics with his mother. They will never be used.

He thinks of resigning his ranger's commission, of sending Franklin some sort of message. But there is no way to send it, in any case.

A ranger is clean. I am not.

A ranger is loyal. I have betrayed . . . something.

What happened?

Baker. His mother. None of this was covered in the ranger training.

I should know what to do.

Something has.

A ranger is.

Something has broken.

Yet still he travels south. To California. What else is there to do?

He checks his compass against the afternoon sun. He knows the day of the year. He knows his relative position to the pole, the magnetic declination.

The needle is seventeen degrees off what it should be.

Perhaps it is just the metal of the train, some stray magnetism. But no. Franklin is right. Something is changing in the earth. Something always certain has come unglued.

The train car Jarrod rides in is over two hundred years old. The windows are broken out and the undercarriage rattles and whines like a hundred thrashing chains. He has never traveled so fast before—near forty miles an hour. It is a wonder that one can breathe. The train is thirteen cars long. Two cars in the front, near the locomotive, hold the militia guard—the Karma Patrol—with a small contingent also in the caboose. The middle boxcars carry trade goods from the north—timber, cloth, coal, iron. Jarrod is one of fifty men and women who are to watch over these materials, to see that Ocean gets his fair trade in Yreka. The patrol will accompany the wine and other California goods back, but Jarrod will not.

I may never come north again, Jarrod thinks.

A half day has passed since they crossed the wide Columbia. Jarrod barely notices the blasted ruin of Portland. The train takes on diesel fuel in that city, and now Mount Hood has grown to a distant white point away north. The Willamette Valley rolls beneath them, and the sun is low and dim through a foggy scud of clouds.

For hours, Jarrod has sat by the window gazing indifferently out, his packful of medicine stowed away above him on the luggage rack. After a time, a man balances his way to the seat next to Jarrod's and plunks down beside him.

"Kelp," the man says, extending his hand. Jarrod now knows the custom of handshaking. He takes the man's hand, and the other squeezes strongly. Jarrod draws back his hand, mildly disgusted at the touch of a stranger.

"My name's Jarrod," he says.

"Well, Captain, you have your twenty-five, and I'm over the other half of the brigade."

Jarrod shrugs, nods.

"Have you heard of the bandits, then?"

"Not much."

"Do you care to?"

"Yes, I should hear it."

"Well, down at Ashland, at the twist of the Cascades and Siskiyous is where their turf starts. The Mother knows how far south it goes after that. Maybe to Mexico. We killed a brace of them last trip up. Cougars, I think. They had an AK-47."

"Automatic rifle? Just one?"

"Just the one that they used."

"Did we get it?" Jarrod feels odd using "we," but let it pass. What does it mean—or matter—whose he is?

"We did." Kelp nods in approval of his question. "Have you ever come up against one before? Back in the woods, there? I've heard what you are, Captain. Some, at least."

Jarrod again shrugs. What I am. "I helped kill a man once who was using one. But he was a fool and let us get behind him."

"How did you kill him?"

Jarrod looks at Kelp, then turns to gaze out the window once again. "I think it was a piano wire," he says.

Kelp lets out a low whistle. He reaches inside his coat and draws out a bottle, uncorks it. "I believe I'll have a bite of the dog." He swigs down a mouthful of pale yellow liquor, breathes out a wreath of alcohol vapor. "Jack Tack, potatoes and corn," he says hoarsely, and offers the bottle to Jarrod.

Jarrod shakes his head no, and turns back to look at the man. Kelp is big and broad-shouldered. The brown and red wool of his Karma Patrol coat is slung upon him like a loose skin. With his brown beard and long brown hair, Kelp resembles a bear that knows how to sit upright. Standing, he'd likely be a foot taller than Jarrod, and thirty pounds heavier. His carbine is resting against his knee, and Kelp idly twirls its leather strap as he sits.

"Did *you* get the man with the AK-47?" Jarrod asks.

"Yep," says Kelp. His hand moves to the stock of his rifle. He strokes it. "I got him." Jarrod looks into Kelp's eyes and sees—nothing.

They speak further of weapons. Kelp breaks down his carbine and shows Jarrod the way to clean and oil it.

"I have a reloader, too, back home," Kelp says, and they talk about the difficulty of finding good gunpowder, the impossibility of making it as pure as it used to be, in better days for guns. "What I'd give to get my hands on some Napa prime," he says. "They know how to make it in that valley."

Jarrod takes his .22 revolver from his pack and he and Kelp look over his ammunition.

"Long rifle," Kelp says. "Maybe not the best."

"These are the last of the cartridges that haven't worn out," Jarrod replies. "Forty-grain bullets. We get the lead from a deposit in the basalts. Probably a glacial erratic." He sees Kelp has no idea what he is talking about. "There were ice ages," he says, "thousands of years ago."

"Whatever you want to believe," Kelp replies. "Though Mother keep you from open heresy."

The train rumbles through Corvallis, then Eugene. Darkness settles over the valley, until only the peaks of the Cascades to the east are still lit with the low sun. They go to the second car for mess. This is an observation car from the old Amtrak lines. Some of the huge plastic windows are cracked and cauterized back together with ugly welts. Most are intact, though, and the regiment eats and smokes rowdily as the countryside rolls by.

Kelp introduces Jarrod to the others, to his two lieutenants and the twenty-three who are under his command. The food is stew, cooked in an iron pot over a fire built down below in what was once the snack bar lounge. Every once in a while, the wind shifts and a puff of smoke rises from the stairwell that leads to the kitchen. But the cigarette smoke of the Karma Patrol is so vile to Jarrod's nostrils that the woodsmoke from below is nothing—not until he remembers that it is chopped trees that the cooks are burning. Killed trees to make this horrible mush, he thinks. But he eats two helpings of stew. He is hungry.

Near midnight, the train pulls into the town of Drain, Ore-

gon, and lurches to a stop. Jarrod has nodded off in his seat, and
Kelp shakes him awake.

"Angry Duck," Kelp says.

"Did you just say Angry Duck?"

"Get a move on, Captain."

They exit the train and step down into a bare dirt yard.
Across another set of tracks, lit by kerosene braziers, is an immense sign. There are no words on it—only an enormous duck,
twenty feet tall, with red lines radiating from its quaking head,
as if it were throwing off bloody perspiration.

But ducks don't sweat, Jarrod thinks. Do they?

Kelp leads him under the sign and into a building made of
rough-sawn logs covered, in places, with sheet metal.

"They brought that duck down from Portland," says Kelp.
"Mother knows how they got it on the train."

"Who brought it down?"

"Aw, the sisters, I guess."

They step inside the building. Despite the hour, it is
crowded. People sit at tables, some of them eating. Most of the
patrons are only drinking, however. Conversation dies down for
a moment as the contingent from the train comes in, but it
quickly returns to its regular level. Jarrod, Kelp and one of the
men named Poppyseed sit down together at a table.

A woman in a short two-piece pink dress approaches them.
Her hair is long, but piled high upon her head, and she smells
strongly of some flower that Jarrod doesn't know. Not dandelion
greenness, though. *That* he would recognize.

"What can I get you boys?" the woman says.

"How about a half hour with *you*, Tiffany," Kelp says. He
reaches out and runs his hand across the woman's buttocks.
She backs from his reach, but does nothing else. That would get
a ranger killed, Jarrod thinks.

"Sorry, sugar. I'm waiting tables till later." At that moment,
she notices Jarrod, and turns to smile upon him. "Well now,
Kelp, what have you drug in with you tonight?"

Kelp rubs his chin, frowns. "Oh you like that, do you?"

"He's a cutie, all right. Ain't seen his like in a while. He's a young and pretty one."

"Young and inexperienced," Kelp says. "What you need is a man who—"

"I'm a good teacher," Tiffany says. "And by the looks of his clothes, he's got the brank to pay for it."

"So do I!" Kelp says, digging into his pocket. He pulls out a wad of crumpled notes.

"Olympia Town brank? That's about enough to buy you a bottle and a place to sit and drink yourself stupid."

"Mothercunt," Kelp mutters.

"I just want some water," Jarrod says to the woman.

"Sure you do, honey," the woman says. She takes the orders of Kelp and Poppyseed, then brushes a hand against Jarrod's bare cheek as she walks away. The flowery perfume she wears makes his eyes tear up for a moment.

"She sure likes you, Captain," Poppyseed says, shaking his head and smiling. "I'd get me some of that if I was you."

"What? Is this place a whorehouse, or—"

"Tiffany'd slit your throat with a butter knife if she heard you saying that," Kelp replies. "She's got a head for trade, but she's a little loopy other ways." Kelp gestures around the room. "This is the Angry Duck House of Drain, and Tiffany and Alexia are Sisters of the Railroad. Proper Birch and Pond sect, all chartered by the oversight committees and everything. Well, mostly."

Tiffany returns with the drinks and food, and again brushes up against Jarrod.

"I think she'll give you the special," Kelp says, and then digs into his huevos rancheros—at least that is what Jarrod heard him order. It looks like amalgamated mush to him.

He drinks his water—only it isn't water, but a golden liquid. Sweet and strong with alcohol.

"What is this?"

"That's mead—the Duck's trademark," Kelp says. "The women make it from out of the beehives out back. You'd see them if it was daylight."

After the meal, Kelp and Poppyseed have a smoke. Jarrod watches the fumes curl up toward the ceiling, winding into dissipation. There is the sound of a metal skillet being thwacked repeatedly.

"Hey, hey," Kelp says. "Time for dessert."

Along with many of the other men in the room, Jarrod, Kelp and Poppyseed line up in single file. They step through a trapdoor in a corner and descend a flight of stairs—into a basement, smaller than the main dining room. It is all of brick, and its walls are hung with smoky pitch-oil lamps that burn yellow-orange. As each man reaches the bottom of the stairs, he is met by a woman, who takes him by the arm and leads him into the room. The women are naked, but for their shoes.

Jarrod finds Tiffany taking hold of him and pulling him into the room.

"Damn the mothercunt, she *got* him," Kelp says, behind Jarrod.

In the far corner Jarrod catches a glimpse of a wooden table, but he cannot see through the press of bodies what is on the table. Tiffany leads him into the room. Her hair is down now, and her nipples are dark. She's suckled children, Jarrod thinks. But she still seems young—maybe only a few years older than he is. Her shoes have heels that put her on tiptoe as she walks.

There is more clanging of pans, and the room grows quieter—although never completely silent. A woman climbs up on the table and speaks.

"Welcome to the Dessert Feast, ladies and gentlemen," she says. "I'm Sister Alexia, and I'll be your server tonight." She bends down and picks up a handful of something that looks like brown jelly. It drips through her fingers.

"Thank the Mother," she says.

From the crowd comes a roar of approval.

"The Mother gives us long life," she says. "If we only eat her bounty."

"Yeah!" yells someone behind Jarrod. Jarrod recognizes Kelp's harsh voice once again. "Yeah, eat it! Eat it!"

Alexia lifts up her hands, covered with the jelly. "We bring to thee this oblation," she proclaims, "which is the very fruit of the Mother."

Everyone cheers in the room, and Alexia proceeds to lick her hands clean. Alexia motions, and a man climbs up and joins her on the table. The crowd parts slightly, and Jarrod can now see that the two of them are standing amid a heap of steaming food. Alexia undoes the man's trousers, drops them, and begins to rub against him.

Without further ado, the women, the sisters of the order, turn to the men and begin to do the same to them. Jarrod backs away before Tiffany can lower his pants. She pushes him back through the crowd and into a wall. There are too many people around for Jarrod to escape up the stairs.

"This is the Feast," she says. "Share the Feast."

"I'm not one of your—"

"Doesn't matter, cutie. You don't have to join." She reaches down and strokes him. "You just have to share."

"Isn't there some place more . . . private? Where we can talk?"

"But this is the sharing time. This is the Feast, cutie. We'll stay here." Now she does have the drawstrings of his pants untied.

With a quick, strong shove, Jarrod pushes her away. "No," he says. "I didn't know about this."

Tiffany looks at him, and he sees that there isn't any anger in her eyes. Only acceptance and determination. She comes back toward him, hands outstretched. He takes her by the wrists, turns her around, away from him.

"Well, if you wanted it this way, why didn't you tell me?" Tiffany says, grinding against him.

"Listen to me," Jarrod replies. "I didn't know." Being rational will get him nowhere, Jarrod realizes. I need a distraction, he thinks. "What's on the table? What is that?"

"What?" says Tiffany, turning around to face him. "That's the Motherfruit. Part of the Feast. We'll all share in it tonight. See? If you're worried about getting a child on me, you needn't be."

She points toward the table.

Jarrod slowly lets her go. She moves to grab him, hold him, but he pushes her aside. He pushes his way through the orgy of the crowd, rubbing against writhing women and men groaning to their task, until he comes to the table.

Fruits and vegetables in bowls, and shanks and haunches of meat, mostly cow meat. And the centerpiece, a large bowl containing the brown quiver of a jellied aspic. Tiffany comes to stand beside him.

"Cutie, if you're *that* shy, there *is* a side room we can use." She dips her finger in the aspic and puts it in her mouth, licks a bit of its amber from her lips. "See?" she says. "No need to worry. It's Motherfruit."

"Motherfruit?"

"Yes. That's what the sisterhood *does.*"

Jarrod suddenly understands what she is saying.

"Whose child is it?" he asks.

"Blessed Mother only knows. We've had three come to term this past fortnight. It is all of them, plus the leftovers from last time. I thought. Why did that man, that Kelp, bring you if you didn't . . . This could be trouble for us all."

"It's all right," Jarrod says. "I won't cause any problems."

Tiffany takes his arm and looks him in the eye. There is a certain loveliness in her blue eyes, her skin as white as young sprouts that have yet to see the sun. As if she's been used hard by life, Jarrod thinks, but not as hard as she could have been. "I hope you are telling the truth."

"I am," Jarrod says. "I'd like to go now, though."

"All right. I'll see you up."

They push back through the crowd and climb the stairs in silence. The dining hall is empty. Tiffany goes behind the counter and finds an apron, which she carelessly drapes around herself, covering only one breast. She pours herself and Jarrod cups of mead. They sit down together at a table.

"Don't you like me?" Tiffany says. She brushes her hair back from her face.

"I think you're very pretty."

"Then why don't you want me? Are you one of them that likes other boys? It isn't our specialty, but we can do something about that with a little time to get ready. On your way back, maybe."

"No. It isn't you," he says. He swallows mead. "How did you get here?"

"Alexia and me took the train down from Portland. Ages ago, seems like. The sisters up there had too many of us, so they sent us out as missionaries. We've done good, I think. We are one of the few houses that turn a profit. The Mothersisters in Portland are sitting up and taking notice."

"Yes. Seems that you're doing fine," he says.

"We take care of our own, you know? The sisterhood does. My girls need me. They need you. Men like you."

"Yes."

"Then why are you so against it, cutie?" She reaches over, squeezes his arm. "You have a cigarette?"

"I don't. I'm not against you, either."

"You may not like the way we do it, but some do." She motions with her shoulder at the closed trapdoor.

"They surely do," Jarrod says. He takes a long draught of his mead, nearly draining the cup. "Well, I think I'll be going."

"Are you sure?"

"Yes."

"I'll let you out, then." She gets up, accompanies him to the door. Jarrod steps out into the wee hours of the morning. Sheet lightning flashes in the southern sky and distant thunder rolls.

"Mother bless you and keep you," Tiffany says.

"And you, too," he replies. "Mother bless you."

"You are *such* a cutie."

He walks over the railroad tracks and climbs back into the Karma Patrol train. In the empty quiet, he is able to sleep with a bit of peace.

At sunrise, they roll out of the Willamette Valley and there are mountains once again. They turn where a spur of the coastal ranges turns inward, joins the Cascades. And it is as if the two ranges were added one onto the other, for the mountains grow taller, and there is Mount Shasta, the great volcano anchor of the southern Cascades. And south of Shasta, a fault-block range— *the* fault-block range—and the uplift is far, far higher still, and these are called the Snowy Mountains, the Sierra Nevada. There is Yosemite, and the Sequoia trees, which are a legend among the Olympic rangers. And there is Mount Whitney, the tallest peak between Denali in Alaska and Aconcagua in Argentina and Chile. Even if there isn't an Argentina, a Chile, anymore, Jarrod thinks, there will still be Aconcagua, Denali, Whitney.

A steady rain begins to pour, and the train smells of hot metal and steam.

The range that connects the coastal mountains to the Cascades is called the Siskiyous, and these are the mountains at the southern end of Willamette Valley. The train groans and smokes its way up them, into them, as the morning brightens to day. Ashland at noon. Then a steady crawl up, up, to the pass that marked the old southern border of Oregon.

For a moment, the skies clear, and as the sun moves to the low west, the train rolls downhill, squealing and rolling—into the state of California.

But not for long. Soon the squealing, braking wheels send out a scream and grind. The train lurches to a halt.

"Damn them," Kelp growls. "Lady damn the mothercunts to Hanford's Fires."

Word passes back from the train crew that the rails have been cut. Immediately, windows are battened with steel plates. Firing slits are opened, and carbines protrude. Jarrod imagines that the outside of the train must look like a cross between a porcupine and a snake. Fortunately, the men ostensibly in his charge know exactly what to do, and all that's left for Jarrod is to take out his revolver and blowgun and find a slit to stare out of. He settles next to Kelp.

"They'll wait till night," Kelp says. "They're likely cutting the track behind us."

"Then we can't get away?"

"We have rail iron enough to make repairs—providing the beds are not too tore up. Mothercunts don't want to stop all the trains for good. Just this one."

"So . . . we are going to wait?"

Kelp glances at Jarrod, but Jarrod cannot read his expression. "Have any better ideas?" he says.

Jarrod looks back out. He sees nothing. Then, *there*—in bushes to the right, the faintest outline of a man's shoulder.

"I see one of them," Jarrod said.

"Where?" Kelp replies. "*Shoot* the mothercunt!"

But now that Jarrod is getting used to the vegetation, he makes out more. A jiggle of twig here, the round top of a head with a few twigs sticking out there. They don't know how to break up their forms, not effectively, Jarrod thinks.

The bandits are clumped together not in the tall trees to the left, but in underbrush, where there is more low cover. He moves to the other side of the train, looks out. Yes. There. It is exactly a position where he would suspect them to be, even if he had not seen them.

He is about to tell Kelp about this, but realizes that the man will immediately begin gunning into the brush, he is so agitated. Or maybe not.

"I see them, a lot of them on this side," Jarrod says. "What do you think about *not* shooting at them now?"

"Not? What are saying, ranger?" Kelp turns to him, letting go his gun, but leaving the carbine wedged into the firing slot, at the ready.

"Will they offer us the chance to surrender?"

"They might. But they'll take high-class prisoners for ransom, then kill the rest of us, is what they'll do." He eyes Jarrod. "You'll live, if we give up," he says. "Unless *I* get a shot at you before they gut me."

"Don't worry about that," Jarrod says. He looks out. Twilight is coming on fast. "Offer to surrender. How do you do that? With a white flag, like the Timberlanders?"

"That's so," Kelp says. "And they'll pay it as much mind as do you greenshit bastards."

"Not so," Jarrod says. "Rangers *never* let anyone surrender. But you just told me that *they* do, whoever the hell *they* are."

"I did." Kelp looks hard at him. "I did say that. What are you thinking, ranger?"

"Give them a distraction. You and I sneak out, come around behind them. Kill a few. Give a signal, and the other men charge."

"And how do you propose we sneak out, Captain Greenshit? Turn into smoke and go out through the boiler?"

"No. I was thinking about the last time I took a shit. I sat over a hole in the train and there it went, right onto the tracks."

"Out the dunghole?"

"Out the dunghole," Jarrod says. "And crawl down the tracks."

Kelp has the engineer hang the white flag out the window of the engine. Jarrod and Kelp go toward one of the rear cars, farthest away from where Jarrod has seen the bandits clumped. They hear the battened window squeal open, and there are one or two random shots, then a yell from the bushes, and the firing ceases. But during the crackle of gunfire and the rattle of ricocheting bullets, Jarrod and Kelp slide headfirst through the hole where a toilet has been removed. They scuttle under the train, down the tracks on their bellies, gravel and sand scraping against their faces and bared arms.

Finally, a quarter mile down the tracks, Jarrod slides over the rail to his right, trying to move as much like a snake as he can manage. Down the slope of the train bed, hoping that Kelp is behind him, and—breathing hard and shaking with adrenaline—into the understory of the surrounding woodland. He sits up against a tree, and Kelp scrambles up beside him, his rifle still in his hand.

"I'll be damned," he says. "Mothercunt and Hanford's Fire, I'll be damned."

Jarrod rises to his haunches. "Well then," he says. "Let's go kill them."

Kelp smiles a grisly smile. He says nothing, but slaps Jarrod on the shoulder. The two men melt through the wood. Although a ranger would have heard Kelp coming from a half mile away, Jarrod is impressed with how stealthy he is for a Mattie. Jarrod, of course, moves noiselessly.

From behind, the bandits are easy to make out, hardly concealed at all. In the twilight gloaming, they stand out perfectly black against the deep blue sky. They are armed with bows and a scattering of guns. One holds only a spear, but then Jarrod notices the bulge of pistol in his belt. All about the ground at their feet are glass wine bottles, stopped at the neck with streamers of fabric, which trail out several inches. The bandits are clothed in skins and tatters of old fabrics.

On their heads are round hats. This is what Jarrod has seen from the train. The hats cover most of their heads, down to their necks even, though leaving holes for sound to get to their ears. There is a bridgework—like strange lenticular antlers—over some of the bandits' faces. Upon each of the hats is the letter C.

"Mothercunt," Kelp whispers in Jarrod's ear. "It's the Cougars."

Jarrod has his blowgun ready. He aims. A bandit shifts, exposes a sunburned red patch of neck. A quick breath out, like someone who's been punched in the stomach, and the dart flies. Jarrod's aim is true, and the dart flits into the neck. The man slaps at it. Grabs it and pulls it out. Looks at it.

"Jabbo," he says. Another man turns to him. "Jabbo, Uk thinkdruh—" The poison hits his bloodstream. He lurches forward. The brush rattles. He sinks to a knee.

Jarrod has reloaded, and blows another dart. This one thwacks against a helmet, deflected. He blows another, and another. Two men are moaning now. There are cries of alarm.

And Kelp starts shooting. His rifle is a single-shot, but he moves with a steady precision in working the bolt and reloading, and he is able to get three shots off in quick succession before he and Jarrod move on to another position. Three shots, and three men hit by them.

And three shots is also the signal to the force in the train to attack. Kelp doesn't waste bullets, Jarrod thinks.

More quickly than Jarrod had expected, one of the bandits orders a group of five to charge his and Kelp's previous position. But the two have moved on to more dense cover and the men find only briars for their trouble. Then the trip wire that Kelp had set. A blasting cap pops.

Karumph! Three of the men are hoisted by an ammonium nitrate petard. Kelp had brought it from the train, strapped tightly to his back, and set the trigger while Jarrod was making his first blowgun hits.

One of the bandits does not fall back to the earth, but hangs, shredded, caught in a broken pine bough.

Jarrod takes out his pistol. He is not as good a shot with it as he is with the blowgun—but bullets will not bounce off the round hats of the bandits. Bullets will go through. Jarrod looks at Kelp, who is loaded and ready. Kelp nods. They fire away into the bandits. Jarrod spots one, two, three, in quick succession.

Two of them fall, moaning. One he misses. A fourth. Jarrod aims for the C on his head. This one sinks without a sound.

Kelp slaps his shoulder. "They see us," he says. Several of the bandits pick up the wine bottles and take them over to a man who has ignited a piece of cloth. They set fire to the ends of the fabric stoppers in the wine bottles.

"Mothercunt," says Kelp. "That's *napalm* cocktails they're going to throw at us. Let's get."

They take up their weapons and move quickly through the forest. We've taken ten or fifteen of them out, Jarrod thinks. How many more can there be? Then the woods around him rattle with the sound of bullets chewing into trees. There is a great *whumph* behind him, and a wave of heat. Jarrod's shadow suddenly becomes distinct. Someone has set off a napalm Molotov cocktail. They run.

He and Kelp duck behind a sandstone boulder. Jarrod's heart is racing. He breathes deeply, slowly, trying to control it. Can't shake, he thinks. Need a steady hand. He looks at his hands. They are trembling.

"Reinforcements should be on their way," Kelp whispers raggedly.

Another flash of brilliant yellow light and the crackle of brush on fire. The Cougars seem to be throwing the Molotov cocktails randomly.

From behind them they hear gunfire, the screams of men. "Well," Jarrod says. "Let's go."

They work their way back more slowly than they'd run away, but no one is waiting in ambush. Apparently all hands are needed back on the front. The Karma Patrol—the half that is fighting on *this* side of the train—has charged into the bandits, and the fighting is now bayonets and hackwork. Several bandits have their wine bottles lit, however, and they throw them at the charging patrol members.

Jarrod watches as a bottle slams into the ground in front of Poppyseed, breaks, and spatters viscous liquid all over the man's legs. Poppyseed bends to wipe it off, but fire flows up him just as he is bending, its force causing him to stand up straight, as if he'd suddenly come to attention. Poppyseed screams, and another in the patrol jumps on him and rolls him over and over in the dirt. The still burning napalm sticks to this man's hands and face, and he falls down screaming as well.

But most of the bandits do not have time to light their cocktails, and they are quickly overcome by the charge. A Cougar turns to flee, and Kelp waits until the man approaches. The bandit is so intent that he does not see Kelp or Jarrod. As he passes, Kelp steps from behind a tree. He wraps a sinewed arm around the man's head, pulling it back, baring the throat, which he then cuts with a hard slice from his knife.

Kelp turns to Jarrod, smiling, hot blood on his forearms, and a red spatter across his face where he has wiped an arm. Soon the fighting is over, with the bandits either dead or run away. But from across the tracks, they can hear shots fired and yelled orders called out. The air flashes with yellow fire and there is the sickly smell of burning gasoline.

"Charge didn't take the bastards," Kelp says. "Waterfall and them must've gotten to the woods, though, from the sounds of it." He turns to the men—they are spread out, on the watch for sniping, but within shouting distance of Kelp. A couple are tending to the wounded, and one is standing, silent, over a fallen comrade.

"Well, let's go help," Kelp calls out. "Bong, you take your troop around the engine. Sleet, yours around the caboose. Three shots is the signal. Got it?" Bong and Sleet nod. Their men look weary, but they raise themselves to a man. The wounded are left to fend for themselves for the moment. The Karma Patrol splits, gathers at either end of the train. Jarrod takes a few steps after the force that has gone to the caboose.

"Oh yeah," Kelp says from behind him. "Another thing. Brother Ocean told me to kill you." A shot.

A stitch in my side, Jarrod thinks. Then Kelp's words register. He glances down. Blood on the green wool of his shirt. Blood trickling down his left leg. And then that leg won't work.

The ground is not leafy, but bare dirt, railroad gravel. He's come too far from the forest. The day smells like hot iron. But that is the train. Dying here, all out in the open?

Jarrod draws his pistol, yanks himself around. Kelp is standing over him. He knocks the pistol out of Jarrod's hand, then clubs Jarrod in the face with the gunstock. Broken. Something broken. Teeth?

Pain jabbing at the back of his eyeballs. The world is dim, but Kelp is bright over him. Is the moon rising behind him? Dark coming on, though. Dark night, and so far away from home.

"He told me to tell you—what was it now?—he told me to tell you that you took advantage of his hospitality. That's it, *took advantage of his hospitality*. He don't appreciate it."

Jarrod doesn't reply. He's not sure he can move his mouth. Anyway, rather think of other things as I die.

"I wanted to show you a good time at the Angry Duck," Kelp says. "Give you a last—"

"Captain? Captain Kelp, what are you doing?" It is Poppyseed, his face a burned and contorted mess—but with two white, seeing eyes in the blistered flesh. He's propped himself up nearby and is looking on, bewildered. Kelp frowns, shakes his head. He turns to Poppyseed and shoots him in what's left of his face.

"Mothercunt," Kelp says, and spits.

As Kelp is swinging the muzzle back toward Jarrod, more shots. Rapid. Evenly spaced. Automatic rifle.

Kelp whimpers in a high voice, like a rabbit, and collapses beside Jarrod. His body is riddled with bullets and his brains are blown out—some of them onto Jarrod.

My clothes are dirty again, Mother, Jarrod thinks. Need a lot of cleaning. More than. He tries to smile, but can't. Hurts too much. Tries to move at all. Can, but barely, stiffly. Slowly, Jarrod crawls back toward the woods. I want to die in the leaves, he thinks, over and over.

But he cannot. Cannot make it. And night falls hard, and there are no stars and not a light in the sky. And then there are no thoughts about the sky at all.

I want to die in the leaves.

# ORF DREAMS

In Orf's dream, the ranger approaches a chasm of rainbow brilliance. No, it is not a chasm but a river. The ranger walks steadily to the bank of the prism-river. He stops at the bank, looks down one way, then the other.

Who are you?

The ranger looks around at the ground at his feet. There on the river bank is a small stone, about the size of a human's head. The ranger sits upon it—perches upon it, really.

The ranger begins to cry. He puts his head in his hands and sobs, sitting on the bank of the wonderful river.

What is wrong?

The ranger sniffs, wipes his eyes.

Who is there? he asks.

What is wrong?

I have no matches, the ranger says.

Are you sure?

I have no pockets.

What will you do?

The ranger does not answer. He stands up and holds out his right hand. He reaches over with his left and wraps his fingers around his wrist. He yanks suddenly.

The right arm comes off at the elbow. A stream of human

blood, red blood, flows forth. It pools in the sand of the bank and trickles down into the prism-river.

The ranger heaves his forearm and hand into the river, after the blood. It floats up for a moment, then partially sinks, and is carried away by the flow, with only the hand above the surface, in a grotesque wave good-bye.

Well, the ranger says. I wish I'd kept the hand until later. Then with his left hand, he begins to tear himself apart. He pulls off his legs, one by one, and throws them into the prism-river. He pulls off his shoulders. He presses down on one hip, then the other, and scoots himself out of his hips. These he rolls down the slope into the river.

He reaches up and grabs himself by the hair. He yanks off his head and throws it away with the same motion.

Suddenly his torso—torso with one arm—is motionless. It topples forward, rolls down the bank, and it, too, falls into the river. It makes a great splash, and each drop is a separate color.

And each drop of water hums a note, as if wind were blowing through a flute. And each drop lazily settles back into the general brilliance of the river, and is absorbed.

Just before Orf awakens, he gazes across the river. There he sees a dark mass, pulling itself from the river.

Ranger?

The shape seems to hear, to turn and face the robot. But before Orf can make out the face of the stranger, he wakes to the smooth glass walls of the den in which he rests.

# AYTCH

The pain in his left arm is only mild as Jarrod rises from empty sleep. Then his wrist aches as if sunburned. But only my hand? Jarrod thinks. When he smells flesh burning, he opens his eyes.

My flesh.

My *arm.*

A red-hot length of iron sliding through his flesh, between the two bones of his left forearm.

With every moment of waking, the pain grows.

Can't I just go back to sleep?

Cannot.

He jerks his arm. It is held firm. He thrashes. He is held. The iron slides farther along its length. It is nearly a yard long.

Why does it have to be so *long* to burn a five-inch-wide hole?

Jarrod screams now, and pain stabs through his jaw. His mouth is so swollen, he cannot open it to scream.

"Yek quiedruhik, guddammit," says the man who is pushing the iron through his wrist. Is it a man who is doing this? No, it is a red and skinned rabbit, its muscles exposed, its pulpy flesh moist. Rabbit with shining black eyes.

Jarrod thrashes again, and another kicks him in the side, cuffs his face. He never knew he could bear so much pain and stay awake. Going back to sleep. Getting dark, sun in my wrist. No sleep, though. Hurt.

The last of the iron passes through, and its end is a needle eye through which is threaded a leather thong. Metal through, and now the three-stranded leather scraping against outraged inner flesh. Fingers clench, uncontrollable. I can still feel my fingers, Jarrod thinks between waves of ache. The sewer takes one end of the doubled thong, and pulls it through. Instead of tying the two ends together, the man untwists each end five turns back along the leather. He splices the two ends together.

Jarrod has a thong two feet long dangling from the hole in his wrist. The man roughly pulls on the loop.

"Hek holdruhuh, Burt."

Have to scream, can't scream. Who is Burt? The other slaps his face. Blood now, on his chin, the side of his neck. He can feel it. He can feel it all.

He feels the sewer, the man with the iron, reach down and

grab his testicles through his wool pants. He feels the hand grow tight, squeezing.

Go ahead. I'm a ranger. They're expendable.

He puts the tip of the hot iron down near them. Jarrod feels the heat, the shriveling heat. He prepares himself, although he knows there is no preparing.

"Yek keepdruhik, Burt," the man says gruffly, and uses the hot iron to burn Jarrod's inner thighs. Two quick strokes. Odor of burnt wool, then burnt flesh. Two new red welts, there forever. Or however many hours I have left to live. Dark brown dark brown dark.

Who the hell is Burt?

He wakes at twilight—how many days, he can't say. He is too thirsty to sleep. There is a bowl of water—a scum on it—nearby. He turns over, tries to open his mouth. Too swollen. But he must drink water. Can't move his left arm. Why? Worry later about it. Lifts his right hand up, puts his fingers on his lips, forces them into his mouth.

Jarrod yanks his jaw down.

Brown. The world goes brown—but he's too thirsty to let the dark come back. After a long time, he rolls over and laps at the water, each movement of his tongue a new pain. When he has painstakingly finished the water, he is still thirstier than he's ever been in his life. No one brings him any more.

He is in a clearing. It is filled with greenwood smoke, the fire crackle of dying trees. Bastards. Cougars. Huts of pine straw, mud daub, rotted swaths of cloth. They are punishing themselves with the way they live. Gone tribal.

He lies in a clearing. A long line of rope is tied in a square knotted coil through the thong of his wrist. The ends of the rope are tied out of reach. No way except to chew through the rope or the leather, and he cannot chew anyway. He won't be able to chew for a long time.

The wound in his side is bound up with a filthy poultice.

What hurts worst at the moment are his seared thighs, but the ragged hole in his wrist flares horribly if he moves that arm. Best to lie still.

I cannot live, Jarrod thinks. My gut must be exposed. Peritonitis. And gangrene. Broken teeth—the worst place for bacteria. Swallowing toxin.

I cannot live.

A dirty, shuffling thing comes out of a hut, moves toward him. Only when it draws near can Jarrod see that it is a woman. He stares blankly at her. She holds a clay bowl, lopsided, not turned on a wheel when it was made, not fired in a kiln. Without hesitation, she reaches down and straddles his shoulders, pulls him up. He almost leaves his consciousness again. She puts her dirty fingers in his hair and pulls his head back.

"Kay, Burt. Opendruhik," she says.

He does not understand what she is saying.

"Opendruhik." She runs her hand over his face. Smells of dung. Grabs his chin, and forces open his mouth. Jarrod weakly thrashes. Her thighs hold him tight. She pours some of the contents of the bowl into his mouth, forces his mouth shut. He gags, but can't spew it out, can't do anything. Has to swallow. The gruel—it is something thick and vile—goes down in a big lump. The woman sees him swallow, opens his mouth again. This time he is ready, and is able to get most of the gruel down in quick gulping motions.

When she has finished feeding him, the woman lets go his hair abruptly and takes a step. She kicks at his water dish, looks down, notices it is empty.

"Lutur," she mutters to herself, and walks away.

Jarrod lies in the dirt exactly as she has dropped him. He is too exhausted to make even the smallest move. Evening, and a moon. It is not long since the train. Maybe two days.

He is tied in the clearing for many days. He's fed, and not spoken to otherwise. This is just as well, for although Jarrod believes these people speak a kind of English, their words are nearly incomprehensible to him.

Women go about chores during the day. There are few children, and all of them are sallow-eyed and quiet. There is no cheer in this place. Men leave empty-handed, return with things—chairs, pieces of machinery, guns, bags of clothing. It is not until the middle of the week that Jarrod's brain is working well enough for him to realize that the Cougars are looting the train, piece by piece.

Each night, he tries to chew through the leather looped in his wrist, but it is hardened somehow, and even if he could muster the strength, he thinks it is probably too tough for his teeth.

The wound in his side begins to smell of death and maggots. Flies gather about him at dawn, and trouble him all the day long. His breath is putrid as the rot sets into his broken teeth.

I cannot live.

But how long to die? That is what he is waiting to find out.

One day a man comes over and kicks him. Jarrod doesn't respond quickly enough, and the man kicks him again.

"Updruhuh, Burt," says the man.

Jarrod struggles to his knees. He tries to rise. The rope holds him down. The man spits. He goes to the tree where one end of the restraining rope is tied and undoes the rope. He walks down its length toward Jarrod. With a yank, he drags Jarrod to his feet. The leather cuts against the inside of his wrist, but the cauterized scar, still pink-hot, will not let it dig down to blood.

The man unties the other end of the restraining rope. Taking the two ends in his hand, he now has a leash about ten feet long with which to lead Jarrod. Lead him by tugging at the leather that runs through his punctured wrist. Jarrod follows behind the man, stumbling, trying to keep up to avoid the pain. He hasn't walked for days, and his legs are rubbery. With every shuddering step his jaw and side ache. His pants, burned through in the two stripes, chafe against the weals of the burns on his thighs.

They arrive at the center of the clearing, where a cart is loaded with items from the train. It has two projecting handles in front, and two men stand by them. Each of these men has leather through a wrist, and each is bound to the car where he stands. For a moment, Jarrod thinks they will make him pull, which he knows he cannot, but the man binds him to the back of the cart, so that he must follow behind.

They stand there for what seems hours. The two men in the front don't look at Jarrod. They don't look at anything except the ground. Jarrod tries to sit down, but the man who brought him over picks up a stone and throws it at him. It hits him in the shoulder hard, maybe chips a bone. Jarrod pulls himself to his feet once again, but the man throws another rock for good measure. Jarrod flinches, turns and takes it on the back.

The day grows hot, moist. Finally, five other men arrive—all in their battle helmets.

"Upamuh, Burts!" one of them calls. He takes a whip to the men who are to pull the wagon, slapping one of them across the shoulders.

Burt. Slave.

The slaves—this is what they are, Jarrod thinks. This is what *I* am—take up the cart. They pull it forward, and Jarrod follows behind. At the edge of the clearing, there is a worn dirt track, just wide enough for the cart to move along it. They go this way.

Jarrod stumbles along through woods of scrub oak and pine. He sees a eucalyptus tree for the first time, with its shreddy bark. The day is hot, and a swarm of flies follows him, gathering at his wound.

Jarrod suspects that the Cougars are taking him north, to try to ransom him off to the Matties. But then the sun rises high, and he sees that they are headed south instead. So. The right way. It doesn't matter. They walk and walk through the heat of day, the buzz of insects. That night, Jarrod is bound hand and foot, as are the other slaves. They lie doubled over, side by side, like killed deer stored. In the morning, every muscle in his body, torn or whole, is sore. The procession plods onward for another day.

Jarrod is yanked awake by the thong in his wrist the next morning. He tries to scramble to his feet, but is not fast enough to suit the Cougar. Pain in his wrist, deep, acute, as if it were thrust into a fire. He moves one way, another, finds the path of least pain, the path the Cougar wishes him to follow. He struggles to his feet.

"Firsttuhsdays aytch," the Cougar says. "Shinguhltun aytch."

He and the other burts are herded together and tied, neck to neck. They leave the camp behind, unbroken, and plod down a forest trail, which leads to what used to be a road. Jarrod stumbles along over shattered and upturned asphalt; when he stumbles or falters he is beaten with a stick.

Near high noon, the road leads to what was once a town. But now it is brick tumble and scrubby undergrowth. There are people here, others dressed like the Cougars, except for the hats. Jarrod is driven along the streets while these people curse at him and throw bits of brick, pieces of wood and glass—whatever they can pick up from the ground at their feet. The only thing that keeps them from casting the bricks themselves is the effort it would take to go and find a whole one. A splinter of glass slices open Jarrod's temple and the blood is wet and good as it dribbles over his cracked lips.

They are taken into a large area that has been deliberately cleared of most detritus. It is a long, dirt field. On either side are viewing stands, and at either end are two poles, connected by a horizontal bar. They form the letter H.

Jarrod is taken to one of these . . . aytches. Ropes are slung over the horizontal bar and their ends tied to his arms, just under his shoulders. Before he can think, the Cougars pull together on the ropes. He is lifted, lifted dangling, until his back grates against the metal of the bar. The ropes are secured below. Then a Cougar climbs up and shimmies out on the bar. He takes Jarrod's left arm and stretches it out, along the length of the bar. He then ties Jarrod, wrist and elbow, to the metal. He roughly slides over Jarrod's shoulders to the other side, and does the same with Jarrod's right arm. The hoisting ropes are loosened, and Jarrod sags down, suspended only at his wrists and elbows. He must labor to breathe.

Through a blur of pain, he watches as the Cougars face off against another group. These wear hats with what looks like a picture of a bird—a raven, perhaps—on them. They have a brown bag. One of them drops it, kicks it into the air. It is a ball. A misshapen ball.

They are playing a game, Jarrod realizes. *Aytch.*

A Cougar catches the ball, and the others mass around him. He runs forward, toward the other aytch, where a man is suspended exactly as is Jarrod. The others, the Ravens, try to stop the man. When Cougar meets Raven, elbows fly, men go down, bleeding. After a moment, though, two Ravens grab the man with the ball. One of them puts his arm around the man's throat, yanks him back, while the other wrenches the ball from his grasp.

He calls out, and the Ravens mass around him. This time the Cougars attempt to chase him down, take the ball back. But sweat is dripping over Jarrod's eyes—the sun is high now, at high noon—(but is sweat red? not sweat, no) and he cannot pay attention. Can only drift into the red haze until—

Something slams into him, hitting him square in the chest.

All breath passes from him, and for a moment he does not think he can suck it back in. He gags on blood, gasps, gags— then slowly pulls himself up, forces the muscles in his arms to work, and takes in a lungful of air. Not much, barely enough. He tries to do it again, but lacks the strength.

Below him, a Raven stands. He has the ball in his hands. That was what hit me, Jarrod thinks. The ball. The Raven throws the ball again at Jarrod. It glances off Jarrod's leg this time. Then a host of Cougars arrive and jump the man, burying him in a pile and pounding on him with kicks and flying fists. Jarrod feels enough strength return. He pulls himself up, breathes.

The game seems to continue for hours. With each breath, Jarrod can feel himself weakening. I am going to suffocate, he thinks. I am going to suffocate on a letter in the alphabet. But after each breath, somehow he manages another.

Twice more, a Raven breaks through and at close range throws the ball at Jarrod. The second time, the ball hits Jarrod in the mouth, and bursts open the festered clump of sores there. The pain is unendurable, and Jarrod loses consciousness for a moment—only to be awakened by the pressing need to breathe.

Finally, the two teams have had enough. The same Cougar who tied him to the bar climbs up and cuts him down. Jarrod falls the whole way, and adds a twisted ankle to his other hurts. No matter. The Cougar drags him, stumbling, to the center of the field.

There Jarrod discovers who has won the game. The burt of the other team is pushed forward, into the center of the circle of men. Pieces of aluminum and wood are passed around. Each is about the same length, and looks made for a man to swing and hit something with. At the sound of a shrill whistle, the men do hit something.

They advance and beat to death the burt of the other team. They do not stop pounding until he is a bloody mass lying in the center of the field—unrecognizable as a human being.

The Cougars, it seems, have won.

Jarrod spends the remainder of the afternoon bound tightly behind the bleachers. There is a trough of water a few feet away, but he cannot reach it. Once or twice another passes by and looks him over—a woman spends a long moment staring at him—but no one brings him anything to drink. In the early evening, he and the other burts are marched back to the camp. They are tied as usual, but Jarrod could not escape if his bonds were broken. He spends the night sleeping as if he were dead, and when he wakes in the morning, he wishes he were.

They are up and moving earlier than usual, and they cover almost twice as much ground as they normally do before making camp.

"Upmakudruhik fuhr luhstime," says a Cougar, as he drives Jarrod farther into the south.

This night, Jarrod feels slightly stronger. He clenches his hands as tightly as he can when he's bound—fighting not to scream out at the strain on his wrist. With a tiny amount of slack to play with, he is able to work his right hand free from its bonds in the middle of the night. He slowly unties himself.

Now the other slaves are staring at him. It is just past a new moon, and their eyes are darkened white, barely visible, but wide. One of them whines. Jarrod puts his hand over his mouth, motions the slave to be quiet. But the whimpering continues, oddly muted. Jarrod realizes that this is all the slave can do. His tongue has been cut out.

He quickly moves out of the camp. The Cougars are lying together in a circle under the edges of the cart. He is nearly into the trees, when one of the slaves gives out a pitiful shriek. Instantly, the Cougars are awake and scrambling about.

But they still haven't seen me, Jarrod thinks. He gets to a pine tree, hides behind its skinny trunk. Back in camp, someone kicks at the fire, stokes it up, swears.

Jarrod wraps his legs around the tree. He feels stronger than he has for many days. He wraps his arms around the tree. With the greatest effort, he is able to pull himself along. He shins up the pine tree—five feet, ten feet.

The Cougars have pulled firebrands from the blaze. They are searching, searching.

One of them spots him. He calls to the others, and they all run to see. He points his flaming brand at Jarrod, now twenty feet up the tree. Jarrod pulls frantically upward. He reaches the first branches.

First they pelt him with rocks. Jarrod ignores these, although several hit him with a solid thud, and climbs higher. Soon he is out of effective range. The Cougars speak among themselves in the guttural tongue. Jarrod can make out nothing that they say. Finally, all but one of them leaves.

Jarrod looks around. There are no other trees near enough to leap to—and even if there were, he could not manage it. I'm too broken up, he thinks. Too weak and broken.

The other Cougars return with dry branches. They begin to build a pile around the base of the pine tree.

They will burn me, he thinks. Do they know how hard it is to burn down a tree? But the pile grows higher, and Jarrod realizes that the smoke alone will be enough to overcome him. Yet he holds tight, does not descend. This is the way to end it all. In the branches.

The Cougars open a bottle of napalm and pour it over the wood. They light their fire. As the fire takes and burns higher, a curious thing happens. Through the smoke, Jarrod can see the Cougars begin to sway back and forth, in rhythm to the flicker of the blaze. More smoke now, great oily puffs of it. Jarrod coughs it out of his lungs as best he can.

The Cougars are swaying. They are singing. It's a tune Jarrod recognizes, and the words too, twisted, drawled.

"Furudjuka. Furudjukuh. Durmuhvue? Durmuvuhue."

A ranger tune. "Are you sleeping, are you sleeping? Brother John? Brother John?" But the Cougars don't finish the chorus. Instead, they repeat those syllables, over and over. They sway and sing. Then all is lost in the rising smoke.

Jarrod is unconscious when he falls, and only the hot coals of the fire awaken him as they burn into his side. He instinctively rolls away, pulls himself from the heat. And that is when the Cougars are upon him, beating him with the firebrands, dragging him back to the camp. But the pain, the outrage to his body, is too great, and Jarrod slips away into a brown, hurting oblivion once again.

He awakes with something in his mouth, shoved back into his throat. He gags, spits it out. He stares at what lies in the dirt before him.

It is a phlegm-covered clump of two human fingers.

The two end fingers of his right hand. He stares down at the stumps the Cougars have left.

How did I not wake up when they did that? he thinks. How? But he did not.

Never mind. Doesn't matter. He noses dirt over his severed fingers, buries them as best he can, bound as he is.

The next day, he trudges for hours behind the cart. The Cougars kick him, and hit him with sticks constantly. And the next day. And the next.

The wound in his side is not healing, his mouth drips a foul green slobber, and despite the kicks and goads with sticks, there are moments when Jarrod physically cannot continue. The Cougars let him lie for a few moments, then two men pull him up by the wrist thong and Jarrod stumbles another few miles behind the cart, only to fall again.

He tries to imagine ways of killing himself, but can come up with nothing.

Won't be long, though. Won't be long, he thinks.

During the heat of an afternoon, the two gouges of the cart track grow wider, the rut becomes a road. The procession arrives at a gate. There is no fence on either side of the gate; it merely straddles the road. The sides of the gate are made of mortared stone, with the gate itself formed from iron uprights. Beside the gate is a little shelter, a guardhouse. A man steps out. He is wearing a long robe, all of a piece. Wool.

"I've already told them that Cougars are here with goods," he says. He looks over the slaves pulling the cart, at Jarrod. "And men."

"Burts," says one of the Cougars. "Wuk killdruh fin yek fuckdruhik wuk."

"There's no deception," the man says. "I signaled them by mirror relay. They'll be here soon enough. You want some water?"

"Nu."

"At least let me give it to those burts."

"Nu. Keepdruh handsikuh buk."

"All right." The man shakes his head and goes back to sit in the shade of the guardhouse. Jarrod sinks to his knees. Green spit dribbles onto the ground before him. He watches it coil in the dirt of the road.

After a long while, Jarrod hears a clattering sound. He raises his head wearily and looks through the iron bars of the gate. At first he sees only a cloud of dust, drawing closer. Then he makes out horses. People riding on the horses. Closer, closer. One of the horses pulls a wagon. All of the people wear the same robes as the gatekeeper.

The wagon rattles to a stop. The riders do not dismount. Two of them turn their horses and go around the gate, coming to loom over the gathering of Cougars. One of the riders, a man with a flowing beard of black and gray, speaks.

"We'll take the burts, of course. As usual."

"Nu," says one of the Cougars, Jarrod couldn't tell which one. "But elik." The Cougar points at Jarrod. "Frekik totamuh thut wagun."

"Are you sure? We want to buy them."

"Yuh. Frekis totmuh thut wagun."

"All right. Him then. And what else?"

The Cougar begins to unload the cart.

"They've been raiding trains again, Uncle," says the other rider.

"So it would appear." The bearded rider motions impatiently to the Cougar. "Let's make this simple. If it's a machine or metal, we want it. We have all the cloth we need, though."

The Cougars unload the cart and strew the contents about on

the road. Seat parts, valves and nozzles that Jarrod assumes are from the locomotive engine. Baggage.

*His pack.*

His pack, in the discard pile.

He tries to stand up, say something. But the sun is too hot, his shoulders too heavy, his throat almost swollen shut with infection. Jarrod kneels in the dust, staring at his pack. He can't remember exactly why he should want it, anyway.

With the terms of the trade agreed, several of the riders dismount. They remove two great oaken barrels from the wagon, each requiring four men to carry it. They set these on the cart. The two slaves look on balefully at what they will have to pull all the long way back. The riders go back to their wagon and get crates full of bottles. The bottles have cloth stoppers.

Napalm Molotov cocktails.

The riders take up the trade items from the Cougars and load them onto the wagon. One of the Cougar bends down to pick up what remains. The first thing he touches is Jarrod's pack.

With a mighty effort, Jarrod jerks himself to his feet. He cannot speak, but a sound of anguish gurgles from his throat. One of the Cougars makes to hit him with a stick, but the younger horseman takes a step forward, grabs the stick end.

"No," he says. "That is ours to do now."

Again, Jarrod forces himself to make a noise. He looks at the pack.

"Well," says the bearded rider. "Let's have that, then."

"Not thuh duhl," the Cougar tradesman says. "Now ukdruh."

The man sits back in his saddle, shakes his head. "No," he says. "Ours."

"Nu."

"Yes."

The Cougar deliberates but for a moment.

"Fuckdruh yek," he says and flings the pack in front of the

forefeet of the man's horse. The horse moves back one step, then stands still.

"Have a care," the man says ominously. "Have a care."

Instead of responding, the Cougar stalks over to the cart. He unties Jarrod, unknots the rope from the leather wrist thong, coils it sloppily and throws it into the cart beside the barrels. He yanks on the leather thong and drags Jarrod over to the horsemen.

"Duhn," he says. This word, Jarrod knows. He sinks to his knees. He may as well; otherwise the Cougar will kick his legs out from under him.

As has been happening more and more frequently since he fell from the tree, Jarrod begins to fade. The hot sun makes his vision blurry, and soon the brownness is flowing over him, into his head. Bright brownness. Somewhere—a long way off—he hears the sound of the Cougar cart starting to move. Wearily, he gets ready to rise, to follow behind, lest he be pulled.

The cart is moving away. He lurches up, takes a step forward.

"My man," the rider whispers behind him. "Stay where you are, my man." Jarrod stops moving, uncomprehending.

"He can't walk, Uncle," says the younger rider.

"Of course not. Have him put in the wagon."

The younger man leans down to look at Jarrod. "Follow me," he says. He stares harder. "Do you understand?"

Jarrod nods.

Still he stares after the retreating Cougars. He gathers all the strength left in him. He carefully works his mouth open.

Jarrod screams after the Cougars in defiance. He screams at them for a long time. The horsemen look on in wonder. Finally, he sinks to his knees. After resting there for a moment, he rises again.

"Come with us," says the bearded man.

Jarrod stumbles after the rider. Strong hands heft him into the wagon. Clattering. All that clattering, he thinks. It seems the whole world is shaking and jostling. And then the brown wash, passing into the brown wash of nothingness and heat. He falls into the brownness leaning against the rough canvas of his pack.

"I don't think we can save him," the voice, a woman's, says. "But we've drained his abscesses and made him as comfortable as we can."

"Yes." It is the richly resonant voice of the bearded rider. "Pity."

Jarrod opens his eyes. A room. A white room. He is in some sort of . . . he searches for the word. Bed. Sunlight streams through white curtains over open windows. The white room is cool.

Jarrod tries to speak. A croak is the result.

"Give him some water," the man says. He is by one of the windows. A soft hand gently touches his face, props up his head. He opens his mouth and water trickles onto his tongue from a rag. After a moment, he manages to swallow. His mouth feels less swollen, but still there is the taste of poison in it.

"Pack," he says. "My pack."

"Yes," says the man, taking a step from the window. "That was very interesting. Apparatus. Alchemical apparatus."

"Blue pills," Jarrod says. "Three a day."

"Pills?" The woman speaking.

Jarrod tries to turn his head to see her, but cannot. His neck has stiffened. There is not much he *can* do with his body now. Curl his toes? Yes. Fingers? All eight of them.

"I'll have to check the inventory."

"Blue," Jarrod croaks. "Three. Day."

The soft hands ease his head back onto something soft. A pillow, it is called. She moves before him so that he can see her.

Hallucination, he thinks. I am trailing behind the Cougars' cart, and wandering off in my mind. He tries to shake his head to clear it, cannot.

A beautiful young woman, dressed in flowing white. Visions at the end. Biochemical fizz. Need to shake her from my head if I want to die like a ranger. He cannot.

The woman in white is still there. She is smiling.

"Welcome," she says. "Welcome to the Napa Valley."

# VALLEY

For two weeks there is nothing but rain. Steady rain outside his window, cool breezes ruffling the white curtains. Jarrod lies in the dim, clean room while the antibiotics slowly but surely kill off the worst of his infections and his putrefactions drain away. The people who have taken him in are in a constant state of surprise at the speed of his recovery. Jarrod still feels the ache of his wounds, and a weakness inside, like an overripe fruit. He will take months to heal completely. But he is young and was in peak shape before he fell in with the Cougars. Within two weeks he is taking short walks between the daily downpours and learning to use his newly mangled hands.

The man who ran the iron needle through his wrist must have known what he was doing, preserving the value of the burt, for Jarrod finds that he can clench and unclench a fist without trouble, and that all of his fingers responds well enough. The hole in his wrist does not caul over, however, and he is given a leather brace that covers much of his forearm. For most things, he must become left-handed now.

The woman is Sarah Bassda Polleta, and she is the daughter of Raphael, the King of the Valley.

The buildings of the compound where Jarrod is kept are extremely old—as old as any of the houses of the rich in Olympia, his mother's city, had been. But these buildings are in good repair. They are covered with plaster, which makes them far easier to patch than Olympia's brick and exposed concrete. But what makes the real difference is the paint: bright yellows and blues and whites. And the emblem of the sun—the signal that Jarrod had seen on the bearded man's tunic—is everywhere.

The sides of buildings are painted with it; suns are affixed to posts and worked into the wooden railings of the porches of the dwellings. If the paintings and carvings were not so cleverly done, Jarrod thinks, this place would be garish. Instead, he feels more at home here than he has since he left the forest. Yet the only tree worth climbing is a gnarled old oak in the center of the compound, and that tree looks as though it would barely hold his weight when he got to the upper branches.

There comes a day when Jarrod is spending more time outside than lying in his bed, and he is too restless merely to sit upon the porch of the building where he's kept, so he walks about the compound until he finds the woman.

Usually he finds her at chores, washing or mending. There is a cow in a field nearby, and this is Sarah's special charge.

"Saint Ann doesn't like all the rain," Sarah says one morning, when Jarrod finds her at milking. "She especially doesn't like the thunder."

Jarrod watches as Sarah grips the top of a cow teat in a pinch between her thumb and forefinger, then, with a waving motion, rolls her hand closed into a fist. As she squeezes, a stream of milk squirts into her pail. Jarrod is amazed at the aplomb of the cow. He imagines trying to milk a doe in this way . . . impossible. Deer can leap twelve feet into the air when they are uncomfortable and surprised.

"I think the rain will go on for a long time," Jarrod says.

"Saint Ann won't like that a bit, I'm afraid. What makes you think that it will?"

"There are changes happening. In the Earth. Maybe in the sky."

"Yes. You and every other wandering holy man says so, so I suppose it must be true. And do you have the cure for this illness the world has? Salvation? A bottle of rexall medicine? That kind always have something—"

"I don't," Jarrod says. "There's really nothing anyone can do. I'm just . . . talking."

"Ah, I see. Do you always begin your small talk with an augury of doom?"

"We don't banter much where I come from."

"And we are a jabbering people here in the south?"

"Well—you said it."

Sarah smiles, gives Saint Ann two quick squeezes, squirt, squirt. Saint Ann moos, gently shuffles a foot. "There, girl," Sarah says. "Thank you, girl."

Sarah stands up with her milk pail. "She gives her best milk in the hotter months, and it's long into autumn," she says.

"You can taste the difference?"

"Oh yes. April and August milk's richer and you can taste the good clover that's gone into it, too," she says. "But Saint Ann's worst is still something special. Nestor's making cheese this afternoon—Edam, I think. He'd already milked the nanny goats before the Lady rose this morning."

The *sun,* Jarrod reminds himself. They call the sun the Lady.

"Do you mix cow and goat milk?" he asks as he walks beside her back toward the kitchen.

"You can, but we won't today. It's just that Nestor will already have everything ready, and I'm sure he'll let me sneak in a hoop for the court."

"Nestor's not royalty?"

"Oh, no," Sarah says. "He's much too old for that."

After the milk is delivered to Nestor, Sarah hurries through her remaining chores and is done by the early afternoon. By this time, Jarrod is feeling weak from following her around, and his side aches dully. As the Lady begins Her descent, the day clouds over once again, and he and Sarah retreat from a misty rain into the coolness of the main sitting room of the big house in the compound—the king's dwelling.

Calling it a palace would be too grand, Jarrod thinks, but it is larger than any house he has ever seen, much larger than the Council Platform in Threecabin. They sit in old chairs covered with woolen upholstery. The weave is different from the wool that the rangers trade for from northern Timberlanders, and instead of being merely and always green, this is dyed with many colors, just like the pullover shirt that Jarrod wears. His other clothes were burned, Sarah has told him.

"Would you like me to read to you?" Sarah asks. "A story? Or an essay? I'm working on Montaigne at the moment, but my collection is in French, so it would be hard to translate and read it aloud at the same time."

Jarrod goes to the bookshelf and looks through the titles. "Where are the books on winemaking?" he asks.

"There's one over there, I think. I have no idea where the others are, or if there are any others," she replies. "That is one of the men's mysteries. Maybe they have all the old books somewhere secret. But I doubt it."

"Why do you doubt it?"

"Because men can't read."

Jarrod finally finds a title that interests him: *Cabernet Sauvignon: Queen of the Grapes.* But it appears to be a big book of faded photographs, with very little information about how the wine is made, the craft underneath the art.

"You really *can* read, can't you?" says Sarah.

Jarrod smiles, but does not look up from the book.

"Well, you'd better not let the men catch you at it, at least not yet. They know you're different, but they might not understand, not deep down." She closed the book she was holding. "It *is* strange to see."

"There's nothing I can do about it now other than gouge out

my eyes," Jarrod says. "Do you think I'm well enough to drink wine?"

"I think you are well enough to join us for supper tonight, if you'd like. Father has the best wine in the valley."

"I would like that," Jarrod says.

They pass the afternoon reading. When the shadows in the room grow longer, Sarah lights candles, and Jarrod puts his book away. He lets her read to him from a book of essays by Thomas Carlyle, a writer he has never heard of. The words are bombastic, and Sarah reads them vigorously, but Jarrod cannot help dozing off. He is almost asleep when the front door is flung open and the king strides, dripping wet, into his dwelling.

"A ranger in the house!" he proclaims, and claps a firm hand on Jarrod's shoulder as Jarrod is about to get up to greet him. "Rain like the Lady's heart is broken, and a ranger appears out of the fire-hearth stories."

"*Dragged* is more like it, Your Majesty," Jarrod says.

The king looks him full in the face. His beard is sumptuously wet, like the coat of a river otter. "Two things," the king says. "Never contradict me . . ."

"Excuse—"

"And the other: stop calling me Your Majesty!"

The king pats him hard on the shoulder and breaks into a great guffaw. Behind Jarrod, Sarah joins with his laughter. Hers is lighter, but somehow darker than her father's.

"I have to get out of these clothes," the king says. "If this keeps up, that quad down in Bolt Cove will surely catch the mold." He heads for a door, spattering water droplets in a trail behind him.

"Have the ranger for dinner, Sarah," he says without turning around. "I think he'd taste best with a turnip and potatoes!" And then the king is gone.

"You'll have to excuse Father," Sarah says. "You know the motto of the Polleta Court is *Carpe diem*. That means—"

"Seize the day," Jarrod says.

Sarah smiles and shakes her head. "So odd. I really didn't think men were, well, capable . . . Pardon me. I don't mean—"

"That's all right," Jarrod says. "Women are the best killers among the rangers. So we men need a skill."

All of Sarah's extended family—the court—sits down to eat in the dining room. There is an oaken table bigger than any table Jarrod has ever seen. It is polished to a dull shine, and Jarrod admires the rough grain of the surface. To meet such a beautiful end almost justifies the death of the tree. Almost.

The meal is delicious, the best food that Jarrod has ever eaten. There is pasta—ground, shaped grain, boiled—covered with sauce made from fresh vegetables cooked in olive oil. And so much tomato to it! Jarrod has had two tomatoes in his life before this—both from raids on trespassing Timberlanders. The sauce is, in turn, covered with cheese, wondrous, subtle cheese, not the overpowering one-flavored cheese of the north. Chewing it, savoring it, Jarrod can almost taste the complexity he has found in the wine. Nothing Jarrod has tasted before has prepared him for it.

Sarah smiles at him, and has a cabernet sauvignon served—fifteen years old. After sipping it, Jarrod cannot speak, cannot think, for a moment. He is no longer in the room, but somewhere else, swimming in the ruddy brown hue of the wine, thinking only of this taste, *feeling* this taste in the wine, then that one, like a man wandering through the woods with a dozen paths to choose from, all leading to a dramatic cliff, a gorgeous waterfall.

I could drink this and live, Jarrod thinks. The food is only an afterthought. Yet the wine doesn't overpower the food, but complements it, brings it up to its own level. Jarrod eats and drinks, and barely hears a word that is said during the meal. He does notice Sarah glancing at him, sees the slight upturn of her lips, a sly smile.

He sips the wine and imagines those forest paths, walking them in the amber sunlight of this valley—never is the sky so golden on the Olympic Peninsula—walking toward a waterfall of sunlit wine, led by Sarah, who is before him, her white dress flowing in a breeze, her calves dark from the sun, rippling with walking muscle.

"Ranger!" the king says loudly, a twinkle in his eye. "Don't get too lost in the wine. Now is not the time, but we would like to hear your story after dinner."

Jarrod sets down his glass, looks up, blinking. "Sure," he says. "I'll tell it then."

Servants clear the dishes and bring hot coffee. Macon Quitman, the man who had ridden next to the king when they met the Cougars, shows Jarrod how to pour a brandy made from the skins of grapes into the coffee.

"Grappa," he says. "It isn't very complicated, but it's good and strong. We try to use everything for something, you know."

Jarrod lifts the cup, takes a sip—and almost spits it back in. The coffee is vile. He forces himself to swallow.

"Ah," the king says, raising his cup to Jarrod. "Good, right?"

All take their cups and retire to the large sitting room where Jarrod and Sarah had spent the afternoon. Jarrod has eaten so much he is full to bursting. He quietly searches about the side corridors until he finds a toilet. He still is not used to this sort of indoor plumbing, and has to think for a moment before he remembers how to flush the commode.

There is a mirror over the water basin, and Jarrod takes a look at himself. Appallingly haggard, but his face is flushed, almost red, from the wine and food.

I'm getting healthy, he thinks. When I'm well, it will be time to move on. Do I want to move on? He has shaved himself without a mirror, and missed a couple of spots on his neck. Getting careless. Bangs are far, far too long. Will I cut them back?

Maybe tomorrow, when he's shaving, he can do it. After a bit of effort, Jarrod figures out the workings of the sink. He splashes a handful of water on his face, then returns to the sitting room.

Macon and the king are in an animated discussion about how to deal with damp grapes after the rains.

"Thank the Lady the main harvest is in," says the king. "Can you imagine if this were late summer?"

"I don't want to," Macon replies. "We have, what? A couple of tons?"

"About, I'd say."

"A hundred seventy-five gallons to the ton. We could lose three hundred fifty gallons at worst."

"Still. And we won't, though. Not unless the world ends. We'll have to invoke the sulfurous spirit for all of it. Have a special gathering."

"Maybe not."

"It's the only way to cure a mold."

"If there *is* one."

"We'll get three hundred gallons. I'll bet my horse and house on it."

After a while, Sarah moves between the king and Macon.

"I thought we were going to hear the ranger's story," she says. "I believe he's recovered enough from supper to tell it to us."

Jarrod finds himself the focus of attention in the room. His side gives him a twinge, and he sits down in a chair. Still seems a strange custom, to fold oneself in such a way.

"My name is Jarrod," he says to the quiet room. "I am a ranger of the United States Park Service, Olympic National Park Division." He looks down at his right hand, puts thumb to third finger. "I'm *still* a ranger, I suppose."

He tells them some of his tale—of the plague in Yosemite and his mission there. Of his ride on the train and the time with the Cougars. For a moment, he thinks to leave out the shunning ceremony, but in the end, he tells that, too. This is the way rangers are; this is what we do. The way I am. He does not mention his mother.

"So that was what was in those blue pills," the king says when Jarrod is done. "These *antibiotics?*"

"Yes. It's penicillin."

"And the alchemical still in your sack—these spirits are made with this thing?"

"That processes them. They're found in nature."

"Ah, like the Stone," the king says.

"No, penicillin comes from a living thing."

"Oh, the Lady Stone is alive," says the king. "It's the *principle* of life. We will have to talk more of this."

"My family are great alchemists," Sarah says. "That's why we are chosen for the court this cycle."

"We will speak of this later," the king continues. "But what a story this man tells. The Cougars are raiding the trains again."

"I thought so before," Macon says. "That metal looked too clean to have come from looting the old factories."

"Yes, yes," the king says. "And the idiots leave the real goods, and loot the inconsequential—" The king glances at Jarrod and smiles. "Except for *you,* sir, that is." He turns back to Macon. "What galls me is that those goods are meant for *us.* We are dealing with the very people who are cutting off our trade with the north."

"What's to be done, Father?" Sarah asks. The king shakes his head.

"Not that you should be worrying about it, child . . . but I don't know yet. But we will do something. Something soon."

With that, the conversation turns back to grapes. More coffee and grappa is brought forth, but Jarrod declines, taking instead a glass of cellar-cooled water. Candles burn low. It is late when all turn to their beds. Jarrod realizes that this night was a special one, and that it was he who kept the company up, telling his tale. Nevertheless, all rise with the Lady, and the compound is empty when Jarrod gets up in the morning, except for the usual retainers—and Sarah.

He wakes to find her beside his bed, watching him. Today she wears an uncolored tunic of light wool that falls to her knees. It is gathered at her waist by a red sash. Jarrod wipes his eyes, reaches for the jar of water that is on a table beside his bed. He cups the jar in both hands, sits up and takes a swallow. She wears brown sandals, laced about her brown ankles. Whether her legs are tan from the sun or her born color, he cannot tell.

"You're waking up earlier every day," she says.

"I used to get up before dawn. It seems a long time ago, though, when I did that."

"You're healing."

"I feel as weak as a twig still."

"Those pills . . . they are miraculous."

"Science," he says. "They kill bacteria."

"Yes, well. I'm going for a walk and I came to see if you'd like to come along with me. Down to the creek."

"Is it raining?"

"Not yet."

"Yes," he says. "I'll come."

He had gone to bed wearing his pants—made of the same undyed wool as Sarah's tunic—and he pulls on a shirt that is woven of many colored threads. He slides his feet into socks and boots. From the corner by the bed, he takes a curved and lacquered walking stick that Sarah has told him used to be her grandfather's. They go out into the morning.

A mist hangs over the yard of the compound and clings damply to Jarrod's skin and hair. They take a trail that leads over a small hill and into a dale, where a stream runs shallow among white, cherty stones. The walk over the hill leaves Jarrod breathless.

"Are bacteria like very small insects?" Sarah asks, letting him rest for a moment.

"Insects are closer to us than they are to bacteria."

"What do you mean?"

"On the evolutionary . . ." He thinks better of trying to explain this to her. "But bacteria *are* small."

"How small?"

"Like a grain of sand to the big oak tree in the yard. No. Smaller, actually. But you know about yeast, don't you?"

"The vigorous element in the must," says Sarah.

"Yeasts are related to bacteria."

"I didn't know that. The fermenting is one of the men's mysteries. I'm not supposed to know about such things, but maybe *they* do."

She sits down on a rock by the stream and begins to unlace her sandals. The sun shines dully through the fog and the morning grows warmer.

"Yeasts are in even that picture book I read about wine," Jarrod says.

One of Sarah's laces snags, and she tugs at it fiercely.

"I haven't read all the books. I haven't read most of the books. Nobody has for a while. There isn't time. I have to choose what I want to concentrate on."

"What is that?"

"History. Literature. I like to read about wars."

"Wars?"

"Battles. Biographies of generals. Politics. Have you ever read Clausewitz?"

"No."

"Machiavelli?"

"No."

"Clausewitz was a military theorist."

"I see."

She takes off her other sandal and steps into the stream. It is just deep enough to dampen the hem of her tunic. Jarrod gazes down at her feet through the water. They are dark shapes; she trails them like slowly moving fish.

"Don't you want to come wading?" she asks.

He sits down on the rock where she had been and leans over to pull off a boot. The effort pains him.

Sarah dips a hand into the flow and splashes water at him. "Well?"

"Give me a second," he says. "It takes me a while to get my boots off."

She returns to the bank and bends down beside him. For a moment, he thinks that she is going to kiss him, but instead she takes his walking cane into her hand. As she rises, her hair brushes against his face. She smells of olive oil soap, which everyone here uses. With the cane as a crutch, she ventures farther into the stream, then turns around and faces him.

"Do you think we're barbarians?" she asks.

He looks down, begins to work on his other boot. "I think that you and your father saved my life twice over. You've freed me from slavery. How could I think you are barbarians?"

"We don't know what yeast is. Not really."

"Like you said. Maybe the men do."

"They don't."

"I thought you said—"

"*I* know what the men know," she says. "Do you think it's all that hard to spy on their rituals? I've read the old Masonic handbooks they use, the alchemy notebooks of old King Boyd. And the charter of the Presbyterians, too."

"I'm afraid I don't know what you're talking about."

"The mysteries. They aren't very mysterious, really."

Jarrod finds himself remembering the Shunning, when Alaph jabbed him in the stomach with the Burly Stave.

"But sometimes they can be surprising," he says. He takes off his socks and tucks them together into one boot. He steps gingerly into the creek. The water is not as cold as he expected.

"We used to know—the court, I mean—that it was all . . . made up. To impress the common people. To give them a deeper reason for living. But we're forgetting."

"*You* haven't forgotten."

"I am a woman."

"So? Yes, I see. It matters here."

"In some things. The wine and gunpowder—that's for the men, and they wouldn't listen to anything I had to say about it."

Jarrod stubs his toe against a creek stone. In regaining his balance, he starts another twinge in his side. "Do you mind if I take back the walking stick?" he asks.

"Oh yes. I'm sorry. You look so much better. It's easy to forget you're not done healing yet." She hands him the stick. Jarrod takes it and leans upon it. The twinge does not go away, but doesn't grow into real pain, either. He steps farther out into the creek. Below he can see shapes darting about. When he focuses his eyes below the water surface, the shapes resolve into minnows and minnow shadows.

Sarah wades farther down the creek. "There are other things about us. Other ways. You may find that we are barbaric yet. *I* do."

"Don't you have to be unaware of your, um, uncouthness to be a barbarian?"

"Not at all," Sarah replies. "Plenty of people are cruel and know themselves to be cruel, but don't do anything about it, don't stop it. Take Genghis Khan, for instance; he positively—"

"I don't know who that is," Jarrod says. "And why are you talking about cruelty? I don't see any cruelty in you, Sarah Polleta."

She laughs her dark laugh. "Don't be so sure," she says, "Ranger Jarrod."

He takes a step after her. "I *am* sure," he says.

She turns to face him once again. Now she is nearly to her waist in the water, and her tunic streams back behind her in the current, exposing the brown of her thighs, underwater.

"That is good," she says. "For we are to mate."

Jarrod nearly falls into the water, so surprised is he. He steadies himself on the cane. "What did you say?"

"Oh, nothing too serious," says Sarah. There is a trace of bitterness in her voice. "And it depends on *your* consent, of course."

"What do you mean, nothing too serious? Did you say *mate?*"

"Yes. That is, copulate." She takes a strand of her own hair in her fingers, twists it. "And now do you think us so very refined and civilized?"

"I hardly know what to think." Jarrod picks up the cane from the water. Puts it back down on the stream bottom, where it was before. Stands still in the current.

"It's a tradition. Tradition is everything here in the valley, in case you haven't noticed. But to be bred like a goat—I can tell you that at times I think that tradition goes too far."

"Why me? I don't. What about the men? What about Macon?"

"Macon? Don't be ridiculous. And in any case, Macon has far more important things to worry about. Macon is not of the court. He's to be the next king in all likelihood."

"But he calls your father Uncle."

"And he calls me sister. We are not related. He's a child of the Quitman court, the one that came before us, the Polletas. Now he's a commoner. I am a Polleta."

Sarah wanders farther down the creek, too deep to splash. After a moment, Jarrod steps from the water and sits back down on the bank. He pulls on his socks and boots and walks after her beside the bank. With the water slowing her, their gaits match.

"So why me? I'm even lower than a . . . commoner, aren't I? Why not another commoner? Are they too lowly for such as you?"

"The commoners," Sarah says without looking directly at him, "are the reason the court exists. My father does not forget this. *I* know it."

Ahead, the creek flows over a small shoal and makes a little waterfall of maybe a two-foot drop. Sarah moves to the side just above it and watches the water as it surges over the rock and into the air. Jarrod realizes that she has been walking barefoot down the creek. The souls of her feet must be leather-tough to step among the creek stones so lightly. Again, Jarrod feels tired. He goes below the little falls to where a log has been deposited in high-water times and he sits on it. They must speak loudly to each other to be heard above the tumble of the water.

"I'm a Princess of the Valley," she says. "A princess is at the whim of the majority of her subjects—the commoners, as you put it. I am their collective will, as far as I am able to be. That is how we live here, how we keep ourselves from becoming like . . . the others. You've been with the others."

"Yes."

She reaches and plucks a twig from the bank, turns it for a moment in her hands, then sets it in the current and sends it over the falls. "At least that's what I tell myself when I think about the Draining of the Lees."

"What?"

"The Lees. It is a ceremony we have every twelve years, the time it takes to make a fine old red. Then all the old barrels are broken and reworked. Everyone comes from miles around, and brings the best of their household. The food—it is unbelievable how wonderful the meals are then. I remember from when I was a little girl. It was music and eating and my uncle Kim whirling me around and around under the lights in the trees."

Sarah's voice becomes softer, and Jarrod must strain to hear her over the water. She is quiet for a while, watching the falls, and then she steps from the water and comes to sit beside him.

"You've spent the morning getting ready to tell me these things," Jarrod says.

"And half the night."

He breathes out long, breathes in moist air. The fog is beginning to burn off, and the creek water sparkles here and there.

"Tell me the rest," he says.

"There is a cave, in the hills, not far from here. The opening faces directly east. It's a very beautiful place just after dawn. We call it the Grotto of the Lady. That is where we go to die."

"What?"

"The entire court. At the end of the Lees. We all drink poison and walk to the Lady's Grotto. Well, some of us are carried, if the poison makes us too weak. But that is a women's mystery that I'm in charge of. I'll make the poison just right so that the timing will work out. Hermes Androgynous. She flows to my bidding."

"Mercury?" Jarrod says.

"Among other things. The Laughter of the Lady. That is the secret name for the poison. No man can know."

"You're telling *me.*"

"And you are a man. I know. You spilled yourself on the sheets while you were in the fever dreams. Before the pills worked against the . . . bacteria."

"I can't remember that. But—"

"It's all foolish ritual," Sarah says. "Like the shunning that has been placed on you."

"But you die. You *voluntarily* die. No one asks this of us."

"Don't they? From the way you describe the life of rangers, you are constantly at war with your neighbors."

"But the fighting is mostly waiting, preparing, getting ourselves fed," Jarrod says. "Mostly, we spend our time in the trees."

"And mostly we make wine and cheese. Grow our gardens. Tend the animals." Sarah stands up, takes a step back toward the water.

"Oh, why am I defending this?" she says. "I told you we were barbarians. I hate it. I love my life and I hate the thought of leaving it, losing it. They put food in the grotto with us, then seal it up for a year. Time enough for the worst of the rot to pass."

"Why don't you run away?"

"Where should I run to? Toward the Cougars and their ilk? Away south into the madness?"

"No."

"And I am a Princess of the Valley. My word is law. One of the advantages of being an aristocrat, in an aristocracy."

"I don't know history as you do, but even I know that kings have changed the customs of their people. Kings are known for doing that."

"No one can change a tradition. Traditions change when enough of the people want them to change."

"I don't agree."

"How old are you?"

"Twenty years. More or less. We don't know the dates of our births." And I did not ask my mother, he thinks. What a strange thing to wish to know, in any case. Useless.

"I am twenty-five. When I was twenty, I was impossible. They would have had to drag me screaming to the Lady's Grotto. They may yet."

"When is the next Draining of the Lees?"

"In five years' time. I think that will be very good . . . for a baby."

"That you *die?*"

"That I love it well during its earliest years, and leave at a time when it can't really know what death is."

"You won't be there. It will know *that.*"

"The next court will raise it as its own. As we've raised Macon and his sisters. It will get a lot of love."

"But not yours."

"Not mine. Unless there is truth to all those silly words that we die to. Reincarnation, the Lady rising in the East. I doubt that, though. I doubt that very much."

When they return to the compound, Jarrod is very tired. He naps until late afternoon comes and with it, the rain. He lies in the white sheets of his bed, listening to the patter on his windowsill. For a moment, there is a tingling in his right hand where his fingers used to be. He reaches over, but finds them still missing.

He takes his meal in the room. The rain continues to fall into the evening, and Sarah comes to him. She carries a candle, which she sets on the table beside the bed. She stands over him for a moment, gazing down upon him. She wears a thin cotton gown, pure white. Her dark hair is about her face, and her brown skin glistens with a fragrant oil.

Her long brown fingers on the fastenings of her gown. It falls from her shoulders. Brown, shining fingers in his white sheets, and she is in bed beside him.

"I've lost . . . so much," he says to her.

"I don't care about that," Sarah says. She runs her palm over his chest, his stomach. "You're beautiful. I like you well enough. I like you very much."

"I've lost a child," he says.

"Make another. Give one to me." Her hand lower, around him. He is hard there and her palm is soft, oiled.

"I still don't—" He gasps as she tightens her grip. Tightens, releases, tightens. "Why me?"

"Because I want you," she says. "And I am the Princess of the Valley." She pulls the sheets aside, lowers herself to take him in her mouth. "You really have no idea how beautiful you are, do you? The sort of figure you cut in the world."

"I've never thought about it."

"It's funny, but I believe you," Sarah says. She licks him gently, draws back. "You're a gorgeous man, Jarrod of the Northern Rangers, and I want your body very badly."

"Oh."

For a moment, he considers resisting. There is much unresolved. Here. Back home.

Home was a place where he fit in.

They have as much of a reason—a use—for him here in the Napa Valley. Isn't the whole purpose of a ranger's life to be useful to those around him? Does anybody care for him more back among the Ho Brigade? Baker? Franklin? This is what they trained me for, Jarrod thinks. This is what they made me.

"What is it?" Sarah says, rising up from sucking him, kissing his chin. "Is this all right?"

"Yes. I'll give you what you want."

She kisses him then, bites at his lip. He puts his hands around her. His two right-hand fingers stroke the back of her leg; his good left hand reaches between her legs to find her, stroke her to wetness. He is nearly a foot taller than Sarah, and she is so small in his arms. Not like long, strong Baker who matched him in a fierce equality when they came together. So different than any ranger woman would be.

He takes her by the hips, slides her onto him. She reaches down, opens herself, and after a moment he is inside her. She kneads his chest and grinds against him.

"In your plan," Jarrod says, and pushes into her deeper. "There is one thing you haven't thought about."

"Mmm, what?"

He holds her still, won't let her move. She is frustrated at first, but then lets him stay there, inside her, motionless, hard.

"I might get attached to this place," Jarrod says. "I might fall for you, Sarah Polleta. I might want to stay and raise my child."

"Oh," she said. "No, you said you had to go on, to take the cure to your people."

"They aren't *my* people. They're just some rangers we know."

"But—"

"I could come back here after I do that."

"To watch me die?"

She struggles against his hold on her, but he keeps her from moving, stays inside her. She settles down onto him once again, sighs.

"Whose plan is this really?" he asks. "To mate us?"

"Ours," she says.

"Who?"

"The valley. The families. And I wanted you. I liked the way you looked, if you must know, so I told Father that I wanted you. We Polletas usually get what we want when we've a mind to it."

"I thought you were the collective will of your people."

"When you are going to die young and you know it, you tend to . . . take as many liberties as you can."

"I'm one of your liberties."

"Only if you want to be, Jarrod."

"Lie down," he says. "Here, beside me."

With a little gasp, she pulls herself from him and does as he has asked. She is not a virgin, but he doubts she has been well pleased by many of those she has been with. And there are most likely few descriptions in her military histories about being with a woman.

He spreads her legs, moves down to her, kissing her dark skin.

It is tawny brown. Now he knows this color. It is the color of the oldest, best wine.

"What? What are you doing?"

"Quiet. Quiet, Sarah." He finds her, parts her vagina with his own lips, feels gently for her clit with his tongue. Finds it. For a moment she tenses. He laps her. She sighs.

"I didn't know," she says. "I never knew a man could—"

And then her words fall away, and he licks her until she shivers and comes.

Now is the time when a women is most receptive to getting pregnant, he thinks. This is the time rangers are taught to avoid doing what Jarrod will do. He rises up her, moving along against her skin. She is limp beneath him, wholly given to what she has felt. He slides easily inside her. He holds himself over her as he thrusts.

Sarah has her eyes closed, and she smiles with a fierce joy as he takes her, as she takes him in. He leans down, breathes her breath as his. The warm air of the valley, healing. Already he is feeling stronger than he had in the morning. Won't be long, won't be long.

When he comes, she opens her eyes. They gaze at each other in the candlelight flicker.

"No one has ever done that to me before," she says. "How did you do that?"

"It's a secret of the rangers," he says. "We can never tell."

"But you can show."

"We can show."

"Show me again."

In a week, Jarrod has regained much of his strength. He is able to spend a day walking without growing tired. He takes his meals with the court, and every night—and some mornings—Sarah comes to his bed. During the days, after her chores, they take long strolls into the countryside, find hidden places in which to make love.

Jarrod cannot at first believe it, but he is coming to love this land of rolling hills, great open fields of grapes, cut with low windbreaks of trees. There are great stretches where the woodland is allowed—allowed!—to grow, usually along the banks of streams. But even near such certain water, the trees are seldom more than a hundred feet tall. This is not a place where a man—even a ranger—could travel from tree to tree. And yet he is becoming familiar with the ground. It does not sway in the wind, but there is something to be said for solidity—especially for a man just regaining his traveling legs.

King Raphael is planning a movement against the Cougars. While it clearly irks the man to ask his daughter's advice, Sarah has kept up with the scouting reports of the valley riders and she seems to have in her head the entire topography of Northern California available for instant recall.

Jarrod watches them one afternoon in a planning session just before supper. While several of the king's men are gathered about, the discussion is clearly between father and daughter. They stand in the middle of the sitting room, a great map of California rolled out on a table before them, its edges held down by empty wine bottles with candles set in them. There is enough light streaming through the windows, but the candles are lit. The people of the valley seem to delight in the sight of candles burning atop wine bottles.

"I still consider directly stopping one of their bandit raids," says the king. "And think of the goodwill this will make for us with the people of the north, the train-runners. We'll get a better price for the brandy this time, of that I'm sure."

"And you can show off in front of an audience," Sarah replies. "I know how you men think. But think about this, too: that is the one moment when the Cougars are fully armed and ready to fight."

"Are you saying that that rabble could stand against us?"

"Any idiot can pull the trigger on an M-16. They're designed that way."

"All right, Princess, all right. Your point is well taken."

Sarah smiles, leans over the map, searches with her finger until she finds a place.

"We want the fewest casualties for our side with the most impact on them."

"Of course."

"Then this is the place to strike. We need only discover the time."

"What would that be?"

"Shingletown Field. At the Aytch game."

"But how can we know *when?* You can't count on a Cougar to do anything on time or right."

Jarrod steps forward from the doorway where he's been listening. "First tuhsdays aytch," he says. "First Tuesday is Aytch."

"There," says Sarah, nodding to him. She turns her attention back to the map, taps the spot. "Two weeks."

Jarrod is finally able to taste and think at the same time—if he concentrates. Often the food and wine call him away, nonetheless, and he suspects it will always do so while he remains in the valley. He is even coming not only to tolerate the coffee with grappa, but to look forward to it to round out the meal. And this night it raises the inside of his mouth to the perfect temperature to melt the chilled tiramisu dessert like sweet butter on his tongue.

"I hate to wake you up from the land of cookie and custard, ranger," the king says. "But I want to offer something you may find enjoyable."

As if you haven't already, Jarrod thinks. He swallows, collects himself.

"What is that, sir?"

"A place with the riders when we strike the bandits."

Jarrod considers. "Revenge," he says.

"Doesn't it make your blood boil, what they did to you?"

"It does," he says. "But I can't blame animals for being animals."

"Animals don't take slaves. Even if they do, animals don't *sell* slaves."

"Would it help you to have me along?"

"You've been to the area."

"I hardly remember."

The king turns his cup up, drains it. A bit of coffee dribbles onto his beard, but the effect is not comic. He only looks the fiercer. "I would *like* to have you along, ranger. Somehow I think you know how to fight."

"Then I'll come because you want it," Jarrod says. "But not for revenge. I'll fight better that way."

"If you are to fight with us, I would like you to be one of us."

"What do you mean?"

"You are too old for an initiation, and besides the next one isn't for two new moons. But I'd like you to join the Animus."

"I don't—"

"The men's society," Sarah tells him. "It's an honor."

"Tomorrow night, we're holding a Thickening."

"A Thickening?"

"It's a traditional ceremony. I think you'll find it interesting," says the king.

"Of course I'll come," Jarrod says.

King Raphael laughs heartily, wipes his face with a napkin. "Break out the ten-year port," he tells the butler. "And mind your boy doesn't shake the bottle, Grotton. We don't want to eat it."

The old servant, who has told Jarrod tales of serving three courts over nearly thirty years, has likely never allowed a cloudy glass of wine to be decanted, Jarrod thinks. Grotton nods without expression and returns soon with a tawny liquid that is the color of Sarah's uncovered breasts.


The night of the Thickening is cloudy and wet, but the ceremony is to take place indoors, in one of the buildings of the compound set aside for that purpose—the Animus Hall. Macon comes for Jarrod just as dusk fades to evening. The moon is covered, but Jarrod knows it is at half of its fullness. They walk together to the hall, and Macon leaves Jarrod there. He goes to change into his ceremonial garb.

Jarrod finds himself among at least fifty men—the assembled males of the court, plus others of rank from the nearby countryside.

The walls and ceiling of the Animus Hall are covered with suns. The suns are made of stamped copper, each as big as an eating plate, and nailed with shining alloy brads in regular lines. The walls are coated with beige plaster and the ceiling is cedar; it retains a faint odor, brought out by the heat in the room. It is sloped upward into a pyramid, and at the top is a chimney opening.

A low fire burns on a hearth under the chimney. It is mostly coals now, and the only light in the room. The suns glimmer in its red light, and the room is tawny. An enormous iron kettle is set over the fire. Jarrod joins with the men in a moving circle around the kettle. In one corner of the room, someone beats a goatskin drum; in another a man blows a single long, reedy note on a rivercane pipe, over and over. With this regular beat, the men take steps clockwise about the kettle and fire. Each man wears a shimmering robe of blue, yellow and gold. The robes, too, have suns brocaded upon them.

Silk, Jarrod thinks. They have spun silk into cloth, just like in books.

The king, Macon and three other men wear hats that rise two feet over their heads and splay out like the leaves in a clump of grass. The king's hat has a sun on it; Macon's a moon, and the three others have astrological symbols for planets. That one is Mars, Jarrod thinks. Is that one Venus? No, Mercury.

When the men have completed a circle around the kettle, the Mars-capped man places his hand into the kettle; after a moment, he takes it out, dripping with water. After five such circles, the man cannot keep his hand in the water for more than a moment. He raises his hand in a signal, and the drum and pipe stop. The circle stands still.

The king motions to the other hatted man, this one with the symbol Jarrod doesn't recognize. The man leaves the circle, and soon returns carrying another kettle, this one smaller than the one with the water in it. He places it to one side of the big kettle, away from the fire.

The king smiles upon the gathered men.

*"Carpe diem,"* he says. He turns to Mercury. *"Lapis invisibilitatis!"* It is both a question and a command.

Mercury speaks: "Wind is air. Air is life. Life is soul."

The men, in unison, answer: *"De res animali, vegetabili, et minerali."*

The king nods. *"Lapis, prima materia, massa informis."*

*"Lapis,"* the men say. "The Lady Stone."

"Go, travelers," says the king. Mercury, Mars and Macon-moon leave the circle. They open a cellar door set in one corner of the room. The moon and the two planets descend into the cellar. The men patiently wait. After a long while, they return, carrying something among them.

It is a large metal platter with two wooden poles affixed to it, so that the planets carry it between them like a litter. On the platter are two red metal cans and a dark blue box. Each of the cans is painted red. They halt at the smaller kettle and set the litter on the earthen floor of the room.

Macon reaches down and unscrews the stoppers from the tops of the two metal cans. In the low firelight, Jarrod can just make out the lettering on the sides of the cans.

*Gasoline*

*10 gallons 40 liters*

*Extremely Flammable*

*Harmful or Fatal if Swallowed*

Macon opens the two metal cans and carefully pours their contents into the kettle. The two planets kneel beside Macon, and the three of them lift the kettle and, with small, short steps, bring it over toward the fire. They gently set the smaller kettle inside the larger one, as a liner.

They're making a double boiler, Jarrod thinks. For *gasoline.* And within moments, the smell of gasoline and rust suffuses the air. One of the men in the circle—this one with no special hat—steps forward and uses a large fan made of oak slats to waft the fumes up and out the chimney. The fan doesn't work very well, and Jarrod's eyes begin to water.

Macon returns to the liter. He gets the box and comes back to stand beside the kettle. Mars has been handed a large stave—

of about the same heft as Alaph's Burly Stave, Jarrod thinks—
and the planet dips this stave into the gasoline.

Macon lifts the box up before the assembled men.

"*Mercurius, cervus fugitivus,*" Macon says. "Return to us."

"Return to us," the other men say.

The faded letters on the box read *Ivory Soap Flakes.*

With formal and precise movements, Macon shakes the
snowy white contents of the box into the kettleful of gasoline
while Mars stirs. The circle of men once again begins to shuffle
clockwise.

*Napalm,* Jarrod thinks. They are making homemade napalm
over an open fire.

This is where the Molotov cocktails that the Cougars used to
burn up Poppyseed and the other Karma Patrol members came
from. That started the fire in the tree when he sought to escape.

The men of the Napa Valley have a sideline in arms dealing.

Each in the circle focuses his attention on the kettle. The
drum and pipe start up once again, and the circle begins to move
faster. Five turns, ten.

The king halts the circle at thirteen turns. Macon signals to
Mars to stop stirring the thickening gasoline.

"He has returned," Macon says.

"*Carpe diem,*" the king says.

"*Carpe diem,*" the men echo.


Later, Jarrod, the king and Macon sip port in the king's dwelling.
The hour is late, and the wine is smooth, soothing. Almost like
it adapts to my state, Jarrod thinks. I can almost believe in the
alchemy of the valley, the spirits and the four elements of nature. I can almost believe that the world is alive and full of purpose. Almost, while I'm drinking this wine on such a gentle
evening.

"Welcome to the Animus," the king says, raising his glass to
Jarrod in salute.

"You're one of us, now, Jarrod," says Macon. "A Man of the Valley."

Jarrod doesn't reply, but returns the salute and drains his cup.

The king clears his throat. "I thought a man like you—a man who could bear those things the Cougars did to you and still keep your dignity—oh, I saw it from the first. I thought such a man would be a good one for my Sarah."

"I don't. You approve of us?"

"Of course." The king chuckles. "I told her to do it."

"I thought she wanted it first. Will you explain?"

"There's nothing much to explain. We discussed it. We agreed on it together. Prevents jealousies among the families. I saw you were the one almost right away, ranger." He drinks down his wine. *"Carpe diem,* I always say."

"What about you, Macon?" Jarrod asks.

"Sarah is like a sister to me." The words sound almost like an incantation to Jarrod, like one of the phrases from the Thickening ceremony.

"Are you sure?"

Macon frowns. "No, ranger, I am not. It doesn't matter. We have traditions here—good ones. I like you. And now, you're a brother."

Jarrod stares at his glass. The night seems less gentle to him now. "Do you think. Does she care at all about me?"

The king looks at Macon, who rolls his eyes, and the king laughs aloud.

"Who can say what women think? And my Sarah is a deep one. She's got a shadow, too, upon her." He pours himself another glass of port. "Maybe," he says. "Maybe she does."

The next day, plans get underway for the raid on the Cougars. The riders drill on a practice field outside the court compound. Macon takes charge of the tactical movements, and hones his riders to a fine precision. The rains continue, and soon the field is churned to mud, but Macon only works the men the harder. Late in the afternoon they all trundle to the little pool formed by the waterfall of the stream, where Sarah and Jarrod had spoken.

Each man takes a turn in the water, while the servants return the horses to the tents that serve as stables, where they clean and polish the tack, getting it ready for the next day's maneuvers. The riders are drawn from miles around, and near the compound King Raphael has set up a great common tent that the men share. Macon moves his bed to this tent. The king himself remains in the compound, as does Jarrod, for Sarah continues to visit him each night in his bed.

The rains do not trouble Jarrod. He is used to far longer ones in the Olympic Peninsula. During the day, Jarrod stays to one side, learning to ride a horse for the first time. It is far more difficult than it appears. The years the valley men have spent riding allow them to control their horses with a practiced ease. Jarrod is most concerned with staying on his mount, a three-year-old stallion named Sausalito, after a region nearby. He had asked for a gelding, thinking that would be more docile, but Macon wouldn't hear of it.

"Best to learn how to swim by jumping in," Macon had said. "Besides, I raised that one from a foal. Sausalito is a smart horse. A smart horse is better than a tame one in a fight."

Much of his balance from years in the trees works to his advantage in riding horses, Jarrod discovers. After some early uncertainty, Sausalito seems to understand that Jarrod is only unpracticed, and not deliberately trying to taunt him with incompetence. In three days, the horse is working with him, and Jarrod is at last able to sit comfortably in the saddle during a brisk trot. He finds that a day of riding Sausalito can be as tiring as a day spent traveling. Riding a horse requires muscles that he's never used before.

While Jarrod feels that he can make the trip to raid with the riders, he does not think he is ready to journey on alone, to the rangers in Yosemite. A little longer, and his chance for success will increase enormously. But people will die because of his delay—of that he has no doubt.

But Franklin sent me as a ranger, he thinks. And this is exactly the kind of choice rangers always have to make.

Toward the end of the first week, there is a day without rain. Jarrod decides to try out his horseback riding in open country, and invites Sarah for an afternoon ride. They wander a long way, through vineyards and woodland, and finally climb a steep embankment. Sausalito is winded from carrying the two of them when they get to the top, and Jarrod sets him to grazing in a small patch of brush.

"Come over here," Sarah calls, after Jarrod has tended to his horse.

He makes his way through a clump of scrub oak to find Sarah seated on a wide, flat stone. Before her is a grand view of the nearby valley. Far in the distance, Jarrod can make out the Polleta family compound, and nearby the red and white fabric of the tent that houses the warriors. Farther still are the coastal mountains, and over those . . . yes . . . no. Yes. A glint of blue between a pass in the mountains.

"That. Is that—"

"That's the Pacific, Jarrod."

He sits down beside her, and she hands him a wineskin that she has brought along. He squirts a draw into his mouth, swallows, and stares at the distant wedge of shimmering blue.

"I never thought I would see it," he says.

"You can't see much of it."

"But now I will always have seen it."

"Yes. You have."

She takes his good left hand and kisses it. She places it on her stomach, which is warm from the sun.

"My bleeding was due this week," she says.

"Has it come?"

"No. It is too early to tell, though."

"Yes, it is."

"Will you be careful when you go with them?"

"I'm always careful."

"Yes. I think you are."

"I thought the idea was not to become attached to your lover."

"The idea is that my lover not become attached to *me.*"

"Too late, Sarah Polleta."

"Too late for me, too, Jarrod of the Northlands. More's the pity for both of us."

Sarah spreads a blanket and they make love on the rock. The day is warm and they slide against each other's wet skin. Later, they lie drying in the sun. Jarrod's skin is growing darker, although he will always be a pale, light thing beside Sarah's lustrous brown.

Jarrod brings out his bone flute, made from the shin of a moose. He has not played it since he left Threecabin. He blows a tentative note, then a short melody. Somehow the flute sounds different here, warmer. Jarrod gazes at the hills and the sea and plays what songs come to him. Sarah leans against his arm, listens to the music.

After a while, he puts the flute away. He drifts to sleep in Sarah's arms. He dreams—as he has constantly this week—of riding Sausalito. Suddenly, there is a great rumble, and the ground bucks under him. He awakes with the feeling that he is flying through the air, thrown from Sausalito, and instinctively cradles his head in his hands, to guard against the impact of his fall—only to find that he is already lying on the ground.

But Sarah is sitting up, startled. And behind him, Jarrod hears the whinny of Sausalito. Then the ground jolts them again.

"What—"

"Earthquake," Sarah says. "Very big one."

"Are you . . . are we safe?"

"Yes. Here."

"Let me get my horse."

Sarah gazes out into the distance and does not answer him. "I can still see it," she says. "But we wouldn't be able to tell from this far away, I don't think."

"The ocean?" He is bewildered.

"No. The compound. There, look. The tent has fallen."

The large tent lies splayed and loose. Even from this distance, the damage is clearly evident.

"We have to get back," Sarah says.

"I'll get Sausalito."

This proves more difficult than he'd thought it would be. The horse is spooked, and as another shock rolls through the ground, he rears away from Jarrod, and he must follow Sausalito into the brush and untangle his bridle from a eucalyptus branch.

"I don't blame you, friend," Jarrod says. "Who's to know if the world is not ending."

Sarah takes them on a more direct route, and they ride back at as quick a pace as they can. As they ride, more tremors undulate through the ground, and once or twice it is all Jarrod can do to hold Sausalito to the path. Sarah breaks her silence to speak kind words to the horse, and they continue on.

A horseman who is by the fallen tent sees them approach and he breaks into a gallop toward them. Jarrod recognizes Macon's mare, Chinquapin. Jarrod feels Sarah's arms grow tighter and tighter about him at Macon's approach.

The rider meets them on the road, and turns Chinquapin in a chuffing of turf and earth, to stand still before them. Tears stream from his eyes, and his face is red.

"Your father," he says to Sarah. "The king. My. Queen."

Sarah slips from behind Jarrod and stands on the road. After a long moment, she falls to her knees. She digs her hands into the ground and stands, her fists full of dirt. She stares at her hands, as the earth falls from her clenched fingers.

A low wail breaks out from her, like the creaking a closing gate might make. It ends in a scream of anguish, as if the gate has slammed shut.

"How did it happen?" Jarrod asks quietly.

"A beam in the house," Macon answers, still gazing in shock at Sarah. "We build them to withstand the quakes. But not so big a quake as this one. I've never felt its like."

Again Sarah wails, but this time she shakes her head, smears what dint remains over her hair. Another tremor passes under their feet. There are creaking and groaning at the compound.

"How many others?" she says.

"We were fortunate. Most were out drilling or at chores. Only one other, as far as I can tell. Old Grotton. Someone heard him cry out 'The wine!' and he ran to the cellars—as fast as that good old man could go . . ." Macon wipes his face with a sleeve. "A cask came loose, rolled over him."

Sarah stands up straight, runs the back of her hand over her face, as if willing the look of anguish there to be wiped away. "Help me up," she says to Jarrod. "And let's see what's to be done."

The walls of the buildings in the compound are crazed, and plaster lies about them like a skirt. But only a couple of roofs have collapsed.

"This place was built long ago. The foundations are deep down to hard stone," Sarah says. "But this has to be the worst shock it has ever taken." She climbs down from Sausalito, stands in the center of the compound yard.

"We must get the big tent back up and move everyone into it," she says.

"I have men working on that," Macon replies.

"Good. And the wine. Are the cellars secure?"

"I haven't seen to that—"

"Do it. The wine is as important as our blood. Maybe more so."

"I'll send a detail."

"Send Feng and Merton," she says. "They are the best packers and shippers. And after that, see to the powder and demolitions."

"I'll see to it," Macon says. "And I'll send you a carriage."

"That won't be necessary. I'll ride with the ranger for the time being."

"All right, then." Macon turns Chinquapin and leaves the compound at a gallop.

"Sarah," Jarrod says. "I—"

"There's no time for that," she replies.

The remainder of the day is spent tending to a hundred different tasks. Jarrod sleeps—or tries to—on a cot in the big tent among a dozen smelly men. Aftershocks continue through the night. For the first time, Sarah does not come to him. But in the morning, he awakes to find her standing beside his cot, trailing her hand against his cheek. She motions for him to follow her outside.

The dawn is breaking, and clouds are gathering for an early rain. They walk down by the stream, to the little waterfall. A fault has cracked a line at nearly a right angle to the creek, and the stream has flowed into it, turned to the right nearly a foot, and then found its bed and flowed out again, on along its usual course. Akilter.

"Hold me, Jarrod," Sarah says. He puts his arms around her and she tucks her head against his breast.

"What's happening?" she says. "This rain, the ground shaking. Plagues all to the south. Is the world coming to an end like the Shastites think?"

"Not because they think it," Jarrod says. "Or maybe it is."

"Do you *know*? Do you know something about it?"

"Not really. Only that the Earth is changing. Whether it is a sign of something greater or a problem with the Earth itself—we don't know."

"We?"

"The rangers."

"Is that why you—what about the sickness?"

"I'm bringing medicine."

"In exchange."

"Yes. For whatever information the Yosemite rangers might have."

"And they sent only you."

"Not many believed there was much worth in the trade."

"Can you tell me anything else? There is no sort of . . . plot? My father died so—"

"It isn't magic, Sarah. Not alchemy. Science. Science doesn't care about kings. Or anyone else."

She says no more, but holds him the tighter. He kisses her hair, and after a moment she turns her face up and he kisses her lips. They lie down together near the water and make love quickly, fiercely, and are done before the first misty drops of the morning rain.

They move under the trees, which offer some protection. Sarah seems to relish the wetness on her face, and Jarrod sits near enough to feel the heat of her skin, the fresh olive fragrance of her damp hair.

"I think you should go," she says. "Today. To find out."

"Sarah, even if we know, there's likely nothing—"

"I'll send Macon and five others along with you, to bring back the news. Or you can come yourself."

"What about the raid against the Cougars?"

"That can wait. For a long time, if need be. I was never convinced it would be effective."

There is a strength to her words that was latent in her speech before, but which now has a full and powerful effect on him.

She has become the queen. It is what she was raised to be and she has moved into it like the stream, which was momentarily disoriented, but found its sure, time-carved course.

"Sarah. When the time comes. The Lees."

"Yes."

"You still intend . . ."

"It's our way."

"You could change that."

"We are hanging on very tenuously here. All of us are. We need to stay with what works. This . . . tradition is part of— we're not civilized in the valley. You know I don't think so. But part of whatever we are. Not like the Cougars. Not like the rangers. Besides, who knows whether any of us will survive until *next week,* the way things are going these days."

"I would like for the child to have a mother."

"It already has a mother—and a father. A mother and father who have to do . . . things that can't wait."

Jarrod holds Sarah's hand. The rain keeps falling.

"I'll go then," he says to her. "If you want me to."

"I do."

"I'll take Sausalito, if you don't mind."

"You'll take provisions and a gun," she replies. "I've ordered everything readied."

Jarrod smiles, shakes his head, and water runs down his nose. He wipes it off.

"As you wish, my queen," he says, and she kisses him, stopping any further words. Soon the rain comes down very hard, and they go back to the tent, back to Sarah Polleta's people.

He sets out that afternoon with Macon and five other riders. Each trails behind him a pack horse loaded with dried food, and wine for drinking and trading along the way. Jarrod chooses a 30.06 rifle, a beautiful old antique that is in perfect condition, with expertly reloaded shells to fit it.

They take old roads, keeping to the southeast as much as possible. Macon declares that they must cut a wide swath between what was once San Francisco and Sacramento.

"We are barely safe there when we send an armed party in for trading. And in Frisco, there's the plagues and fevers to worry about."

Once or twice, Macon checks a compass.

"Something wrong with the damn thing," Macon mutters. "Thirty degrees off."

Jarrod does not tell him that the compass is working—that the *Earth* is wrong. What would be the use? After a third look, Macon flings it away, and finds the way by memory and dead reckoning.

They pass through small villages, some inhabited, most not. Elmira. Ryde. Terminus. And then they turn east, across the great empty flatness of the San Joaquin Valley. Even in places that are usually called flat, the land has rises, a gentle curve. Not in this place. This valley is as flat as still water, and it goes on for mile after mile.

Twice they are set upon by bandits, but a few rounds fired from rifles and especially the boom of their lone shotgun scare the bandits away. After weaker prey. If I were alone, on foot, there would be a different story, Jarrod thinks. But I would be traveling by night, and finding what cover I could. Still, Jarrod is very glad to have the armed company along with him.

After a week, Jarrod begins to miss Sarah greatly. He finds himself suddenly short of breath, thinking that he will never see her again. The episodes only last a few minutes, but they come upon him many times a day. At night, asleep by the fire, he dreams of a deep, deep sky, completely blank of stars. He dreams of falling up into that sky, up and up, forever, falling.

The earthquakes continue, and the rain showers become thunderstorms whose like Jarrod has never seen. Crashing gusts of wind, the whip of rain that often as not becomes hail. Once they are caught without shelter in a storm with hail the size of a fist. The men take cover under their horses, and the poor animals take a beating.

During the storm, Macon's pack horse lets out an awful horse scream and collapses under the barrage. It is still living after the storm has passed, but unable to rise. Macon quickly puts a pistol shot into the beast's head.

They ride on.

Waterloo. Cooperopolis. Nearing Tuolumne River bridge, south of Groveland. Up this river is the site of the Hetch Hetchy Massacre, a legend among the rangers. The Yosemite forces, combined Park and Forest Service rangers, blew up the dam and freed the river once again—killing the greater part of the infamous Sacramento Army of the Light, which had once ruled Northern California. But the rangers were cornered in their newly created valley and the remainder of the Sacramento forces wiped them out. Half of the Yosemite contingent was lost that day. But the park was held, and that was all that mattered. Some said Forest Service treachery had been involved in the war, but nothing was ever proven.

As they approach the Tuolumne, one of the men spies a cloud on the road behind them. Jarrod turns to look.

"People on horseback," he says. "Riding fast."

Macon gazes at them. "More than us. Those sons-of-bitches that we scared off must have gone and gotten reinforcements."

"Are you sure it's them?"

"No. Let's get the hell out of here."

The men spur their horses to a gallop, but the pack horses slow them down, and the bandits—if bandits their pursuers are—gain on them.

Ahead is the Tuolumne River—and the bridge. The company gallops across and Macon immediately calls a halt. At first, Jarrod thinks he means to make a stand here, but Macon runs to one of the pack horses and digs in the saddlebags. He comes out with two wine bottles with loose cork stoppers. He yanks out the stoppers. Nailed to the bottom of each of the stoppers is a length of fabric. Wicks for napalm Molotov cocktails. There are more bottles in the saddlebag.

"Help me," he says.

Jarrod and the other men get down and each takes two bottles. They run—as carefully as they can—back onto the bridge. Below, the water runs fast and looks to be deep. A horse could swim it, Jarrod thinks, but it would be slowed way down. If the rangers hadn't blown the dam those many years ago, the river would be only a shadow of what it now was, and its crossing an easy matter.

The bridge is formed in an arch over the river, concrete resting on steel spandrels.

"Save four bottles and break the others, here"—he points to the center of the bridge, the crown of the arch—"and here." The near end of the bridge, which their pursuers will cross first.

"All right. Get back to the horses. I'm going to light the far end, and—"

"I'll take the middle," Jarrod says. "I'm pretty good at climbing on things."

"Fine, then," Macon says, giving him a crooked smile. He reaches into his pocket and hands Jarrod a little box.

"Here's some matches," he says. "You *do* know how to work them, don't you?"

Jarrod takes off his shirt and bundles his two bottles of napalm into it, then fixes it over his shoulder like a sling. He swings out over the edge of the bridge and toes his way down the side until his boots rest on a ledge—more a crack than a platform—of a half inch or less that is formed where the rusty steel of the spandrel protrudes from the crumbling concrete covering of the bridge. Above, Jarrod can hear the other men running to the bridge's far haunch.

The climbing is easier than he'd expected. He hears the pounding hoofs of the approaching pursuers. He can hear the bandits' yells, too, and one of them fires a gun into the air.

At least that bullet won't be in my chest, Jarrod thinks.

He experiments with holding on to the bridge's side with one hand, then looks across to the shore and sees that Macon is also getting into position, but with less steadiness and speed. Just as Jarrod glances over, one of Macon's bottles comes loose and falls fifteen feet or so onto the ground below him. It shatters, but does not burn. Macon doesn't try to grab for it. Good, Jarrod thinks. You still have one.

"Damn it," Macon calls to Jarrod. He carefully removes the other from his makeshift sling. "This will have to do." Macon waves the bottle in his one free hand. "I think I can light it. Can you light yours?"

"Think so," Jarrod calls, and quickly gets to work. He undoes one sleeve of the shirt sling and carefully swings it around in front of him, keeping it looped around his neck. He takes out the matches and puts a handful in his mouth, then drapes both wicks of the napalm bottles out of the sling, one to the left and one to the right of him. He rises up on his tiptoes and looks over the side of the bridge.

The bandits are almost on the bridge. Jarrod looks over at Macon. He, too, has matches in his mouth.

Jarrod hears a hoof beat on concrete and he scratches the match box against the tips of the matches. They flame up and acrid smoke flows into Jarrod's nostrils. No time to worry about that. He drops the match box into the river, takes the matches from his mouth and lights the wick of the Molotov cocktail. It flames smoky and yellow.

Jarrod reaches down, and with the wick of the first bottle, he lights the wick of the second. For a moment, his eyes water over from the match smoke, and he spits them out violently.

Clatter of many hooves.

He tosses the first bottle up and over the bridge. He hears it shatter while he is reaching for the other bottle.

A thick, solid explosion.

Jarrod tosses the other bottle onto the bridge.

The screams of horses and men. He does not try to look at

the conflagration. Instead, he sees Macon, with his one bottle lighted, tossing it over the end of the bridge. A bright flash and crackle.

More screams, these not of surprise, but of pain.

They've trapped at least some of them on the bridge.

Without another thought, Jarrod launches himself back and away from the bridge. He falls for many feet. Slam of water like the ground jolting him. But ground that gives way and he's under, a long time under. He's prepared himself and doesn't lose his breath. The current is strong and it carries him swiftly downstream.

Jarrod swims as hard as he can with the current—thankful that learning to swim in ice-cold Crescent Lake was part of his ranger training. When he glances back, he sees the bridge engulfed in flames. He'd never known napalm was so . . . effective. A burning man dances about, trying to get the stuff off himself, but he cannot. Suddenly, a horse and rider, both on fire, leap off the bridge and plunge down like a meteor into the water below. But even in the water, the napalm sticks. The rider floats motionlessly, but the horse continues to writhe and burn.

Jarrod takes a moment to be sure he is swimming to the correct bank of the river, then makes his way over and drags himself out of the water. A little way down from him, Jarrod sees Macon doing the same thing. Macon picks his way up the river bank to stand beside Jarrod.

"Good thing you brought napalm," Jarrod says. He wrings out his shirt and puts it back on.

"Yes," says Macon. "What a waste of good horses, though."

Suddenly, bandits that were late in arriving appear on the abutment. There is huffing of horses and shouting, as they rein to a stop.

"Let's get out of here," says Macon.

"I agree."

They work their way up and through underbrush to the road

and, a quarter mile down it, meet up with the other men. Sausalito recognizes Jarrod and gives him a whinny.

They ride on.

That same day, they are inside the boundaries of the National Forest. Jarrod looks around for telltale signs of rangers, but sees none. The trees begin to change from deciduous oaks and eucalyptus to evergreens. They are a day in before Jarrod is among the tall trees once again—ponderosa and Jeffrey pines. The air is full of their fragrance, which is even stronger and sweeter after the daily rains.

Then Jarrod sees them—the first grove of giant sequoias. It is afternoon, and the air is full of their fragrance. A storm is gathering, but Jarrod pauses among the trees, touches the ropy bark of the tallest.

"Hello, grandfathers," he says. "Hello, grandmothers."

They ride on, and the next day strike the junction of State Road 120 and the way up to Tioga Pass and the High Sierras. The road is marked on Jarrod's vellum map as a dotted line, its exact path uncertain. Uncle Nab could not have known the true state of the road, copying from even older copied maps. Yet the roadbed has not been so thoroughly destroyed here, and the going is easier for the horses.

They come upon another grove of giant sequoias and Macon decides to make their camp here. Wrapping his hands in cloth to avoid splinters, Jarrod climbs into one of the trees. The sky looks as though it will rain. He has brought his bivvy sack with him, and he drapes it over him as a makeshift roof. Jarrod sleeps in the crown of the tree.

That night, the sentry is startled by sounds in the brush near their camp. He wakes the camp. Jarrod's sequoia is far outside the perimeter of the valley men's camp, and the intruders have made the mistake of gathering right under him. Have some of the bandit pursuers tracked them down, or are these other men?

Jarrod cannot tell. Their attempt at hiding is abysmal—worse than the Cougars. They are not rangers.

Jarrod descends from the trees like a hard rain.

He fires once, twice. Two of them fall. He shifts around the bole of the tree and comes upon the other three while they are still looking in the direction where they've seen Jarrod's muzzle flash. He shoots another, knocks one man down with his gunstock, then knifes the third in the heart. He strides quickly forward and uses his gunstock to crumple the skull of the fallen man.

"All right," he calls out to Macon. "All done."

The men follow the sound of his voice and gather around him, around the carnage.

Macon shakes his head in wonder. No one says anything to Jarrod. They carry the bodies a few hundred feet away and pile what stones they can find upon them, while Jarrod cleans the blood from his hands and shirt.

Jarrod climbs back up into his tree. He has defended the forest. He feels more like himself than he has in many weeks. He feels like a ranger. Jarrod doesn't know at all if he likes the feeling, if he wants it back. It *is* back, though. He sleeps quietly and deeply in the twisting branches of the giant sequoia, breathing its ancient incense. The dreams of falling into the sky are gone. He is in the mountains again, among the trees.

Out of storms and great cataclysm, Jarrod enters into the great valley of the Yosemite. The lode needle of his compass is uncertain in these uncertain days, but he has found the way all the same. Behind him walk Napa Valley men, all on foot now, leading their mounts up the road beside the Merced River. On the back of Jarrod's horse is his pack, brought down from Washington State, full of medicine. El Capitan rises to the north, Bridalveil and Illilouette Falls to the south. And ahead is the giant face of Half Dome, its granite face no different than it appears in pictures taken nearly three hundred years before that are now in the library at Threecabin.

But this is real, Jarrod thinks. I am here, in Yosemite National Park.

Many have died from the plague and are buried in the acrid piny soil around the makeshift infirmary set up near Yosemite Falls. But many more live, covered with buboes, breathing ragged breaths that they think will be among their last.

Jarrod finds park headquarters. The rain grows harder. Macon and his men go to find shelter for the horses, while Jarrod walks to the main building to make his report. He enters the room, gently sets down his pack in a corner. He is met by Beatrice, the chief ranger, who is barely older than he is, but who is the oldest Yosemite ranger who is well. She nods at him as he comes to stand before her desk.

"Jarrod, third scout with the Ho Brigade of the Olympic National Park Service, reporting, ma'am."

"Welcome, ranger," she replies.

"I came as quickly as I could," he says, "but I met up with a few delays."

# ORF DREAMS

The harder the robot works, the more he dreams. Sometimes the dreams are about the work—of the voices that surround him, the beings that cannot be seen, and that are everywhere to be seen. Geographies, he has thought of calling them, but has settled on a name, a pun name, really: terranes.

The Olympic terrane, Skykomish, Orf's first friend. Impetuous, young. Its near neighbor, Farallon, almost eaten up and subducted, but once the greatest ocean of them all—Tethys—and there is wisdom in the riddles it spins. Broad North America, speaking in many voices that are one voice saying many things. Very difficult to comprehend, but worth the effort.

The chatter of the microterranes. Less worthwhile translating, but necessary at times.

And the others, large and megalithic, small and solitary floaters. The gathering at the core, where a great project is underway. Where something is happening, *someone* is becoming. Orf is a part of the becoming. It is his suggestion that the terranes speak to humans, somehow involve them in the project. Speed the project up to a human time scale.

This would also benefit the terranes, for the slow, cold area near the crust is also the place where the terranes' rationality is centralized. They are mostly subconscious beings, moved by strange, nearly incomprehensible feelings. Their reasoning is obscure and arcane. In speaking to humans, they would also begin to think clearly.

And then the becoming could flow and flower. The *one* could be born of the many.

Years Orf had spent developing understanding, moving deeper through the layers, the swirling algorithms of magma and metallic flux.

More years patiently explaining to the terranes about humans. Learning the path of the terranes' consciousness, so that, when the time comes, Orf can truly translate, and not butcher the nuances. But always the words are not right, or they become mathematics—and Orf is lost. He is not that kind of a robot.

Sometimes he dreams of the schemata and equations of Asia, the Great Calculator. But they are disassociated, meaningless representations. Sometimes he dreams of the secrets of Antarctica, the strange bones buried beneath the ice that have no DNA. The cold memories of a cold race that danced down the dry valleys when the winds blew their fiercest. Somehow, the two types of dream are connected, or in need of connecting. Must consider this.

But mostly, he dreams ranger dreams.

The dreams are so frequent and so intense, that Orf begins

to wonder if they might have meaning. Surely a robot's dreams are merely off-line sparks and embodied machine-language microprocessing. But this ranger has a face—a face that Orf has never seen before, but that he would recognize in an instant were he to encounter it.

Only once a revolution about the sun does he got to the surface. One dark night a year.

Maybe that's what the dream—his unconscious self—is trying to tell him. That being so long underground he is losing his humanity. It is easy to get sucked into the languid, meandering thoughts of the terranes, to spend weeks mulling over a small idea, an odd fact. Is this rock greenish-white or whitish-green? Where will this magma flow if I squeeze just so? Or so?

The terranes have all the time in the world to think about such matters.

Humans are out in the weather. They wear away.

Andrew. Laramie, Little Bulge. Orf remembers.

They die.

He dreams of the ranger, dying.

The ranger hung on a pole against the sky, sucking fetid air into his lungs.

Get me down.

I can't. I'm not there.

Then kill me. End it for me.

I cannot.

The ranger moans, looks up into the sun. Blood flows from his face like sweat. The skin peels back in places, exposing the red, dry striations of muscles.

My mother killed me, he says. She killed me by having me. Can't get back. Tried. Have to live now.

Around the pole on which the ranger is hung a square appears, dark blue, iridescent in the bright sun. The sun. It has been a hundred years since Orf has seen it. I must go to see the sun.

The blue square frames the hanging post, so that the ranger's agony is like a painting of agony. The square grows brighter still, glows hotter than the sun.

The ranger screams. He screams a long scream that is impossible, for a human would run out of air. It goes on and on and on. The longer he screams, the brighter the blue square glows.

And then, in an instant, the square closes in on itself, collapses in on the ranger. Exactly as if someone has turned off a monitor screen.

Closes down to a dot. Nothing. And only then does the man's scream fade away to a low whine of sorrow.

The sorrow remains, like a distant meshing of gears.

It stays with Orf, even after the robot wakes up and goes again to work with the terranes. For weeks, the low whine stays with him, and makes him sad.

# CALIFORNIA

The radio sings. It whistles and chatters like a marmot.

"Batteries are low," says the radio operator. "Haven't had the sun to recharge them. But they should do."

Three tries, and another half hour to find Franklin. He has been sick with a cold. His voice is stuffy.

"Jarrod?"

"Yes."

"What do you know?"

"Some."

"All right, then."

Cracklehum. The radio operator presses a small button, twice. The black number on the gray readout changes in the last digit. The signal strengthens, clears.

"Better," says the radio operator.

"Gravimetric data. They have a good setup you ought to see, sir. The poles are *flipping*. Happens every few hundred thousand years. North becoming south."

"Well. But this quickly?"

"Even in the past it may have happened this way. Fast. The question was never settled."

"So. No asteroid is making it? Nothing like that?"

"Their observatory is amazing, sir. They've been looking. Nothing that they can find. There is something else, though."

"What is it, ranger?" A sound that might be a sneeze.

"There is a pattern to the movement of the poles. Harmonic. It's been very steady. They've done some math I don't understand. They have a computer, Uncle Franklin! They've done some projections and there is going to be something really big. The fault. The San Andreas fault. It is *transferring* from the San Joaquin to the Owens Valley. It's moving *east* of the Sierra Nevada. Do you understand?"

"San Joaquin to Owens Valley? That's . . . hundreds of miles."

"It's going to join the fault line that runs up the eastern side of the Sierras, the one the mountains made when they rose. Going to *become* that fault line."

"I see. I think I see. What do they suppose will happen then?"

"The main stress point of plate tectonics for the North American continent will suddenly and completely transfer itself many miles to the east. It will be the biggest earthquake humankind has ever experienced."

"We'll feel it up here."

"Oh, yes. There will be dozens of ancillary quakes. Tsunamis all over the world. The Juan de Fuca, the Farallon plates—they'll definitely be affected up there. It's going to be big, Uncle Franklin. Very big. They are talking about basalt flows erupting like the one east of the Cascades, in the Columbia Basin. Giant dust clouds thrown into the atmosphere. They are talking about mass extinction of species in the Western Hemisphere."

"God. Damn. A long night is coming."

Jarrod waits; the signal remains steady.

"We'd better get ready," Franklin says. *"Can* we get ready?" Franklin is asking himself this question.

"Franklin, another thing," Jarrod continues. "They know *when.*"

"When?"

"Yes. They've narrowed it down to *two days.*"

"How could they do that?"

"They have seismic sensors all along the fringes of the National Forest. They know when a herd of deer passes. They've sent an expedition to the Tejon Pass north of Los Angeles, and along the Big Bend, where the San Andreas splays out and the Garlock fault runs east. The expedition didn't come back, but they radioed in their data before they disappeared. It'll switch over to the Garlock, then move up the east side of the Sierras. The Sierras are about to join the Pacific Plate."

"Understood, but—"

"And they use chaos theory. They've got a real old-fashioned geophysicist or two down here, I think."

"Does anyone know why?"

"Sir?"

"Does anyone know *why* this is happening?"

"Because the poles are—"

"Yes, but why is the Earth's polarity flipping?"

"No, sir. No one knows. It just *is.*"

"And they're sure it will?"

"Yes."

"So. They've not gone native after all."

"No, sir. They've concentrated on math and physics, though. Not much biological or chemical knowledge. They were worried about *us* having going native."

"They should. Maybe they should worry about that. All right." Franklin is clearing his throat. "Which two days?"

"A month from Tuesday. A month from *next* Tuesday."

A very long silence. Jarrod glances at the radio operator.

"Still got him," the radio operator says.

Finally, "Ranger?"

"Yes, sir."

"Have you delivered the medicine?"

"And set up the distillation equipment."

"Very good. What's the situation?"

"Bad. It's a full-blown epidemic."

"Plague?"

"Both types of buboes."

"I see." Another silence. "Ranger?"

"Yes, sir."

"Jarrod, what is your state? What state are you in?"

"California, sir."

"All right, ranger."

"I have had a hard time of it. Banged up, sir. Chewed down."

"It is risky coming back. I could reassign you down there, son. Might be for the best. I'm not sure what you'd come back to, anyway. Do you want to come back?"

Now it is Jarrod's turn to be quiet. Franklin lets a good deal of time pass, then says, "Son?"

"Yes, sir."

"Take all the time you need."


To the east, Mount Whitney is a sheer face, a wall of granite scowling back over the continent. Approached from the west, Whitney is a gentle slope, the long back of a giant, strewn with boulders and lichen. Jarrod spends two weeks traveling south down the High Sierras, along the old Pacific Crest Trail. He climbs Whitney from the west at first, the Kern River down a long slope behind him.

Then he circles around south of the mountain and meets up with the old trail blasted into the sheer face of the peak by the Conservation Corps, over three hundred years before. It is still as flat and passable as ever. Nothing grows in the solid rock. Three hundred years and a blink of the Earth's eye. Nothing much has changed.

Storm clouds gather at noon, and he takes refuge among some overhanging rocks high above a wash. In the afternoon, the wash is deluged, and Jarrod hears enormous scrapings and grindings as tens of tons of granite boulders are moved a few feet farther down to the valley. The night sky is full of fire and wind.

Today is Monday. Tomorrow will be Tuesday. First Tuesday. *The* Tuesday.

He wakes hours before dawn and eats some dry bread, drinks a canteenful of water. The climbing goes well, and by six in the morning, he is on the curve just along and below the southern shoulder of the peak.

He climbs the last stretch, a rocky path through larger granites and by seven he reaches the summit of Mount Whitney, 14,494 feet above sea level. Very little air. Enough. He is feeling better—as good as ever.

I could go on climbing, Jarrod thinks. I would like to go on climbing up into the sky.

But he has run out of mountain, and he must stop. He takes off his pack, gets a shelter ready. He takes out a can of kindling and builds himself a small fire with flint and steel. He makes hedge nettle tea. Then he walks to the edge of the world and has a long look away east. He can see for hundreds of miles. Jarrod gazes over the basin-and-range emptiness of Nevada and sips his tea. The Sierras are the westernmost of a stack of dominoes, fallen against one another all the way back to the Rockies. Who lives in that jagged desert land now? No one knows. People do not come out of there. They do not speak.

Jarrod takes out his bone flute. He plays old ranger songs, then settles in and waits for the cataclysm.

He sits for an hour. Two hours. Clouds begin to gather, and the view is obscured. The sun dims. Thunder sounds and echoes in the peaks behind him, distorted, monstrous. He waits. A single bolt of lightning strikes not a hundred yards away. The crackle is loud, bone-shuddering. The adrenaline surges to his heart, and he catches his breath in a gasp. Hold still. Still.

Still, he waits.

Behind him, there is a rumble, a growing rumble and tumble, as if boulders are being thrown this way and that. So. It is time. The rumble grows. Grows deafening.

Stops.

All is quiet for a moment. But there is something. He feels *something*.

Slowly, Jarrod turns around.

"Hello, ranger."

Glint of metal and the soft white of ceramic plating. Something like a spider, a nine-foot-tall spider. Nothing like a spider. Nothing like.

"You've been in my dreams," the robot says. "I didn't expect to meet anyone up here. Least of all *you*."

"Orf," Jarrod says.

A sensor turns, a camera lens irises. A foot stamps.

"Yes. That is my name. Orf."

"The friend of Andrew Hutton."

"He was my friend."

The robot pads toward him several more steps. Jarrod has to keep himself from flinching, so imposing it is. It stops a few feet from him.

The robot speaks. "As long as you're here, there's something I'd like to ask you."

"Ask *me*?"

"Yes. Have *I* been in *your* dreams, too?"

"I hardly ever remember my dreams," Jarrod says. "Mostly, I dream of climbing—or falling."

Another lightning bolt sizzles down a crazed path and crashes nearby. Jarrod starts.

"It isn't safe for you here," Orf says.

"It isn't safe anywhere."

Again the footpad stamps. Annoyance? Laughter? Can it feel anything at all? But the robot says it dreams.

"I can make you safe," Orf says. "If I hold you."

"What do you mean?"

"If I hold you suspended with my ceramic pincers, and keep the metal of my other pods grounded, I'll form a Faraday cage. A bolt of lightning could strike me full on and it wouldn't get to you. At least, theoretically. I've just read about it being done."

"I have a shelter ready. Over there."

"That isn't going to hold up. Not with what's coming. Something enormous is coming."

"And you will hold up?"

"I will. I suppose I will."

"And you know what's coming?"

"Yes, I know what's coming," Orf says. "I helped make it happen."

Jarrod looks at the robot. After a moment, he stands. The robot holds out its arms. Jarrod takes a breath, steps into them. The pincers close about his waist, his shoulders.

And he is drawn up and hanging. Three feet from the ground, suspended, with six long legs about him like the supports to some metal gazebo. He is a bit uncomfortable, but then Orf shifts him about, and he breathes easily.

"There. Now I'm not so worried about losing you," Orf says.

"How long?" Jarrod asks.

"Not long now. Very, very soon."

They watch.

The sky darkens. To the east, cracks open in the land. To be visible from here, they must be so huge, so . . . And red, red magma, the Earth's blood. Earth's wine. Sarah, he thinks, Sarah, I hope Macon got back in time to warn you. He had plenty of time, but who knows? Macon is a good man.

*Sarah.*

"That's the fault along the Grapevine and Funeral ranges," Orf says. "Death Valley is going to be coated with lava fifty feet thick. Maybe more."

The ground moves.

"The Inyos are sinking. They have to give." The ground *screeches.* "Here we go."

Jolt after shudder jolt. Rocks fly into the air, fall back, only to rebound off the elastic ground. Orf holds on, fends off the boulders that come their way. Jerk, jolt. Until the heat of the movement melts the fault-line rocks, lubricates. The jolts become rumbles. The movement steadies. But never smooth. The Earth always moves in fits and starts. That *is* plate tectonics. Fits and starts.

I would have died, Jarrod thinks. Now I would be dead.

The ground *rises.*

He can feel it. He can *see* it. He is rising in respect to the horizon.

"The Sierras are going up," says Orf. "Twenty-three feet in three minutes. Nothing like it for millions of years. Andrew would have loved to see this. Victor, too. Laramie with her camera would—oh. Hang on."

Lurch. Jolt. The sound of a million trees, breaking in the wind. Jarrod holds his hands over his ears. Lightning flashes and flashes—until the sky is a white blaze, until the moments of darkness are like the flicker of a bright candle. The wind howls, a hundred forests falling. Somewhere, they really may be falling.

The dark ground rises into the white-hot sky.

Rises. Blue on white, it rises.

It is the longest three minutes in the history of the world.

Jarrod at first grips the robot's arms. But then he cannot think to do this and his hands go slack. Orf does not let him go. Jarrod forces himself to keep his eyes open, to see this, but the afterimages peak up and down his nerves. Pain and release. Pain. He closes his eyes. Long enough to take the edge from the pain. He opens them. The ground is still rising. Lightning begins to strike all around him. It blasts rocks, and pieces of granite shrapnel clang off the robot's legs. If one gets through. Dead.

But I made it so far, this far. To the end of the Earth. Made it to California.

Grinding, screaming, slowing. The sky clamps down. Inches now. Slowing. The mountains have grown as much as they will. Slower.

A shower of sparks, as a lightning bolt hits them, is funneled around Jarrod. Leaving Orf to shine with a moonglow hue. St. Elmo's fire. The ground becomes the ground again.

The robot glows against a pitch black sky. The ranger dangles in the robot's arms. Both have survived. Both are alive at 14,517 feet above sea level.

Storms continue to the north and south, but the fire in the sky seems to have moved away for the time being. Orf sets Jarrod upon the ground. The ground seems to hum beneath his feet, to resonate with the dying ring of a bell, but he cannot tell if this is his muscles or the granite itself.

He sits down on a rock and watches the red flow of liquid basalt away to the east, clouds and lightning above it.

"Why?" he asks. He shouts, but the wind is unexpectedly calm, and his own voice startles him.

"To regulate the heat flux around the Earth's core, and to speed it up," says the robot.

"But—"

"I have *friends*. Down there. That is where they live. They *are* that flux."

"People have died. A lot of people. Maybe all."

"No. Not all. I am sorry."

"Sorry," Jarrod says, blankly. "Sorry."

"They are becoming something new. My friends. They are beginning a great task. And they want to talk to you. They want to talk to people. But they think so slowly when they approach the surface. Hundreds of years to the sentence. This will help. That's partly why we did this. So that they can speak to you."

"It had better be important, what they want to say."

The robot taps its foot upon stone. Tap, rattle, tap. It is laughter. A peculiar kind of laughter.

He sleeps in the robot's arms, swaying as if he were in the upper branches of a tree. They have descended a way, to the entrance of a cave, a carved passage into the side of Mount Whitney, where none was before. This is where the other part of the robot—the thinking, digging part—has remained.

Jarrod awakens to a dark morning, full of storms from horizon to horizon. He reaches into his pocket and finds his old compass. The red needle points south. The poles have reversed.

The robot has told him that the passage that they are in leads down, into the Earth's crust. It can lead to where Jarrod wishes it to lead, Orf has told him.

He can go home. Back to the Rangers.

Or to Sarah.

He can go—

is she dead?
she will be soon
she will drink her death
she will be a good queen
five years

Five years with Sarah, and then she will die. Will kill herself. I won't be able to talk her out of it, Jarrod thinks. I'm no good at talk.

Five years
no time
what is living but dying all the time?

is there a child
growing in her womb
His?

Yes. Someday I will come for that child. It is half mine. I won't let it die. *But Sarah—*

He loves her
dead, alive
forever
in her Lady's cave

Give me a sign, Jarrod thinks.

Lightning flashes in the sky. The ground rumbles. The world is full of portents; the world is *only* portent.

"Are you all right?" the robot says.

"Yes. Put me down."

The robot lowers him, releases him. He steps away, outside the cave. He leans against an upthrust pillar of dull white granite. The air smells of electricity, burnt wood. He runs the two fingers of his right hand over the roughened surface of the stone. Something smooth there. Lichen. Algae and bacteria mashed together into the vein of the rock. Blue-green, tight in the declivities. Together. Alive.

"You had better come back," the robot says. "You aren't safe there."

I am
not
safe
here
Earth
be
careful
of what
you have made me


When a ranger goes renegade, he is a far greater peril than
an ordinary man. A ranger knows how to do things. A ranger
has great competence in the world.

A ranger is

A ranger is
dangerous

when a ranger knows
that even if the Earth speaks
even if the Earth gains a voice
nothing can be said

*nothing* is all
a ranger ever hears

*This* ranger

*this*


The storm is moving away. Jarrod understands storms, and
he can feel it. He knows what it is like to be outside, in the
weather. A sheet of rain falls, spatters man and robot, moves on
across the landscape, a traveling curtain. He watches it flow.

"I'm tired," Jarrod says. "I'm tired of it, up here."

"On the mountain?"

"Here. Above."

"I see."

"I think I want to go down with you," Jarrod says to the robot.

"All right."

"I think I want to go under the ground with you," he says, "and not come back up again. Ever."

The robot is quiet for a time. The sheet of rain, only a few feet wide, billows and folds along the granite.

"I'll take you, then," Orf says.

A traveling rain. Rain, dry and bright before, dark and wet behind. Limning the vastness of California. Away. Jarrod turns away.

The rain keeps moving and falling. Saying only that the world is full of might. Saying only that the world is empty and full of might and empty.

# THE NEW EXILES
# OF CALIFORNIA

# THE GREAT KNEE SATORI

I am writing this in English so that no one will read it. If and when the Chunk makes its way to Earth, and we either perish or overcome it—and if I survive—then I will translate this, the little memoir of the last trip I took to the surface, into something more accessible. Or maybe not. I am caring less and less whether anybody listens to what I say.

Getting old—I don't know. Turning into something either daft or incomprehensible to other humans. I'll never know for sure which. But they *did* listen. They did listen one last time to what I had to say. And soon we'll know whether it will do any good.

When the Chunk arrives.

Whitney Forester—the woman who began the saving of the Earth—once wrote (also in English), "My competence in being in the world brings the world to be in that moment."

This is from *The Exiles of California,* which is one of the founding books of the dear old sect I was brought up in, the Ecstatic Tributarians—Tribs for short (although some call us ETs). It's funny; the more competence I acquire, the less settled and certain I am. If Whitney Forester is right, well then, it is the *world* that is an unsettled place, and my state of mind is both a reflection and part of the cause of the unsettledness.

"Another way of saying this," Whitney Forester writes, "is in this way: *The gathered stones are where they have fallen.*"

Now, what she means by "competence" is a discussion that fills many scholarly tomes—all to the good, I suppose, and some of that scholarship is mine. But as I neared my fifty-fifth birthday, I could not help but feel that all this talk, all these words, were beside the point. Of course, every good elucidator of Whitney Forester admits as much. Her way is a way of realization, not revelation or study.

But California Zen cuts two ways. I don't know, maybe the

ancient masters—Dogen, Rinzai and the rest—found peace in their satori, a release from the illusory world. But if we are an expression of the essential unity of the universe, then we're also products of the crazy diversity of things. All those rocks, lying all over the universe. It gives my essential unity a headache just thinking about going out stone gathering.

Whitney Forester was a Californian. Her way is a turning inward—some would say an unhealthy obsession with one's own navel. Books, by their very nature, are *outward* things. The very fact that they are *things* at all makes them so. So when all is said and done, the books only have half a truth, and it isn't a lot of good without the remainder.

Understanding the "unsayableness" of everything is quite a different thing from knowing it in your bones. I think this is because it takes some time to know your bones. When I turned fifty-two, I can definitely report that I began to know *mine*. Something gave in my right knee when I rose from my bed one reveille. I was getting up, and then I was suddenly on the floor, with what felt like a knife inserted in the top of my knee, behind my kneecap, and out the bottom.

Now I say "suddenly on the floor," as if I had no perception of the moment between intending to get up and go about my workday and of being knifed and writhing—but I do; I remember it very clearly. Actually, I should say, *it* remembers *itself* very clearly and this *it* implanted itself in me at that moment, and has been slowly growing and taking over the body of Noah Noahbronen, the Trib shaman and symbologist who used to inhabit that body—to the point that the "it" who was born in that moment is the very man who is writing this, an account of my travels.

Which is to say that in moments of realization, it is not so much an idea that is born, but a *new person* to surround the perception. After all, the information has most likely been around for quite some time and it's only new to you.

This new Noah leapt from my old perceptions and with a

"hmm" of mild interest, he looked down and saw a middle-aged man's body giving way after a great deal of use over time.

"I'll be damned," he said, "that must hurt like a knife in the knee. Glad it's not me that feels that way."

But in fact, though he'd not intended it, the pain sucked the new Noah right back into the body from which he'd come and—accessing the old memories and realizing who he was supposed to be—the new Noah grunted and called to the Skykomish errand intercessor algorithm—Hermes—to please send medical help that knew a lot about knees.

Later, I was sitting at my desk, trying to finish a piece for *The Downagain* on the aesthetic implications of the coming Chunk, but my knee perversely went on aching. This was a difficult piece to write, because I had to find a way of putting all the transformational aesthetic symbology into plain words. I wasn't sure that *I* understood the symbology, and I'd come up with most of it. The Chunk was clearly coming for a reason that had to do with aesthetics.

It would be an incredible coincidence for the thing to show up just at the point in human history when we first awakened to the fact that the universe is held together as much by the symbology of beauty as by the equations of physics. The very reason that we know the Chunk is coming is because of the disturbance it is setting up in Trance City and along the beauty lines. My paper had to do with the "aesthetic shadow" the Chunk was beginning to cast on us. While we might not know *why* the Chunk was coming to Earth, we could damn well sense that whatever the reason, it wasn't going to be good for us.

But my body was aching, and I abandoned the attempt at work and gave myself over to wallowing in knee pain misery. After a while—and out of sheer boredom, I think—I lay down in bed and tranced into my terrane—my otherself—to talk about the pain I was feeling.

Now you may think the Skykomish crustal plate would have better things to do than cheer up an invalid, and you'd be right, but the mind of a terrane is not something that does one, two or three tasks at a time, but many thousands. It isn't like an AI algorithm, existing as a single entity within the thermoflux of the magma and timesharing its attention out.

Instead, Skykomish parallel-processes its thoughts. That is how we—the rest of us conjoined to it—are all something like *parts* of its consciousness, yet, of course, we are all very much individuals. It isn't collective consciousness, like a beehive or what have you. Terranes are sentient *ecologies*.

"I wonder if this pain is randomly visited on me, or whether I deserve it," I asked the terrane.

*How would I know? What did you think of that pretty rock I left for you the other day?*

"That was nice quartz. The pink in it was nearly wine red. But listen, haven't you ever been hurt?"

*Yes. Once really a lot. I was thinking about gathering a lot of those rocks and making a—what do you call it?—a sculpture for your room.*

*Also, the Pure Water humans give me a headache.* The terrane's thought-manner became almost conspiratorial. *I know where a lot of those rocks are.*

"I'd like a sculpture. Don't make it too big, though. Sometimes you forget about how small I am." Once Skykomish "traveled" out to the desert and made me a magma intrusion in the shape of a flower—down under the Chisos of Texas. We'd both gotten in trouble with the crustal stability people over that.

*Okay, I'll make it really small. I remember that I got scared when I was hurt.*

"When you first met the robot? When the Mohole got blown up and Orf was sealed underground?"

*Yes, that was when.*

"What was it like for you to feel that way?"

*I can't tell . . . I can show you, maybe.*

"All right." I got my mind ready for a *flash*—that complete moment of union with the terrane that galvanizes the mind like iron filings about a powerful magnet.

And then, instead of the flash, everything faded for a moment. It wasn't as if Skykomish and I lost our reverie-connection. It was more like a disturbance *from somewhere inside us.* As if our *beings* were repelling each other, and even themselves, blowing us apart.

This is a difficult feeling to describe. It is as if *being* were withdrawn from you, yet you *still exist.* Like the feeling you have when you've been busy for a long, long time and haven't taken a moment for self-reflection in ages. Alienation, you might call it, but the feeling goes deeper than that, down even past nothingness.

The tide has withdrawn, leaving ripples in the sand, but there is no water and no life there anymore. Only dry markings that once were an ocean.

Then, it all came back. Came back like a rose blooming in my heart.

"That was the Chunk," I said.

*Yes.* Skykomish was distracted, didn't really want to acknowledge what had just happened. Frightened. *Now it's gone. Are you ready, Noah?*

"Yes. Go ahead."

For an instant my consciousness went white, as it irised out to encompass the terrane's thoughts. It can be quite a rush, but I was used to it after thirty years of being conjoined. As usual, there was a time of confused imagery, as my brain figured out how to associate and present the incoming thoughts. What I ended up with was a vision of *me*—a little man, of a millimeter or so—climbing about on my patella, making geodetic observations with barometer and sighting compass and then—whack, whack, whack!—setting a marker inscribed with this information right into the soft spot where a tendon joined a bone.

"I am *causing* the pain," I said aloud to myself. That knee was just as much me as the suffering old academic trying to write an informative article for the general population on the coming doom. "I'm causing *and* suffering the pain," I said.

*It's funny when humans think that all they are is a brain in a skull. You can explain it to me, but I never really get it.*

"You want me to flash it to you?"

*I don't think I really* want *to get it.*

So that was how I began to grasp, literally in my bones and joints, what Whitney Forester meant when she said that the gathered stones are where they have fallen. And I began to question what I was going to do with the rest of my life if my knee kept hurting the way it was hurting for the *next* fifty-four years.

The pain *did* stop in a couple of days. Something that my healer hadn't been able to find popped back into place, and there was my knee—given back to me, by myself. Except with the caveat that it could be taken away again in an unpredictable instant, and that I'd better learn to live with that fact.

Of course this *was* a predictable midlife crisis, as old as the time humans have been living past forty. But the new Noah— the post-trauma Noah—refused either to find a place in the old Noah's psyche or be a good fellow and off himself. Instead, over the next few months, he insisted on taking more and more of the old Noah's mental resources, until the *old* Noah threw up his hands in frustration, defrocked himself of his Trib scholarly finery, and cast it at the new Noah's metaphorical feet.

"All right, if you won't let me write and teach, then *you* figure out what we are going to do with this body," he said, and stalked off to a little room he kept at the bottom of our frontal lobes. As far as I know, he's sulking there still, and will be until the day that we die.

## PROFESSIONAL HELP FROM A TRAINED COUNSELOR

Meanwhile, I was in a quandary. I felt simultaneously like an old man and a teenager. I was suddenly experiencing everything *viscerally*—cool door buttons against my fingers, the rustle of my bed sheets, the long echo of Downtown's tunnels, the heartbreak of a colleague who'd lost her partner after an illness. I was grinning maniacally at small revelations and sobbing at odd hours over what wouldn't have seemed like much not long ago. Yet I was also completely detached, observing myself as I had when I fell, from afar.

"Hmm," I might say. "That man is crying for no apparent reason. Curious." And the man was me.

That phrase, the "gathered stones" phrase, haunted me—after a while, it was all I could do to go a half hour without thinking it, or even saying it aloud. I began to fear I was losing my mind, that I was getting stuck in some neurotic do-loop like a malfunctioning algorithm, and that it would grind my brain to meal.

This was when the Abbot Hisamatso retired and I became Tributarian Barwarden—the major shaman of the Ecstatic Tributarians.

I was put up for the post (without my consent or knowledge) by a cabal of my former students, who, though they had only the best of intentions, did me something of a disservice, since the last thing I wanted to do was sit on the Assembly and listen to the terranes reflect endlessly on very little of human concern.

(Sometimes I still wonder if the terranes are consciously aware that a very ominous *Something* from outer space is on its way—at faster-than-light speeds—to try to eat all of our beings—that the Chunk *means business*. Skykomish just won't or can't grasp so many things. How odd that we can now walk and talk with a god and find that it is very like holding a conversation with a child. Well, actually, a bunch of children all capering about at once and not really paying attention to a single word you say.)

But the Chunk was nearing, and the times called for action as well as thinking, even from the most inwardly directed of us, of which I surely was a prime example. So I took the job of leading my sect, even with my misgivings.

Misgivings that proved to be well founded. More and more, I lost my ability to manage my workdays—my life!—effectively. At any moment, I could drift off into a mystic state of wonder— my knee satori—and every day was a turning wheel of elation and despair. I felt like Camus's Sisyphus, returning to his rock with sorrow one time, joy the next, but always and forever returning to that damned rock and having to push it up the hill again. Only I am not a twentieth-century Frenchman, and so received no great rush of freedom by expressing my withering disdain, as Camus would depict Sisyphus as doing. I can see him (and I always picture Sisyphus as looking like Camus in his tan raincoat) walking back down the hill to shoulder his load once again. "Those dirty, stinking Olympians and their so-called divinity; it is I, *I*, who do their nasty work for them. I spit upon them, pfft!"

I am an American. We are a practical people. All the pointless emotion I was heaping on myself only made me weary, but I could not seem to do anything about it.

Furthermore, it was one thing to throw away my so-called career—which I never had much use for as a concept in any case. But to endanger *others* bothered me. The Assembly was facing momentous decisions; the Tribs were in a perpetual state of confused activity, everyone wanting to do *something*, with no one really knowing anything to do. The Chunk was coming.

Finally I put my personal problem to Skykomish once again,

more out of a sense of obligation to the Tribs than anything else. I hadn't much hope that the terrane would be of help.

Yet, while this was far from anything the terranes was interested in or knew about, I'd reached the end of my resources, and *any* ideas would be welcome. As it happened, the terranes often have a kind of simple wisdom that is surprisingly deep (if they are childlike, they are also immensely *complex* children), and Skykomish did exactly the right thing. It delegated the problem to someone else. Or, more precisely, it put the problem up for grabs in its trance ecology. I got an offer of assistance from one of my Skykomish trance relatives.

And that was how I came, as the ancients put it, to seek professional help from a trained counselor.

It is perhaps a strange thing to go physically *inside* one's psychologist, but that first step inside the main unit of Orf was somehow comforting to me.

He'd had a big, overstuffed chair set up in a corner. There were several cameras around the room with which he could view his clients, but there was no one place for us to look at him. After the initial disorientation, I liked things this way. There were no facial tics to read, no silent encouragement or discouragement evident on the other's face. The other *had* no face. Orf was just a voice to me when I was inside him.

"How have you been, Noah?"

"All right," I said, fixing myself a cup of Earl Grey tea. The bergamot suffused the chamber with its dark, bittersweet odor. I felt at home enough to do such things by now, and had even become adept at working the archaic tap water dispenser and heating element. For the past several weeks I'd been coming to sessions every three or four days. "I've been thinking about the Chunk. Thinking about Becker. And I've been rereading Whitney Forester's *Travels with Orf* this week."

"I've never read it, I'm afraid."

"Well—why would you need to?"

"Is it good?"

"Good? Yes, I suppose literarily it's a fine piece of work for what it is. We—well, Tribs, I should say—don't really read it for the story, you know. It's more, well, *doctrinal.*" I took my tea and sat down in the big chair. It had wide wooden armrests, and I set the cup on one of them to let it cool a bit.

"I wanted to ask you," I said. "What was she *like?*"

Orf was quiet for a few moments. "It's been a long, long time since she died," he finally said. "She was a good woman."

"It was your ranger dreams that gave her the idea for the first trance. The idea that the terranes were aesthetic resonators."

"Only part of the idea. She figured the rest out without me."

I sipped my tea. Perfect.

"What about *you* this week?" Orf said. "How would you like to use the time? Has your son called you?"

"No, the Pure Water folk can't—or won't—do that. It's the art for art's sake thing. And Skykomish won't conjoin with them. It likes them, but it says they bother it, some way or another. Becker won't communicate *through* a terrane in any case—you know about their means and ends arguments—so how else is he going to call me when I'm sixty miles underground? And Tanabe's not much company."

"You two are having problems?"

"Not exactly. It's just that she's tranced to Lepderon for the next six months."

"What's Lepderon?"

"Some planet. We're not exactly sure *where* it is."

"So you'll live alone for a few months?"

"She told me to sleep around while she was gone, but I won't."

"She isn't Becker's mother, right?"

"No. Becker's mother and I split up years ago. She's working at the South Pole."

"What will Tanabe do on Lepderon? Something diplomatic?"

"Well, for Earth's sake let's hope so," I said, and laughed, thinking of Tanabe's blunt way with me in bed. *Put it here. Yes. No. Like so. That's right.* And my hands on her saffron skin, there and *there*—Tanabe is as Asiatic as any of us gets these days. Would she instruct the yants as to just where they could put their collective consciousness? "She's a cultural emissary," I told Orf. "All of the off-planet trancers are in one way or another. But I don't think you could ever call her *diplomatic.*"

"I see. I really don't know much about Lepderon. I'm rather old-fashioned and I don't get into Trance City very often, much less to other planets. Can the inhabitants help us with the Chunk?"

"You can't ask questions like that in Trance City. It doesn't work that way. But some of us have gotten the feeling from several of the beings that you meet in Trance City that people— beings, I mean—*know,* but that somehow they can't or won't *tell* us. But they do let us know that the Chunk isn't a good thing to have happen to you."

But I really didn't want to talk about the Chunk, or Tanabe. I was irritated at her for going off without me, but I understood it perfectly well, and I wished her the best. She knew she would always be number-one wife to me, as one of the nomad kings of the twenty-second-century coastal epics might put it. The only thing that bothered me was that this might be *it;* I might never see her again.

But we had long ago decided not to let the Chunk rule our lives.

"I was thinking about going away myself," I said.

"I thought if you were on the Assembly you couldn't be permanently tranced."

"I was talking about somewhere on Earth."

"*On* Earth? You mean the surface?"

"Yes."

"Where?"

"Whitney Forester's route to the Napa Valley. My son is there, in Saint Helena."

"As a—"

"A pilgrimage," I said. "I'm supposed to be the shaman of the Ecstatic Tributarians. We don't really believe in vision quests, like the River Way does. But a quest can't hurt, I suppose. Anyway, Becker hasn't spoken to me for over a year now, and I'd like to see him."

"Do you really think that's wise—to go, I mean?" said Orf. "Here, now? Keep this to yourself, please, but you are one of the more reasonable voices on the Assembly, Noah . . . in my opinion, that is."

"Thank you, but I'm not feeling very reasonable these days."

"But that would be quite a trip."

"Yes."

"The Chunk could be here in a matter of months."

"I know that."

"Are you really seriously considering this?"

I sat back, drank more tea. "Do you mind if I smoke?" I asked.

"Just a moment," Orf said. A fan burred into activity somewhere nearby. "Not at all. Go ahead."

I took out a pack of cigarettes, thumped one free, and walked over to the heating element, where I lit it. So odd not to be in a place where you could call up fire or cold from a wall on command. I returned to my chair, took a long drag.

"I'm leaving tomorrow for the surface," I said.

"Have you ever seen the sun?" the robot said.

"A few times," I replied. "I spent a year topside as a grunt on the New York project. That was 3011. I was what? Twenty-one, twenty-two. That was the last time. Back when I was young."

"You still *are* young," Orf said, although it sounded for all the world as if he was talking to himself. "You know, I went on a vision quest once."

"Did you have a vision?"

"Oh yes. A powerful one. I saw the end of one world and the

beginning of another. And I found my totem spirit animal, too."

"Really? What is that?"

The interior of the robot *rattled* slightly, as if a minor tremor had passed through. It had taken me a few sessions to realize that this was Orf's laughter.

"It was a human being," the robot said. "A ranger."

I had a good long pull on my cigarette. "Well, I'm thinking of this more as a—what was the old word?—a vacation."

"Would you like some company?" the robot asked. "I've been wanting to go up, to have another look . . . just in case—"

"The Chunk gets us?"

"In case the Chunk gets us."

"Well, you're welcome to come along."

The robot was silent for a time, and the only sound in the room was the fan, carrying my smoke away to be disintegrated by nuclear fusion. Orf seemed so primitive at times. So goddamn *old*.

Finally, he spoke. He said, "I think that I will, Noah Noahbronen. I'm about a hundred years overdue for a vacation myself."


## PLENIPOTENTIARY SESSION

The actual room from which the world is governed is shaped like a blob and isn't very big. There aren't that many of us who attend the Assembly meetings: The abbots, goodmothers and shamans of the seventeen sects, roots and offshoots; ten-odd terrane and AI voice proxies—human volunteers picked by the others for verbalizing anything that needs couching in human terms—and a couple of attendant robots to do whatever the wall service algorithms physically can't (such as bring you a glass of water).

What would you see if you attended an Assembly meeting? Not much. You might think you'd walked in on a roomful of mental patients conducting a campfire service to the gods of obfuscation. There are grunts and squeaks from this or that member. In the center of the meeting space, Goodmother Singh may be smiling and nodding her head at nothing in particular, and sitting along one of the curved walls a couple of abbots of the minor sects will simultaneously be delivering long speeches about entirely unrelated issues. What's going on is the overtrance, when we turn our thoughts inward these days and try to arrive at a collective course of action.

If you are part of that inward trance, everything is different and—I won't say it makes sense, but I will say that it isn't all confusion. Communing through the terranes, we don't achieve a collective consciousness. Humanity has had enough of that doomed attempt. Instead, we achieve a symbiosis, an ecology of governing. When you're overtranced, the deliberative processes appear as patterns that you *feel* elide and collide; the decisions are both outcomes and continuations of this swirl. It is rather like sitting outside through a dramatic thunderstorm. There's a definite arc to its development, its unfolding and its completion. And it's that arc itself that is what governs Downtown, as much as we can be said to be governed at all.

"It is an indisputable truth that living planets are art, and that for something to be art, it has to be appreciated."

"Here, here. The River Way is entirely in agreement—"

"Art implies a buyer."

"That's symbolically clear. The equations are firm in that regard."

"And the River Way claims that we appreciate ourselves, that *we* are evolving into the buyers, if you must call them that."

"The buyers are coming." This voice is me—Noah—in a way. And in a way, it is everyone in the Assembly.

"Tribs are such millenarians. Always looking for judgment day and the Final Auction."

"If the buyers are coming, where would the buyers be coming from?"

"We don't know. Elsewhere."

"All buyers are one buyer!"

"Thank you, Barwarden Braun."

"So the question we will think on today is whether or not the Chunk is a kind of buyer."

"It means to hurt us! Listen to what people say in Trance City!"

"We don't *know* anything for certain."

"You can *feel* it. Everyone can feel it. Look at what it does to the terranes . . . the drop-thoughts, the washouts. *Time* is affected. *Being* is affected."

"There is that. This is true."

"Damn right."

"We don't know that the Chunk is anything more than an errant gas giant."

"Moving faster than light?"

"Affecting the *trance.*"

"And there's that, too."

"The Chunk has something to do with the beauty lines."

"Yes, but what?"

"It's evil."

"Thank you, Barwarden Braun. Maybe you should let some of the younger Grayrock Brothers be present next time—"

"The Chunk is evil. I can feel it."

"Well, whether it's evil or not," I found myself saying, "I think we've attracted its attention."

"Very well for you to make a pronouncement, Noah Noahbronen. You'll soon be skipping off topside and away from all this."

"Not away, Goodmother Singh," I replied. "Trying to get on

top of it. To clear my head so I'll have something constructive to contribute at these meetings." I stub a spent cigarette against the wall and it is absorbed and annihilated by a quick pustule of magma. I light up another from the heat. "I'll be back before you know it."

## UNDERTAKING

"You gather what *is* by spreading through it," wrote Whitney Forester. "The *gather* is the spread of *you, aware.*"

After her "death" in the Napa Valley, she spent ten years living with the rangers of the Olympic Peninsula, the people who were the beginning of all of us humans underground. She is the one who led the first group of visionaries down, on the new-moon night, when Orf rose from the Earth to mourn Andrew Hutton, the first chief ranger. She showed them the path that Orf took, and once they were inside, arranged for the terranes to regulate the temperatures so that those immigrants could survive sixty miles under the Earth, here in Downtown (though it wasn't a town then, only down), where we live.

She told them that they would meet her father down there, but that she wasn't going with them because she and her father had had an argument, and weren't speaking at the moment, and maybe never would again. Whitney and Jarrod loved each other fiercely, but they never got along very well. She was words and ideas and he had something mute and elemental about him that could hardly be touched—much less persuaded—by talk and reason.

It must have been quite a surprise for those young rangers to meet someone living under the Earth whom they knew, but who everyone thought was dead.

And with Jarrod, they began the Undertaking—the union

with the terranes and the aesthetic outreach into the galaxy and beyond that is continuing still.

## OUT THERE

Orf and I emerged in the Olympic Peninsula, near a little stream that fed into the Ho River. Since I was with Orf, I did not use my hopper pack, but rode on top of his carapace. We rolled along an old path made by the local aborigines many years ago and later abandoned when they grew tired of playing neolithic tribal games and decided to go back down and trance out in the city. Almost all West Coast abos and their descendants were permanent Trancers these days, and they were very good at it. It was as if they had discovered something in the hunting and gathering that was also supremely useful in the trance. Of course, dissertations had been written about this, and we still didn't know what it was exactly.

The son of one of these ex-abos was my best friend, Hercules Gammonofax. Hercules was currently a tranced regimental lightbreeder in some star cluster in Andromeda. I'm not exactly sure what lightbreeders do, or what sort of regiment he belonged to; Hercules always got a glazed look in his eyes when I asked and gave me vague answers about his work.

It's a long trip to the stars and the way lies through beauty. There are no ships that will take you there, and it isn't your rationality that travels—it is your *consciousness,* which is different. You walk the beauty lines, the traceries of pattern and purpose that are folded and dimpled into reality as surely as are gravity wells and electromagnetic fields. The universe—at least our local area—is teleological. It moves toward a purpose, toward a becoming moment. We have no idea what that purpose is, of course. But *assuming* that there is one, meditating on the becoming of that purpose, and joining together in the resonating mentalities of the terranes—that's how Trance City arises for humans, and how we reach out to . . . the *others*.

Trance City is the hubbub and bustle of the meeting bazaar, and it is the peace and quiet of the parks. These *feelings* are what the place *is*. Trance City isn't anything *but* zones of feelings and the transitions and wild and beautiful mixtures of feelings. You might think of it as something like the local cluster of galaxies' big art museum. But we aren't looking at the paintings—we're living, working and playing *within* them.

Trance City is all the sentient life of the local cluster communicating to one another through pure feeling.

It's the only way to break the speed of light and have contact with other inhabited planets and systems within individual life spans. At least, it's the only way humans know of at this point in history.

Hercules told me that describing what it was like being a lightbreeder was a lot like telling somebody your dreams; it was pretty boring to the listener, since there was no shared understanding of the little things that could and couldn't happen. But, in the most simple and the most profound way, what he did was to help in the difficult births of stars. He was a sort of midwife and artisan.

There is an arrangement of luminous bodies in the heavens that is more pleasing than others. While I can show you the symbology and explain why this must be so to fit the observations, the understanding of how intergalactic sentience actually influences the painting of the starry fields—the working craft of making the night sky more beautiful—is a mystery to me. Hercules always said that you had to *do* it to understand it, and that you couldn't do it without giving your life to it, so talking about it would always be a letdown. I gathered from the conversations that we did have that he and the others of his regiment—whoever or whatever they were—moved along the beauty lines with a kind of intuitive logic and gave a nudge here and there across the threshold of meaning and into the physics of newborn stars. It was all about having the right touch, the right feel, and not something that could be communicated in words.

What Hercules *did* love to talk about was the foibles of his West Coast abo parents and abo ways in general. Even he had to admit, however, that coming from an abo family was the very reason he was the best cook ever to blanch vegetables on Eurasian magma (the only magma for cooking, in his own humble opinion). Abos knew from long experience how to make the most unlikely raw substance into something delicious.

But the abos were gone underground now and tranced away, and the Olympic Peninsula was all wild, from sea to Sound, and filled with giant old-growth firs, hemlocks and cedar that grew to enormous diameters sucking up the two-hundred-inch annual rains. All wild, that is, except for the overgrown decay of ancient cities, and the carefully preserved historical reconstruction of Threecabin, the hidden village of the rangers. Orf and I rolled into Threecabin near sunset, and his mobile unit, the mu, and I set up camp under the immense gnarl of a five-hundred-year-old cedar tree.

"Whitney Forester had terrible disagreements with the leadership of the rangers when she was here," I said. "She wanted them to institute *marriage.*"

"She got things in her head," Orf said. *"Usually* rational things. She had read *everything* and could be very argumentative. Jarrod used to say she was a lot like her mother."

"But did she persuade anyone with her arguments?"

"Not about that, as I recall."

"No. The histories say she didn't. At least not about reinstituting marriage."

The mu turned its cameras to the foggy sun, beginning to set over a distant ridge. "The light here is different from anywhere else on Earth," he said, using the mu's speaker. "It's *lustrous.*"

"The air glistens," I said.

We watched the sunset.

"Do you know, there was a time just before you were made when aesthetics had nearly died out as a philosophical discipline in the . . . what did they call them . . . the universities," I said.

"I hadn't realized that. That's practically all anyone does these days. What were people thinking?"

"Well, if they thought at all, they thought the Earth was some kind of living thing, a kind of giant cell, I suppose."

"Yes, I remember that vaguely. There were books."

"But to be alive means to compete for survival. What does the Earth compete with? Other planets? Hardly."

"But the Earth *is* alive, in a way. What about the terranes?"

"Sure. But what is the Earth *more* like?"

"Well, I know the answer you are looking for. A painting."

"Yes. Or any sort of art." I felt like I was slipping back into teaching mode, but Orf certainly didn't need instruction in the Shaman's Way. Really it was I who wanted to hear the Truths aloud once again. Something about the amber sunset had made me think again of those simples and, for a moment, of the Chunk, out there on the edge of the Oort cloud's orbit. Some connection. Vague. Luminous. "What does art compete with? Other art? Only in a crude way that doesn't really matter in the long run. And it doesn't evolve; it just changes. Nobody thinks Sophocles or Aeschylus is *primitive.*"

"Who is Sophocles? Some ancient Greek?"

"Some ancient Greek."

"And that's how you trance around the galaxy—feeling through the terranes."

"Aesthetic resonance. Not worship. Not intellectual contemplation. It's the state of artistic rapture while contemplating the ecological unity of the terranes. Their aesthetic balance. And from there, out along the beauty lines—"

"To Trance City."

"Yes." Darkness had seeped under the trees of Threecabin. Fog was in the air, and all sound was hushed. "During the sunset. A moment there. I saw the edge of something. I don't know what."

"*I* saw that it was pretty," Orf said. "There was something there."

I moved under the tarp for the night, and settled into my blankets. I fell asleep on friendly ground.

## HUMMING DOWN THE COAST

The next day, Orf went underground for better traveling along the ways he knew (the ways he had dug, long ago) and I flew my hopper down the coast of Washington and Oregon, and into California. The sun was bright this day, brighter than I'd ever seen it, glinting off the watery back of Nep, the Pacific plate terrane.

The hopper was little more than a ceramic block—the reaction mass—with an electromagnetic transceiver built in. The power that held me aloft was geothermal. It was sent to me in a tight little laser beam from a station in the eastern basalt horseshoe range of the Olympics. It was as though I were a speck on the end of a giant sky-writing pencil—but in this case, the speck controlled the movement of the pencil. Over the Oregon Dunes, I switched reaction channels from Skykomish's beam to Nep's strong signal—originating from the ocean floor—and the pencil got more stubby.

All day long, I thought about that moment, just after sunset of the previous night. What *was* it that I'd felt?

*Sunlight through the trees.*

It had been years since I'd seen trees. Whitney Forester had made this trip down to California on foot. She was going home, back to her mother's people. As she passed through the forest of the Northwest, she began to think about trees. I called the piece she'd written up from my Hermes algorithm, who was patched into the hopper, and, while I was eating lunch on a great rock jutting into the sea near Brookings, Oregon, I reread the part of her essay that eventually led Whitney Forester to her first trance with a terrane:

Symbiosis.

The curl of two facts around each other. And: there are trees! Trees with limbs branching out willy-nilly, but which all stop and spread so that they can collect the most amount of sunlight and transpire the right amount of water into the air. And the crowns of trees are like individual tree limbs. They are limited in how big around they can become because other trees are nearby, and these trees take a portion of the available light and water.

There isn't any tree intelligence at work, no consciousness. It isn't like a giant mind. What is it really like? Mighty like the human unconsciousness, mighty like the relations of the ter-ranes to one another. An ecology of imprints, algorithms, life forces and—don't forget—soil, air and water.

Nature on Earth is a collection of things and facts in sym-biosis. It's an ecology. So is culture. Culture is the shaping of our minds to nature. It's our response, as a species, to being here. That's why you can't get world peace by imposing order. It has to *grow*. Look at the sad history of the twentieth century— or worse, our own twenty-first-century madness. People *trying too hard*.

But after the growing is over, what do we do then? When we're children, we *get* our culture—and our culture gets us. That's what individuals are. We are the meeting and melding of culture and nature. We enter adulthood as the biological sur-vivors of these two processes. But nature and culture go on in-teracting long after we've survived. Long after Darwin has had his say.

Then you have art. Art is culture and nature attempting to project itself beyond itself. That's where war and strife come from, perhaps. That's definitely where beauty comes from.

Beauty is something new. It is something other than you and something other than the world, but it is made of nothing else but you and the world. It is the universe humming a song.

When the hum of beauty grows to a full symphony, you cannot break out of the hum, become only you again. You are unable to stop getting it. It gets *you,* and releases you only when it—the hum—is done singing itself. The moment of release is determined by the particular song. That's what awe is. When *you* are singing and being sung by the world.

## THE FATHER OF THE MAN

I arrived in Saint Helena in the Napa Valley in late afternoon. I set down a mile or so out of the enclave and stowed my hopper in some scrub oak on top of a prominent hill, then walked the rest of the way in. Becker's Tributarian offshoot sect—the Pure Water—didn't approve of any algorithmic translations of the terranes' revealed glory—for example, using modulated geothermal lasers to power a back hopper. Art for art's sake, and only art's sake.

Which is part of the reason he hadn't talked to me for a while.

It took a bit of asking around, but I finally found Becker in a barn, tending to the sore leg of something that looked very like a deer, but with sturdy legs and uncloven hooves. The Pure Water had no philosophical problems with genetic engineering.

He saw me when I came in and saw that it was me, but didn't pay me any notice until he was done tending to the animal.

"Well, Papa," he said, standing up and wiping ointment

from his hands onto a white rag. "What brings you up from the bowels of the Earth?"

"For one thing, I wanted to see you," I replied. "I thought I might not get to again."

Becker frowned, as if he'd just bit down on something sour. Pure Water folk don't believe the Chunk is coming to harm us. But since they don't go to Trance City, they don't know the feelings of dread and trepidation the others are sending our way concerning it. All they know about the Chunk is secondhand—and it is information from folks whose judgment they don't trust that much to begin with.

"Let's not talk about it," he said.

"All right," I said. "What do you want to talk about?"

"I want to *eat,*" he said, throwing the rag aside. "Ling is making supper tonight. Want to join us?"

"I love Ling's cooking. Even Hercules used to rave about it."

"Hercules. It's been a long time since I thought about him. How's the old trancer?"

"Fine, I suppose. He was two days ago."

"Good. Well, come on then."

"There's one other thing, Becker. A friend is going to show up, some time today. He's kind of large, so you can't miss him. His name's Orf."

"*The* Orf?"

"That one."

"Now how would *you* come to know Orf?"

"He's my shrink."

"I see. And I'm the president of Mexico. Come on and eat."

We walked down the main street of the enclave. The houses—all made of stone—were decked out with streamers and flowers.

*It's spring,* I realized. No wonder the trip down the coast had been so pleasant.

"Some kind of fertility rite going on?" I asked Becker, pointing to the decorations. "I know how you people like to have a party if you wake up in the morning and realize that there's *air."*

"That's a pretty good idea, come to think of it. Breathing is good." Becker looked at me, smiled wryly—the way he had as a child—and melted my heart. "But actually, about noon today, some old robot showed up and started asking around for you. Seems the sisterhood council is throwing a big celebration in his honor. Tonight, after everybody eats supper."

I couldn't help myself. "I thought the Pure Water didn't approve of artificial intelligence," I said.

"That's disembodied algorithms we don't approve of. And come on, Papa, it's *Orf,"* Becker replied without irony. Well, without much irony. "For him, we make an exception."

Ling had made a spicy vegetable curry and raita, with yogurt and cucumbers, which was delicious. We drank lassi with it, and, although I enjoyed it, I thought about what a shame it was that the Pure Water folk didn't believe in alcoholic beverages. They didn't even grow grapes, except for juice and raisins— here, in the Napa Valley!

But, of course, the valley's history was pretty much lost to them, living in the moment as they did.

After supper Ling excused herself to go help get set up for Orf's welcome. Before she left, she gave me a big hug and told me she was glad to see me, and that Becker had missed me more than he let on.

I hugged her back, and after she'd left I looked over the table at Becker.

"What I really miss is our interminable arguments," he said. "Can't get enough of *those."*

"Well, you shouldn't have joined the Pure Water then. All this frisking and gamboling is bad for your constitution."

"Oh, we argue well enough," he said. "We just resolve ours. How's Tanabe?"

"Fine. Tranced to Lepderon."

"Tell her hello when she gets back."

"I will."

"Do you ever see Mom?"

"Hardly ever. She's in Antarctica."

"The dead aliens."

"Or whatever they are. I believe the current theory is that they're . . . eggshells. It was a nest."

"And what hatched out?"

"Nobody knows. But I read something your mother wrote about it for *The Downagain*."

"Yeah, I saw that."

"You get the . . . oh, a paper copy."

"I keep up with your and Mom's work, Papa."

"Then you know she thinks that the *terranes* are what hatched down there. If that's true, that means they aren't native to Earth."

"I know it."

"But you don't believe it."

"I don't believe anything, Papa. I'm trying to *live* things."

"Yes, that Pure Water distinction. One day I'm going to understand why you want to split those hairs."

"Papa, please."

"All right."

"All right, then."

We drank more lhasi, then; since Becker knew my likes, he heated me up some tea. The Pure Water folk only drink it for breakfast. Some superstition about the caffeine keeping them awake at night. It never did that to *me*. I didn't even bother asking if I could smoke a cigarette.

I looked around my son's place. Ling's artwork was on the walls, and a couple of Becker's ceramic sculptures were poised on a shelf, where the smallest earthquake could have knocked them off. On one wall was a bulletin board with the cryptic message: "get hornet's nest," written in Becker's scraggly hand. He saw what I was looking at.

"I noticed it when I was out running yesterday," he said. "It's from last year. Just lying on the ground now."

"How far?" I asked.

"About a mile and a half."

I thought about Becker growing up, how I'd showed him the wonders of Downtown. The flicker glow of the tunnels' capillaries. Crystal Cave and Eleveny's Deep. The slosh and ooze of magma behind fused walls many yards thick and colored with all the hues of stained glass and rainbows. We explored, found things together. Intricate windings where water had been forced deep, then carved its way back toward the surface. The gnarled roots of mountains. I'd tried to show my son all the things that I thought were beautiful under the ground.

I drained my tea, stood up. "Shall we have a look?" I said.

"You want to go and get it?"

"Can we make it there and back before the celebration?"

Becker nodded. "Let me get my shoulder bag," he said.


## NOT STUNG BY HORNETS

We walked through the greening countryside along a wagon track. It was actually in the direction where I'd left my hopper, but I didn't say anything about it as we passed its hiding place. We turned down a side trail, and after walking about a hundred yards, we found the nest.

I would have tapped it once or twice just to make absolutely sure that it was empty, but Becker scooped it up without a moment's uncertainty. It was the size of a person's head—mostly gray-brown, but with a few ribbons of green where the chloroplasts from the chewed leaves still remained in the dried pulp.

"Beautiful," he said, regarding it.

"It is," I agreed.

At that moment something black crawled out of one of the folds of the nest paper and onto Becker's hand. I started back, but he just laughed and brushed it off. It was only a beetle.

*Only a.*

I stared at the nest in my son's hand.

*Something I. Something I remember. Something that I remember that I couldn't possibly remember.*

Becker looked at me strangely for a moment, then shook his head and put the nest into his bag.

"Ready to head back?" he said. "We're going to miss the celebration."

"That's it."

"What?"

"The Chunk," I said.

"What about it? Papa, let's not get into that discussion—"

"It's a collector. That's what it is."

"Papa, the Chunk isn't sentient. We've been through this. A collector?"

"An art collector."

"What are you talking about?"

"You know the big argument between the Ecstatic Tributarians and the mainstream River Way—surely I pounded that into your skull when you were little?"

"That living planets are art, and that for something to be art, it has to be appreciated."

"Art implies a buyer."

"And the River Way claims that we appreciate *ourselves*, that we are evolving into the buyers, if you must call them that. Tribs are millenarians. They think the buyers are coming . . . from elsewhere. And the Pure Water—in case *you* were wondering—says that everyone can have everything. That all buyers are one buyer."

"What if we're *all* right?"

"Papa, it's all so much useless talk, if you ask me."

"Time makes the difference."

"I'm getting tired of this—"

"Becker, bear with me a moment, a moment." I was thinking furiously.

The Chunk. Time. Aesthetic symbology. The buzz of the last Assembly meeting. How tiring it was to attend sometimes. The way my knee had twisted and hurt. The way it still ached. The Chunk.

The Chunk sent out a time signature traveling before it. That's why all those trances are picking up interference.

Trancing *is* participating in a timeless moment. But if you are a person, and not a god, you need *time* to define timelessness. It needs to be gathered about you, like darkness gathers about a pool of light, so that you can remember who you are in that moment of ecstasy. The symbology is quite clear in this. Being requires time. Being unfolds in time.

The Chunk was going to drain all our time away.

The gathered stones are *where* they have fallen. But not *when* they have fallen.

That thing wanted to stop us in our tracks. It wanted to freeze us in place, shellac us over, and stand back and regard its nice little find, the Earth.

It wanted to hang us on a wall like a pretty picture. But take us not out of space. Out of time.

"How do you make time?" I asked my son.

"No one can make time. That's why we die."

"Think about it another way. Where is that tranced time going?"

"I don't—"

"Back into itself. Harmonic resonance. We buzz. We *hum*. I can show you the symbology."

"Please don't."

"We have to scare it."

"How are you going to scare a gas giant?"

"We don't know what its physical being is, not really. The surface is just accumulated atmosphere from its travels. It's moving in and out of space, like a dolphin. That's why it's getting here faster than light can."

"My question remains."

"Like the hornets scare people."

Becker shook his bag. "See? There aren't any hornets in this nest."

I stomped my foot. For a moment he thought I was mad at him, but then I pointed down. "There *are* in this one. Our nest. Would you have picked up that nest if you thought it was full of hornets?"

"Of course not. But not from fear. From reverence for life."

"Come on, Becker! Remember what the terranes say about Pure Water folk? They trance out, but they don't go anywhere. It can be very unpleasant to them."

"They've never said that to *us.*"

"Skykomish did."

"Well, it's the only one who did."

"That's because the other terranes don't know what it is they're feeling. But Skykomish does. It is the only terrane that's ever felt direct, concrete pain. And Skykomish won't have Pure Water conjoints. It says you give it a headache. But what you're giving Skykomish is a *time* ache. You're causing it aesthetic pain. Like bees crawling around under its skin."

"I still don't see what you're talking about."

"I knew coming to visit you would be a good idea," I said, and patted Becker on the back. The hornets' nest rustled in his bag, and once again gave me the willies.


## THE GATHERED STONES

When Whitney Forester returned to her birthplace in the Napa Valley, no one believed it was she who had come back. After all, they'd seen her walk into the Lady's Grotto. They'd seen the entrance seal, and they knew that the cave was solid rock in the back and sides. There was no way out. The queen died. She was planted in the ground. She came back to life through the grapes, the greening land.

Yet here she was, walking among them, down from the north. Still flesh and blood.

"It's over," she told her people. "The old way has been broken. You can hold on to it and watch it wither in your arms. You can wither with it. Or you can turn away and let it die peacefully and alone. As for me, I'm alive, and I'm going to keep living for as long as I can."

This year happened to be the fullest crop since before the dark years after the poles had shifted. Thirty-five years had passed. The Quitman king was very sick and the Polleta who was actually running things—Whitney Forester's first cousin— at first arrested her and locked her in a wine cellar, afraid that the people would flock to her and neglect the harvest. But that night there was a great rumble heard and *felt* in the ground, and in the morning, the Polleta steward found Whitney standing by the great oak of the compound, explaining to the court teenagers why her mother had insisted she didn't take the surname Polleta.

"My mother, Sarah Polleta, was a great queen, and very proud of her house," Whitney told them. "But I was only a kid when she died. I couldn't know her, not really."

" 'I'm going to be the last,' my mother said. 'I won't let Jarrod stop me from doing this.'

"My father had come to her, knowing that the time for the Draining of Lees was in a few days. He had come out of the Earth, where he made his home. He'd offered to take her with him. To take her down under the ground where she could live. My mother had refused.

" 'We must remember the seasons and calm the earth beneath us,' she said to me. 'For me to die with the turning of the year is the way to do that. It's *my* way to do that. I know that now. I'm a Polleta first, and I'm the queen. But you are *Whitney*, first and always. Something new in the world. Jarrod will come for *you*. We've agreed. He'll come for you when they seal you into the Lady's Grotto. Jarrod will come for you through the Earth, and you won't die.' "

The teenagers scattered as the Polleta steward brought a force of men and jailed Whitney Forester again. But the next day, the same thing happened, and the steward found Whitney once again in the courtyard, talking to the teenagers. Finally, he begged his cousin to please go away, that she was going to ruin everything. That she did not fit the way things were and that at the next Draining of the Lees, all would be lost. That the people would be thrown into poverty and hunger if they listened to her, and the land would become barren.

"Well, if it's the harvest you're worried about," Whitney said, "I have a friend who can help you with that." And she spoke into a radio transceiver and called her friend, whose name was Orf. For the first time in a hundred years, the robot came forth into the sunlight. And with blade and bale modified by the men of the kingdom, he and the people got in the grapes.

Even though there were harvest times with better weather and more abundant grapes, the reds from that year were said by the old to be the best in living memory, and their grandchildren never tasted a better run for as long as they lived.

"The only difference between those grapes and any others was that the people who picked them did so knowing they would never again have to kill their queen to get a good harvest. You tell me that didn't make a difference and I'll tell you bullshit, it *did*," Whitney Forester wrote in *The Exiles of California*. "You gather what *is* by spreading *through* it."

And so, we are trying it. We are going to try to scare away the Chunk with a burst of sheer beauty. All trancers have been called back, and everyone—everyone who could be persuaded into it—will go into trance, all at once. But not to Trance City. Not *through* the terranes to the greater galaxy.

We will stay mentally at home. We will buzz like a nestful of bees. For a spell, we are going to shine with time the way the sun shines with light.

Becker and Ling came back Downtown to stay with me for a while. Becker has joined the Big Trance.

"It doesn't go against any Pure Water doctrine," he told me. "And even if it did, we make exceptions for helping out our fathers. At least, *I* do."

So I did not raise a son who was inflexibly doctrinaire after all.

And here we are, in Downtown. Here I am. I'm finishing up this record on a table here in the Assembly Room.

I know it is presumptuous and perhaps sacrilegious, but I have added to Whitney Forester's *Exiles of California*. But it's just one word, so maybe you'll forgive me. I've hooked on a little algorithm to this tablet, and my addition will automatically append itself at whatever point this memoir ends, and so you will know—that's all.

The terranes are actively present here, their awareness gathered in the immediate vicinity. All the continents, microterranes and exotics of the Earth. The walls glow with the rainbow luster of terranes and humans, conjoining. Getting ready. My counselor is nearby, inhabiting his mu. He will trance, too, after the rest of us have done so. He was the first to meet the terranes, and he'll be here at the end—or at least the culmination, one way or the other.

"Well, Orf, it's a good time for humanity and terranes, even if all of us are about to die."

"And enthalpic robots."

"And robots."

*The Chunk is getting pretty near.* Skykomish's message in my mind. There is also an emotion—a sort of blue-green feeling—half buried in the words. The terrane is frightened, but trying not to communicate it too forcefully.

"We're ready," I say.

"What?" says Orf.

"I was talking to my terrane."

"Oh."

"Can I ask you something? I've asked Skykomish, but it never really gives me an answer."

"Go ahead," says Orf.

"You're over a thousand years . . . oh, never mind. Forget it."

The mu rattles for a moment; one of its legs stamps.

"I can tell you the answer," Orf says.

"But you don't ever know the question."

"I can tell you the answer."

"All right."

"The answer is that I have no idea what it all means," says the robot. "But I know that there are good and evil—and beauty. I know *those* are real."

"Maybe beauty will save us."

"Maybe we'll save ourselves."

"They're the same thing."

"Yes."

*The Chunk is here.*

We keep striving. We're already saved. We keep striving.


The gathered stones
are where they have fallen

singing

# ACKNOWLEDGMENTS

My family is full of geologists, entirely by accidental faulting, subduction and plate elision. On our gigantic vacations around the North American west, my father, a cartographer, would drive us from fault to caldera to fossilized sand dunes and back to Alabama again. Later, my Aunt Maria and Uncle Gene Bottoms would talk California geology as we looked down on L.A. from their perch in the San Bernardinos.

But a lot of people help you out on a slow-going second novel that takes four years to write. On Vashon Island: Joan Kirshner, Jim Dorsey, Dietrich and Josh Ayala, Dru Church and Josiah Palmer. In Seattle: David Myers, Scott Stolnack, Richard Clement, Katie Esser and Chris Resleff. In Prague: Marta Plášilová and Josh Ayala. In California: Maria and Gene Bottoms and Kevin Mims. In Alabama and Georgia: Louise Montgomery Poe, Emmett and Myrtice Daniel, David Whitney, Kurt and Carol Schreiner, John DeWitt, Lisa Paterno, Ed Hall and Michael Bishop. In New York: Jack Womack, Michael Taylor, Ellen Datlow, Andrew Wheeler, Ellen Asher, Dy Robinson, Margaret Cino and Jessica True. In Dallas: Jerry, Martha and David Daniel and Danny Daniels. Christine Wenc was a steadfast and lovely critic for three years. All these people gave me great succor in time of need. And, in Atlanta, Nicole Williams swerved and saved my life.

I talked to many geologists over the years, and I thank them. There's a bunch of them, and I didn't write down all their names. Particular thanks to consulting geochemist Richard Wharton and to geophysicist Gary Mitchell of Hunt Oil Company in Dallas. Thanks to John McPhee for his beautiful essays on the forces within the land of America.

Gardner Dozois edited the original pile of scree into a

novella and Greg Cox helped it extrude and metamorphose into a sort of novel. And always around, showing me how to be a writer, was Lucius Shepard, who is an exotic terrane unto himself.